# STANLIN *and* SYLVIA

CYNTHIA HEY

ISBN:      1477420908

ISBN 13:   9781477420904

Library of Congress Control Number: 2012908625
CreateSpace, North Charleston, SC

*To Andreas, Ray and Linda, and Milton and Ruth*
*Your exemplary living, your support, and your love have given me the*
*strength to spread my own wings. I love you!*

# Acknowledgments

I thank my entire family and all of my friends for their heartfelt encouragement for this project. A special note of gratitude goes to the Millman family.

I also thank the following very helpful people: Lauren Pape, Esq., for having the keen eyes to notice many stylistic errors while still appreciating the story; Jen Rosenfeld, CSW, for information about the child adoption process and perspectives about social work cases; JMU career counselor Denise Meadows, for describing global business management consulting careers; Professor Scott Vollum, PhD, for answering my criminology questions; Laura Abate, MSLS, for leading me to important medical resources; and authors J.K. Rowling, Dean Koontz, Sandra Brown, Stephen King, and Sharon Pape, for inspiring me with your incredible talents.

# PART I

THE FORMATIVE YEARS

# Spring, 2002

## CHAPTER ONE

"Nixar said he wants me to go with him to his planet," Julie divulged to Shelby. For the last half an hour, she had been describing the alien's visits to see her. "And I kind of want to go! I've felt...connected to him. I can't really explain it. You know how much I love Jim, but there's also this weird part of me that wants to be with Nixar." She lowered her face into her hands and wept softly.

Shelby, aghast, was silent. She and Julie, now in their mid-twenties, had been friends since childhood. They had always talked openly about everything together. But now, Shelby looked at her dear friend with deep concern. Snippets of what Julie had said raced through Shelby's mind: bald-headed, blue alien man; large, dark, mesmerizing eyes; strong, slender build; of a unique density: not really solid like humans, though not transparent like a ghost—somewhere in between. And this "Nixar" had explained to Julie that, regardless of their different densities, his species, known as Ramponts, had internal organs and systems very comparable to humans.

Julie had shown Shelby a book, too, filled with stories of other people's alien encounters. Evidently, to Julie, the book legitimized Nixar. To Shelby, it only proved that people with delusional disorders could experience similar phantasms.

Shelby sighed, devastated. Her poor Julie was feeling connected and strangely attracted to an utter fabrication. It was going to require tough love, but Shelby knew she had no choice: She would have to bring Julie to the psychiatric hospital.

**Note:** For the purpose of sharing this tale, all Rampont discourse has been translated from their native language, Paritam, into English.

Meanwhile, in the Andromeda Galaxy, on planet Capton, Nixar was daydreaming about Julie. He found her hourglass figure and flowing red hair entrancing. She looked nothing like all of the lanky, blue, bald Ramponts. But her beauty was only a portion of her appeal. She was also intelligent, witty, and kind.

His fluency in English, acquired during Capton's rigorous, expansive language courses, enabled them to converse, and talking with her engaged and exhilarated him. Technically, he and Julie were friends; there had been no physical contact between them. And yet, he sensed that she was attracted to him, too.

He loved seeing her on Earth, but what he wanted most was to bring her to his homeland. He vividly pictured it: In the same way that Ramponts brought entities from many other planets to Capton for visits, he could embrace Julie and instantly transport her body along with his.

Only about a year earlier, the Ramponts had begun communicating with distant entities—occasionally transporting them to Capton. In prior years, Ramponts had transported alone, simply to silently and invisibly observe activity on other planets. They really enjoyed learning about other cultures. Often, they would incorporate the novel customs and rituals they witnessed into their own lives. From Earth, they had adopted winks, hand-shakes, hugs, kisses, and marriage.

But as a morally evolving species, the Ramponts had recently decided that communing more with the rest of the universe would be better than mere observation. Real interactions would enhance love, joy, and peace in their own lives, as well as in the lives of others. So they'd started reaching out, becoming friendly with beings from faraway worlds.

Their pursuits were cautious. Unless they were bringing a being back and forth to visit Capton, they each transported alone, figuring that for-eigners might be frightened by seeing many Ramponts manifest at once. To protect themselves, each Rampont interacted with only one specific being on any given planet, privately. They thought that if a species was hostile, a group would probably attack, whereas a lone being would be less likely to strike. On the positive side, if an entity was kind, repeated one-on-one visits with the same Rampont could foster genuine friendship.

To this point, interactions with the humans on Earth had been mini-mal, and no humans had been transported to Capton yet. Nixar was eager for Julie to be the first. He had already posed the idea to her, suggesting he could bring her back and forth as often as she'd like, or he could even bring her to Capton for good. Julie really seemed tempted, but torn with guilt—because of Jim, her human boyfriend.

Nixar clenched his teeth in frustration. Jim was inattentive—a work-aholic by Julie's own admission. If only she'd ditch Jim and give *him* a chance. He would show her what it felt like to be priority number one. He would never take her for granted, would never neglect her.

"You're really quiet," Nixar's friend Munin commented, breathing heavily from exertion. He and Nixar were jogging along their favorite path, listening to the upbeat, flute-like music spouting from a tiny, square radio wrapped around Munin's wrist. The path below them was made of small, black, shiny stones, and the plants to either side of them looked like verti-cal, white, wavy sticks. The sky above sparkled with a rich, purple hue. "What's on your mind today, buddy?"

"I'm just thinking about Earth," Nixar replied, trying to sound casual. "I've been visiting it lately."

"Yeah, I like the plants and animals there. And those humans, they're an interesting species, eh?"

"Uh-huh." Nixar tried to think of a good transition to ask what he wanted, but couldn't conjure one up. So much for subtlety. Hopefully Munin would regard the questions as curiosity-based, and nothing more. "Have you heard or read much about romantic relationships there? Are they stable, or is it common for the humans to, uh, switch partners?"

"From what I've heard, the humans' relationships generally aren't stable. Boyfriends and girlfriends split up a lot, and marriages fail about half the time."

Nixar worked hard to suppress a grin.

Munin glanced over at him. "What I want to know is, why are you glad to hear that? And why do you care about relationships among the humans?"

Nixar felt his face becoming hot. He forced out a pretend cough. "I, um…" he stalled.

"Have you been visiting a human female? Maybe one who's involved with a human male?"

Nixar still didn't know what to say. "Possibly," finally trickled out.

"You can't get her out of your mind, can you?"

"No," Nixar admitted begrudgingly, looking at the black pebbles as his feet rhythmically pounded on them. Munin was sharp as a tack.

"Have you sensed that she's attracted to you, too?"

"Yes." Nixar's gaze was intense as his eyes veered upward to meet Munin's.

"Don't get flattered by that," Munin said flatly, breaking their eye contact and picking up the pace of their jog. "She's probably a compassionate human, and you're a compassionate Rampont. I've read that compassionate thoughts have a particular frequency, and that beings of any kind with similar thought frequencies can feel emotionally connected—and often physically attracted, too."

"It's more than some physics properties!" Nixar retorted sharply.

Munin sighed, shaking his head. "You're smitten, aren't you? You wish she'd leave her boyfriend for you, don't you?"

Nixar grimaced, fixed his gaze straight ahead, and jogged onward in silence. It was maddening. Munin knew him entirely too well.

"You're not offering to transport her to Capton, are you?"

Nixar craned his head abruptly and stared at Munin, hardly believing what he'd just been asked. It was as if his best friend could read his mind, for goodness sake.

Munin took one look at Nixar's face and challenged him. "Aren't you concerned that that's never been done with the humans before?"

"Surely they can be transported here by a hug, like so many other beings have been, and the mathematics in Cadence's article say that a human's resonant atomic frequency should be adaptable to our atmosphere," Nixar answered defensively.

"'Should be' is the operative phrase. I've read the article too. I didn't see any flaws in it, but her calculations are brand new. With the other entities so far, the elder Council members have evaluated the research and initiated the transport. What if the elders don't feel the human physiology is understood well enough yet? Why not wait for their call? Don't you think it could be risky to do this on your own?"

Nixar paused as he grappled with Munin's precautions. "No," he replied at last. "I combed through that paper. You know me. I can pick things apart better than most. Her research is sound. A human would be fine traveling here. Have you noticed that no other beings that have come have been hurt? And don't give me grief about the elders, either. It wouldn't break any laws for me to initiate the transport."

"No, it wouldn't break any laws," Munin conceded, "but it would be against precedent. And no, no one has been hurt yet, but what if..."

"Even if she had some weird negative reaction, I'd just bring her right back to Earth," Nixar interrupted. "She'd recover instantly, like the Plexitronian did."

Nixar knew Munin had heard of the incident two months earlier, when a being transported from planet Plexitron had acclimated poorly to Capton's atmosphere. He couldn't see clearly and felt shaky and dizzy, but he normalized completely after prompt transportation back to Plexitron.

Munin's demeanor softened. "Hmm. It's a good point that the one negative reaction was reversed so easily. And, knowing your fastidiousness, I agree that you'd have caught any flaws in Cadence's research. Heck, I was pretty critical in my analysis of it, too. I guess there's no real danger with bringing the human girl here."

"That's right," Nixar touted, feeling quite satisfied—until he suddenly realized that if Julie didn't wish to take the trip, all of their chatter was wasted breath. "If she keeps dating that Jim man, she won't even want to come here with me anyway," he grumbled.

"Ah, the mystery: Will she or won't she stay with Jim? What does the future hold?" Munin playfully dramatized.

Nixar stopped in his tracks and gaped at his friend, who, in turn, stopped jogging. They stood facing one another.

"What is it?" Munin asked.

A sly smile spread across Nixar's lips. "What's the one way that we, *as Governmental Council members,* can peek into the future?"

"We can look into the Probability Sphere," Munin answered matter-of-factly.

Nixar raised his brows and smiled wider.

Munin nodded. "OK, I think I see where you're heading."

"Isn't it brilliant? The Sphere just might show us if Julie's still with Jim in the future!"

"No guarantees what it'll show, but yeah, you might find out. Regardless, I'm sure it'll be interesting. Already, I've learned one fun new tidbit. Her name is Julie," Munin teased.

Nixar sighed with chagrin. "Let's just go to the Sphere." He transported himself, and a chortling Munin followed suit.

# CHAPTER TWO

The Governmental Council Headquarters Complex was constructed of large black boulders, strategically placed with spaces in between, serving as windows. With Capton's mild climate and absence of insects, open-air buildings like this were the norm. Inside, were Council members' offices, a computerized surveillance room, the Council's meeting room, and one very tiny six-by-six-foot office, which housed the Probability Sphere.

Nixar and Munin each manifested directly into the small office. The Sphere sat in the room's center, and the surrounding walls displayed elaborate blueprints of the Sphere's internal machinery. Otherwise, the room was barren of furnishings. For several moments, the two Ramponts gazed upon the large, round, technological masterpiece in wonderment. It was shiny and cream colored, about four feet in diameter, and was situated within a stand of coiled, transparent wire.

The Probability Sphere could reveal images of the near future. It was accessible exclusively to Governmental Council members, thirty-seven of whom had collaboratively created it to foresee and stave off dangers. The device was new, still in testing mode. As the most recent and youngest members of the Council, each twenty-eight years of age, Nixar and Munin had not yet used it themselves. They had both observed a few senior colleagues dabbling with it, though.

Ready to get things underway, Nixar broke their silence. "I need to look into the center of it, picturing Julie in my mind, right?"

"Yeah, I think so," Munin agreed. "But remember, from what we've seen, the Sphere will show you what it wants to about your topic. You could see just about anything in Julie's future."

"I know, I know. It might not tell me if she'll stay with Jim, but it's worth a try!" Nixar said, brimming with excitement.

Munin squeezed in a jesty precaution. "You know, once you do this, it'll be enshrined forever in the Sphere's records. Anyone will be able to check the logs and know that you were looking in on the future of a human girl. You sure you want to go through with it?"

"Who's going to check those logs anyway? Why would anyone care?" Nixar quipped.

Munin chuckled with amusement.

Nixar rolled his eyes.

"You're probably right. Why would anyone look back?" Munin accorded, becoming serious again. "So go on. Let's see what it says."

Quickly gathering himself, Nixar looked into the Sphere, mentally focusing on Julie. Munin's eyes were fixed on the Sphere, too, but he cleared his mind—the device could only respond to one Rampont's thoughts at a time.

After a moment, a succession of disturbing images appeared: a brick building with the words "Vernon Valley Psychiatric Hospital;" a doctor's notes, reading, "Ms. Julie Abler is having delusions, saying she has seen a blue alien man;" and Julie crying while a nurse holding a cup of pills rubbed her shoulder in consolation.

The pictures faded away, and words appeared: "Tomorrow, with 98 percent certainty."

Nixar and Munin knew that because no future outcome could be 100 percent guaranteed, each prediction from the Sphere was followed by the numerical probability that it would come to fruition. Nixar was appalled that, at 98 percent certainty, Julie's awful forecast was practically a shoo-in. Momentarily stunned, he watched with a dropped jaw as the Sphere blurred the words and returned to its usual cream color.

He covered his mouth, and stepped backward. Julie was perfectly sane. She did not belong among the mentally ill. He was at a loss for words. His troubled eyes left the Sphere and met Munin's.

Munin's face was wrought with concern. "We know she's not crazy. This is bad," he said.

# CHAPTER THREE

The Capton Governmental Council had its next session three days later, and the friends decided they would discuss the Sphere's findings with the rest of the Council.

The large meeting hall in the Headquarters Building was filled, as usual, for the weekly gathering. All seventy-seven ruling authorities and the eight specifically selected scholastic instructors were present. As was the protocol, they handled Capton updates and happenings first. Then they addressed issues relating to their galaxy. When the meeting reached its third and final phase, intergalactic matters, Nixar raised his hand.

"Yes?" Bartholith, that week's orator said, pointing and nodding to Nixar.

Nixar spoke with a hint of a quiver in his voice. "Like we all have, I've been visiting other galaxies and meeting different beings. A human on planet Earth in the Milky Way has been my favorite so far." Nixar could feel his heart beating fast and hard in his chest. He cleared his throat. "I was…curious about my human friend. I thought I might learn more about her by looking into the Probability Sphere." His heart felt like it was going to burst right through his rib cage. "But when I did, I saw something upsetting. The girl was in a psychiatric hospital, because the other humans did not believe that she had met me—an alien." Nixar breathed heavily, profoundly relieved to have finished delivering the essentials.

Low sounds of "Oh" and "Mm" resounded. Some Ramponts shook their heads sympathetically.

Munin raised his hand. "I was with Nixar. We both saw those images and talked about it afterward. We don't want our visits to Earth causing problems for the humans. What can we do?"

Sillu raised her hand. "Last week, my human friend told me she was afraid to tell anyone else about me. But at the same time, by not talking, she felt like she was going to explode."

Several other Council members nodded in apparent commiseration.

With sadness, Sequentor said, "For a while, I visited a four-year-old child on Earth. We played games together, like when my son was small. But one day when I arrived, the boy was crying. He said his neighbors were calling him a liar and a baby for having a make-believe friend."

Bartholith's eyes shone with empathy. "This needs attention," he muttered. After pausing to contemplate the shared anecdotes, he raised his voice and commanded the room. "With so many planets to contact, I understand that not everyone here has traveled to Earth. But if you have, and you've spoken with a human, please rise."

About one-third of the Council members stood.

"Please remain standing if the human you've visited has ever expressed distress to you about being spurned by other humans."

Only one of the standing members sat down.

Bartholith's eyebrows rose as he realized the prevalence of the problem. He murmured, "Hmm." Everyone present displayed similar reactions. Slowly, the standing Ramponts seated themselves.

Renito's hand shot up. "Clearly, some of the humans have bonded with some of us. Cadence's paper supports that they can adapt to our atmosphere. Provided that the safety is confirmed, should our human friends *ever* be transported here? Or, should that be off the table for good now, seeing how common social disruption already is when they're only *speaking* with us?"

Chatter rose, and Lithantor glared around the room. Thrusting his hand into the air, he snorted, "No one has mentioned the crime statistics on Earth. Have any of you reviewed them? I'll send out a detailed memo right after the meeting. The humans are violent! They lie, cheat, steal, assault, and kill each other. Their society could never subsist with our law enforcement procedure!"

His colleagues, now silent, were well aware of the procedure he referred to: The Interrogations. With the aid of portable lie detectors, Capton Police, at their own discretion, periodically and spontaneously questioned the citizens about their behaviors. When unlawfulness was uncovered, the offenses were relayed to the Governmental Council, who then determined the appropriate punishments—typically prison sentences of a decade or less. But imprisonment and crime in general were rare on Capton. Since the Ramponts overall were an ethically evolved species, the infrequent, randomized interviews were sufficient to keep order and peace.

Lithantor continued hotly, "Even with the human police constantly watching over the people, Earth's prisons are overflowing. How is getting so tight with the humans going to affect our continued moral development? I say, we'll start absorbing their negativity!"

Lively discussions erupted. All of the issues raised weighed heavily upon the hearts and minds of the Council members.

Bartholith gazed at his fellow colleagues. "Yes, there is a lot for us to consider. Earth visits and interactions with the humans are very complicated—more so than any of us realized. Our policies need changing. Until new, satisfactory rules are in place, all Ramponts will abstain from traveling to Earth," he pronounced.

Nixar was extremely disappointed, but he understood the reasoning behind the temporary restriction. He noticed Munin giving him a sideways glance, pointing his finger in a mock, stern warning.

Nixar smirked and nodded as if to say, "Yeah, yeah, I'll behave." But he knew he couldn't stay away from Julie for very long.

# CHAPTER FOUR

The Capton Governmental Council met three more times before confirming the new policy about the humans. Nixar was not at all pleased with the changes, but at least they had finally lifted the ban on visiting Earth. It had been nearly a month since he had last seen Julie, and he missed her terribly. It was maddening to think that he would not be able to talk with her ever again.

According to the new Non-Interaction Law, all Ramponts were forbidden to interact with the humans. While they were allowed to observe silently, they had to remain invisible and wear plugs in their auditory openings. These measures were meant to spare the humans the social stresses involved with seeing Ramponts and to shield the Ramponts from the negativity of human discourse. And the new law's corollary, the Educational Prioritization Standard, specified that Earth's landscapes, climate, animals, and plants were worthy of study, but human observations held little academic value. Worst of all, law transgressors would be sentenced to a year in prison.

Nixar's contempt of all of this notwithstanding, he was eager to go to Earth to check on Julie. Was she home? Or had she been forced into a mental ward like the Sphere had shown? He had to know. He inserted his auditory plugs, became invisible, and crossed his arms over his chest. Thinking intently of Julie's home on Earth, he instantly transported himself there.

He arrived in her kitchen. It was empty and quiet, but something on the counter near the phone caught his eye. He went over to take a closer look. It was a notice with letterhead from the Vernon Valley Psychiatric Hospital. He avidly scanned the paper for the pertinent information and read, "Patient Julie Abler: discharged," and, "lack of medical necessity for continued inpatient status." Grinning, he thrust his invisible fist into the air with revelry.

Practically strutting out of the kitchen, he began searching the house for his lovely Julie. He found her sitting on the den couch talking on the telephone, and his heart leaped in his chest. With red curls framing her face, she looked radiant in her form-fitting green jumpsuit. He watched her lips move as she spoke, but his auditory plugs blocked the melodic sound of her voice.

His smile faded as the harsh, restrictive new reality began settling in. He clenched his teeth, trying to fend off a mix of anger and despair. The Non-Interaction Law was an utter nightmare. His special bond with Julie, which had never had the chance to fully blossom, was now destroyed forever. Gone.

His only consolation was that she looked content and cozy sitting there chatting lightheartedly. Just seeing her at peace gave him a small bit of peace, too. Gazing at her with deep affection, he mentally bade her farewell. "Good-bye, my beautiful Julie. I wish you a joyful life. You deserve it. You are a kind human. Every time we talked, my day was brighter and my heart was happy. I will always remember you." His eyes brimmed with tears.

Feeling choked up, Nixar transported back to his private office on Capton and flopped down into the chair behind his desk. From all of their prior conversations, he knew that Julie genuinely cared about other people and tried to do right by them. She also cared about the Earth itself: environmental issues, conservation, recycling, and the like. It wasn't fair that people like her were lumped in together with the dregs of human society. The Non-Interaction Law didn't discriminate. *All* human discourse was dubbed "potentially immoral and dangerous." But that simply wasn't true, and he and Julie had to pay the price. He wondered if the extreme new law might, at some point down the road, cause more problems than it prevented. Or was he only wishing it was a mistake because of his personal bias?

Needing a break from his torrential emotions, he shifted his thoughts to more factual terrain: the Sphere. It had worked. It had been correct. Julie was released, but she had been admitted to the Vernon Valley Psychiatric Hospital, just as it had shown.

Nixar was so impressed that his spirits lifted a little. He resolved to tell Munin and the rest of the Council about the on-target forecast.

In the following weeks and months, the Council members experimented more with the Sphere, and shared more stories of its accurate predictions at the meetings. Everyone grew so excited about the new technology that they planned to expand its usage and produce many replicas from the prototype.

# A Brief Look Ahead to Autumn, 2032

# CHAPTER FIVE

Ned Chambers sat down by the television. The newscast that followed thrilled him. The disease was killing millions. Infected people traveling by train and air were spreading it to every state and to countries throughout the globe. Animals were dying in droves, too. Ominously, and with terror, the news anchor concluded, "The incubation time and potency of this influenza strain are unlike anything doctors have seen before. I'm sorry to say, everyone is at risk."

Feeling vindicated, Ned got up, walked outside, and looked up at the sky. Now he knew, undeniably, that both his father and God were proud of him. This mission was truly his calling; he would continue on with it until his final breath.

# Summer, 2021

# CHAPTER SIX

He was not wearing a helmet. Had he been, his life would have been immensely different, immeasurably better. But alas, when his bicycle was struck by the car, his head was totally unprotected as it slammed against the pavement. Seven-year-old Ned Chambers was knocked unconscious for several minutes from the impact.

To make matters worse, the driver of the car did nothing whatsoever to help. She was a teenager, high on drugs, who had taken the family car without permission. As she sped back home, hoping to return unnoticed by her parents, she rationalized that she'd barely brushed the young boy on the bicycle.

When he regained consciousness, groggy and dazed, Ned slowly got up onto wobbling, scraped legs. He noticed his arms were scraped up, too. He saw his bent bicycle lying on the ground nearby. It looked as if he'd crashed it.

"What the…" he murmured in bewilderment. He didn't remember crashing, but at the same time, he understood that he must have taken one heck of a fall. It was craziness. He'd ridden this section of Jet Street a lot and could easily handle its twists and turns. It was like the street had somehow changed itself and tricked him. Jet Street had become Freaky Street.

The side of his head was really, really hurting. He gingerly touched it and then looked at his hand. Seeing bright red blood on his fingers, he started crying.

Thankfully, his dad wasn't there to see it. His father was always saying that real men were strong and never cried, but Ned was unable to control the tears right now. So he couldn't go home just yet.

He didn't want to hang out on Freaky Street, either, so he walked, wheeling his dented bike next to him, toward the neighborhood creek, a few blocks from his house.

When he reached the water's edge, Ned rested his bike against some bushes. He sat down on a large rock and took off his sneakers and socks. First aid first.

He had learned about the importance of tending to bleeding cuts. A few times after his dad had been rough with him, his mom had balled up a cloth or some tissue paper and pressed it down on the cuts until the bleeding stopped.

Ned used his socks to repeat the technique on his head. It worked, but it took a very long time. He didn't bother with the scrapes on his arms and legs; they weren't bleeding as much. And he was getting impatient. He was more than ready for a dunk at this point.

He stuffed one sock into each sneaker, stripped down to his underwear, left his clothing on the rock, and went into the water. While wading, he softly cried again. It was so good to be alone, with no Dad there to scold him. The cool, gentle waves were starting to soothe him. He closed his pale blue eyes, held his breath, and dunked under, carefully fingering through his dark, bloodied hair. Surfacing for air, he began lightly rubbing the wounds on his knees and elbows to release the dirt.

Unfortunately, his quiet alone time was short lived.

Tim and Jack, two nine-year-olds from the neighborhood, were walking alongside the brook, hoping to find turtles, fish, or frogs. As they approached and saw Ned, Tim also spied the clothes and sneakers on a large rock a few yards ahead of them.

"Check it out, Jack," Tim said, heading toward Ned's belongings. He picked up Ned's dirt-stained shorts and T-shirt.

Jack picked up the sneakers. The socks were stowed so deeply inside that he didn't see the blood on them. "Ned's goin' home in his undies tonight!"

The two friends cackled voraciously.

"Hey, Neddy; these yours?" Tim taunted, waving the clothes in the air. Jack was slapping the sneakers against each other, eyeing for Ned's reaction.

"Come on! Put 'em down! Put 'em back! Come on!" Ned yelled. But as soon as he started toward the shore, the older boys bolted, still clutching his things. By the time he had gotten himself out of the water, the boys were out of sight.

Ned sat down on the rock where his clothes had been, leaned forward, and rested his forehead upon folded arms over his knees. He wondered if things could get any worse. His physical pain mixed with humiliation and anger. Hot tears streamed down his cheeks.

As he sat there, a frog hopped over by his feet and croaked loudly.

Ned winced, extremely irritated by the noise. It was grating. Caustic. Unbearable. With haste, he reached down, grabbed the frog with both hands, and squashed it.

It made a crunching sound. Slowly, he opened his fists and stared. It was a big, dead thing. Way bigger than flies and spiders, the only things he'd killed before. This was very different; weird was more like it. Why had the croaking been so annoying to him? Why had he squashed the frog that fast, without even thinking about it? And why had the killing felt good?

# CHAPTER SEVEN

It was dusk when Ned came out of the creek for the second time. He had cleaned off the frog guts from his hands and more of the blood and dirt from his head and body.

He figured the warm summer air should dry him off pretty well by the time he got home. Since he had no other option, he walked in his underwear, praying that none of the neighbors would be looking out their windows when he passed. He wheeled his bent bicycle next to him. It might still have been usable, but it was hard to tell, and Ned didn't want to risk having another fall.

He dreaded going home. It was going to be awful trying to explain the rough, mystery bike crash and what the bullies had done to him. Hopefully his dad wouldn't be drunk. That would only make everything worse. It always did.

Ned arrived at the house, laid his bike down on the lawn in the back-yard, and crept inside through the unlocked back door. Lacy, the family cat, slinked in with him. It occurred to him that if he could just sneak up to his room to put on some clothes, he could totally skip telling his parents about Tim and Jack. He made his way to the staircase and stepped up as quietly as possible.

"Neddy! There ya are!" Ned's mother, Delia, called out when he was just two stairs shy of the top. "Where're yer clothes?" she asked. "Oh my gosh! You're all scraped up!" She stood at the foot of the stairs, concernedly squinting her dark eyes up at him.

Standing next to her was Aunt Cora, his mom's older sister. She visited often, especially since she'd told them about Uncle Reed cleaning out their bank account and running off with his secretary. "Are you OK, Ned?" she asked in a high-pitched squeak.

"What's all this ruckus?" Ned's father, Thomas, came out of the kitchen and stood on Delia's other side. At six foot four with a stocky build; a dark, stubbly beard; and piercing dark eyes with thick, furrowed brows, he had a frightening appearance to Ned—and to everyone else. "What'n the hell happened ta you?" he bellowed.

"I was in the creek, and Tim and Jack took my clothes as a joke," Ned said, trying to sound light about it, though it burned him up inside to say aloud what they had done.

"You need to toughen up, boy. Looks to me like they was pickin' on you."

Ned felt tears beginning to sting his eyes, but he fought them back. His dad was disappointed in him. Again. He turned his head and huffed in frustration.

His most gruesome injury was in full view for the first time.

"Oh, dear Lord!" Delia exclaimed.

"We need to take care of that!" Cora urged.

They hurriedly climbed the stairs toward him, with Thomas following very slowly behind.

"Jeeze, they took yer clothes and they beat ya up," Thomas sneered.

"I got scraped when I fell off my bike! They didn't beat me up!" Ned practically shouted. He hated thinking or talking about that confusing fall, but his dad had to be corrected. Ned would not be thought a wimp for a fight that never happened.

"Fell off the bike, eh?" Thomas rubbed his beard.

"Yes!" Ned replied through gritted teeth as Delia and Cora brought him into the bathroom. They sat him down on the closed toilet seat while they soaped up some washcloths. Thomas remained in the hallway.

Ned winced when his mother started blotting his head. She asked, "Is this really hurtin' ya?"

Since his dad was still in earshot, and, in general, the more Ned whined the more his dad got upset, Ned thought he should try to ignore the searing pain. Eventually it would get better, whether he complained or not. "It's alright," he lied.

She continued blotting, and Cora busily soaped up Ned's knees and elbows. After they had thoroughly cleansed all the wounds, Delia got out ointment and bandages from the cabinet.

Cora watched Delia dab the salve on Ned's head, and her body stiffened. "Oh! The other week, I saw this medical documentary about a man whose head was slammed to the ground during a fight—and his wound looked just as bad as Ned's does." She squeezed her hands together tightly. "But afterward, he started getting really angry and aggressive, so his wife told their doctor about it. The doctor did some tests and found out that the man had a serious concussion of his temporal lobe."

"What's all this medical gobblety-goop?" Delia quipped impatiently.

"I'm just thinking you should keep an eye on Ned for a while, make sure he doesn't start acting out, doing bad things. On the show, they said that the temporal lobe is on the side of the head, and that's where the man and Ned got injured. If that lobe gets really damaged, the person's whole personality can change. The man in the show got violent, but they said that kind of injury could also cause hallucinations and even weird religious obsessions."

"Becomin' obsessed with the word wouldn't be so bad," Delia joked as she linked large bandages together to cover the head wound.

"I'm serious!" Cora shot back. "You really need to watch him, and you need to take him to the doctor."

"Neddy's always been a real fast healer. Whether it's cuts or sicknesses, he's back to himself in no time flat. Strong as an ox. He'll heal from this just fine, too." Delia's voice lowered. "And last year, Tom's company took the insurance away. We can't afford no doctors anymore."

Cora bit her lower lip and fastened a bandage to Ned's knee.

"But I'll watch him. I'll watch him. Neddy'll be fine. Strong as an ox. You'll see," Delia asserted confidently.

Ned was very pleased. He hadn't been all that interested in their conversation, but when his mom talked about his strength, that had caught his attention. At least she knew he wasn't a weakling. Maybe someday she could convince his father of that, too.

"I wish I could pay for Ned to see a doctor," Cora said. "But after what Reed did, I can barely pay my bills." She shook her head bitterly.

"I'm gonna take ya campin' with me," Thomas said. He had stepped in front of the bathroom doorway and was standing with his arms folded across his chest. His eyes were fixed on Ned. "You'll learn to be a man. We'll go as soon as the off-season starts, an' we can hunt."

Tensely, Ned nodded. His dad had never taken him out alone before. Maybe this was a good thing? But then again, there was a sternness in his father's voice that sounded as though the trip might be meant for punishment more than for fun. Ned didn't know whether to feel happy or frightened.

# Autumn, 2021

# CHAPTER EIGHT

Infants were born a foot long and grew into six-foot-tall adults. Aside from their difference in size, young and old Ramponts on Capton looked the same.

Three-year-old Stanlin was no exception. His faint, blue body was airy, but not transparent. He was completely hairless. His head was egg-shaped, tapering at the chin, and his oblong eyes were large and dark. He had a small, human-looking nose and mouth and tiny auditory openings where human ears would have been. His physiological systems, slender torso, arms and hands, and legs and feet also roughly paralleled a human's.

His intellect was not so similar to a human's—it was far superior. All Ramponts were exceedingly smart. Stanlin could already speak and read Paritam fluently and grasp complex concepts.

Now, he was sitting up in his bed, eagerly waiting for his parents. It had been a fun day. He and his mom had picked and eaten fresh fruit from the family garden and had taken a walk together afterward. His dad had been at work, but he would come in for the nightly reading ritual in a minute.

Stanlin reached down and grabbed the Rampont Reader off the floor near his bed and plopped it into his lap with a big grin on his face. The Reader was a one-foot square white box with a round hole, about the size of Stanlin's fist, in its center. Cylinders with all different types of literature could be inserted into that small hole. With a cylinder in place, the Reader produced a hologram of one sentence at a time, directly in front of itself, for the Rampont to view. It could also read the sentences aloud, if the viewer asked it to. Stanlin never did. He always wanted to read the words aloud himself. His parents liked him to read aloud too, so that's what they always did. The night before, they'd read a wonderful fantasy story. Tonight, they would begin something new. He tingled with anticipation.

"My sweet boy," his mother, Karilu, cooed, breezing in and sitting next to him. She softly smoothed her hand down his back. "Tonight, we'll start reading from Capton's oldest and most famous work of literature. How does that sound?"

"Great! Great! Great!" Stanlin bounced up and down.

"Hey," his father, Andrigon, said, striding in merrily with a cylinder in his fist. He affectionately tapped Stanlin's knee, and sat down on Stanlin's other side. His gaze grew serious. "Our reading tonight is very special. It's different from what we've read before. It's not a story, and it's not a description of facts."

Stanlin's eyes widened. "Mom said it's old and famous."

His voice infused with respect, Andrigon said, "It's called, *Captonian Wisdom*." With deliberate care, he handed the cylinder to Stanlin.

Stanlin looked at the cylinder and then up at his father. "If the literature isn't facts, how can it give us wisdom?"

"The wisdom comes from the words and the decrees of The Highest Authority," Andrigon explained.

Stanlin's parents had already taught him that The Highest Authority was the one in charge of the entire universe. "*He* put *His* wisdom into that cylinder for *us*?" Stanlin asked incredulously.

Karilu smiled. "Not exactly. Long ago, some of the earliest Ramponts received the decrees from Him. They verbally passed on those messages over and over again through the years. Once the Rampont Readers were invented, the messages were encoded in cylinders."

"That means Grandma and Grandpa learned about this, too, right? And so did their parents and grandparents?" Stanlin inquired with vim.

"Oh yes, and on back for over ten thousand years, from what Capton's scientists can estimate," Karilu said.

"Who knows? All of our ancestors might be looking down on the three of us with this right now." Andrigon pointed at the cylinder in Stanlin's hand, glanced upward, and then looked at Stanlin. "Remember how we told you that Rampont spirits live on, even after our Rampont bodies die?"

"Yes," said Stanlin.

"Well, that's just one of the hundreds of great lessons from *Captonian Wisdom*." Andrigon tapped the Rampont Reader lying in Stanlin's lap. "Are you ready?"

"Yes! Yes! Yes!" Stanlin inserted the cylinder and began reading. "Chapter One: Special Decrees. The Highest Authority has informed us of several important guidelines, which He designated as decrees. If we follow these decrees, we will live in His favor. If we do not, The Highest Authority will be displeased, and it will impact His Life Records for us.

"Decree Number One: Free Will. All creatures of the universe are meant to make their own choices in life and must learn from the consequences of those choices. Entities are not to command the course of anyone else's life but their own. Decree Number Two..."

Karilu's hand covered the hologrammed words. "Whoa! Hold on there, speedy. Your father and I want to discuss every decree with you."

"Reread the first decree, think it through, and tell us what ideas or questions it brings up for you," Andrigon instructed.

Stanlin was very glad that his parents liked it when he asked questions. Questioning was something he was good at; even at his young age, he was aware of this. Giving answers was another story. Explaining stuff was always tougher for him.

After he read the Free Will Decree aloud a second time and paused for a minute of contemplation, he asked, "What about giving advice? Is that the same as telling others what to do with their lives?"

"I'd say, giving advice is not the same as commanding others, but I still don't think it's a good habit to start," Andrigon answered. His eyes shifted from Stanlin to Karilu. "What do you think?"

"I wouldn't start the habit either," she said. "Advising can sometimes lead to pressuring, or worse, controlling. It can be a fine line, and when it comes to obeying The Highest Authority, we don't want to take any chances."

"What if you're advising someone to try to help them?" Stanlin pressed.

"You probably wouldn't anger The Highest Authority with that. Although I think He would prefer if you listed some different options and then asked the other what they thought they should do," Andrigon speculated.

"Yes. If you inspire others to think for themselves, you'll be abiding by the first decree every time," Karilu said, smoothing her hand down Stanlin's back again.

Andrigon gazed at him proudly. "What else is on your mind?"

Stanlin reflected on the decrees more broadly and asked, "Since The Highest Authority controls the whole universe, does He give His decrees to everyone on every planet?"

Karilu and Andrigon looked at each other blankly—and then at Stanlin with awe.

"That's a very creative question, honey," Karilu said softly.

All three of them were pensive for several seconds before Andrigon spoke. "We have been visiting and interacting with beings on other planets for two decades. There are thousands of cylinders describing the different cultures. Maybe some of them mention whether The Highest Authority has communicated with, or has given decrees to, the other beings."

"Uh-huh." Karilu nodded at Andrigon. To Stanlin, she said, "In school next year, you'll be reading many of those cylinders. I imagine you will find out who else has communed with The Highest Authority, and much, much more. When your father and I were students, there hadn't been as many interactive visits yet, so there weren't as many resources as today. You'll get to learn all about other planets and their inhabitants. Even better, you'll be visiting them, and sometimes interacting with them yourself."

"Wow!" Stanlin exclaimed, bouncing up and down. He felt like he could burst from joy. He'd known the universe was filled with other planets and beings, but he hadn't known that his schooling would teach him so much about their lives and take him out to meet them. Were some beings out there anything like him? If yes, how? Or how were they different? What inventions did they make? What did they do for fun? What did they read? And, of course, did they read from and obey The Highest Authority?

Stanlin gratefully peered down at the Reader in his lap with the most special cylinder inside it. After reading and talking about only the first decree, he was already more excited than ever to learn about all the life in the universe. *Captonian Wisdom*—it was extraordinary! He brought the Reader to his chest and hugged it.

# CHAPTER NINE

Earlier in the day, Thomas and Ned had been to the shooting range together. Now they were several hours from home at a huge state park with trails, campgrounds, and specified hunting areas, and they had just finished setting up their tent.

"Whoowee," Thomas sighed as he sat down at the picnic table on their camping plot.

Ned sat across from him.

"Go an' get that cooler from the car and bring it here, will ya?"

Ned did as he was told and sat back down.

Removing the lid from the cooler, Thomas said, "It's good you been stickin' up for yerself at school lately."

"Yeah," Ned agreed. He had picked four fights over the last few weeks. His dad had assumed that Ned was only defending himself each time. Ned hadn't clarified the truth; the few snippets of praise he'd been receiving from his father were too precious to chance losing.

"You did alright at that shootin' range, too," Thomas continued. "Holdin' yer own at school, shootin', campin', and we'll be huntin' our dinner tonight. You're really becomin' a man, son."

Ned beamed.

"Let's celebrate with some brewskies." Thomas retrieved two Budweiser cans from the cooler and cracked them open.

Ned didn't like that his father got angry and pushed him around some-times when he had been drinking this stuff. But maybe, if he had some of it with his dad, it would be different. His dad was smiling now, which Ned didn't see very often. So he took one of the cans and drank from it, while his father drank from the other.

"Ha! There ya go! Whaddaya think'a that?"

Ned thought the flavor was gross, but, trying to please his father, he fibbed, "It's good."

"Ha!" Thomas chortled and reached across the table to slap Ned's shoulder affectionately.

Ned glowed.

Thomas reached into his shirt pocket, took out his cigarettes and light-er, lit a cigarette for himself, and offered one to Ned.

Again, Ned tried to partake, but he coughed every time he took a puff. Smoking wasn't as easy as it looked. He grunted in frustration.

"You'll try 'em again another time," Thomas said, laughing lightly.

Ned tossed the cigarette under the table and stamped out the ember. Determined to make more headway with the beer, he managed to drink a quarter of the can. Whenever his dad was watching, Ned forced down a few horrid sips, but each time his dad's head tipped backward to take a gulp, Ned quietly poured some out into a small bush behind him. Finally, his can was empty. He clanged it down on the table, breathing, "Ahhh."

"Good job!" Thomas praised, finishing the last swig of his third beer. He got a plastic bag from the car, gathered the four empty cans, and put them into the bag. "Come on with me." He led Ned a few dozen yards from their campsite and tossed the plastic bag into a large metal bin. "Ya see? Ya put the food and drink trash in here and close up the lid. Then the bears can't smell it."

Ned nodded. They walked back to their plot.

"Now, we're gonna hunt us some dinner!" Thomas said excitedly, getting his rifle from the trunk. "I'll show ya how it's done. Come on."

As Ned followed his father into the hunting section of the woods, he thought that this day was turning out to be one of his favorites—ever.

# CHAPTER TEN

Nearly an hour had passed. They were still looking for deer, but having no luck.

"I'm hungry," Ned whined.

"Ya think I'm not?" Thomas snapped.

Suddenly, they both heard something rustle in the bushes across from them. Thomas aimed the rifle and shot, and they heard something fall. They hurried over to investigate their prey.

"It's a fox, Dad!"

"Dammit!" Thomas gripped his stubbly chin with his fingers and paced back and forth. He groaned, "Hmmm," and paced some more. At last, he resignedly grumbled, "I'm sure they eat this in some parts. It ain't like we're findin' much else. Let's bring it back."

They were weak with hunger, and it was a long walk, but together they carried the fox. With his rifle under one arm, Thomas held the animal's rear while Ned supported its front end.

When they arrived at their campsite, they set down their conquest, and Thomas stored the rifle in the trunk of the car. He got out his knives, two large plates, paper towels, and some plastic bags and set them on the picnic table. "Now watch me real close," he said. He showed Ned how to skin the fox and how to separate out the edible parts from the scraps. Carefully, he laid the good cuts of meat onto the plates. He discarded all the scraps and used paper towels, bloodied from wiping his hands and the knives, into the plastic bags.

Ned wondered why he didn't feel sad, seeing an animal being cut up like this. But all he felt was fascination. He guessed it was because he was learning how to be a real man.

When Thomas finished preparing the meat, he reached into the back pocket of his jeans, retrieved a pocket knife, and handed it to Ned. "You watched real close, just like I said, so that's fer you. Next time we hunt, you'll use it an' help with the cuttin'."

"Th-thanks," Ned stammered. The mention of a future trip was as shocking as the gift. He practiced opening and closing the knife several times before gratefully storing it in his own back pocket.

Thomas placed the plates of edible, carved meat in the center of the picnic table and eyed them with obvious satisfaction. "See that? Not half bad."

"Yeah," Ned agreed.

"Now take the scrap bags to that trash I showed ya."

Ned discarded the bags and returned.

"We've gotta gather us some wood to cook over. Go an' get us some sticks. Put the little ones in the fire pit an' the big ones next to the pit fer later," Thomas instructed.

Ned happily obliged.

Thomas retrieved some utensils and extra plates from the car and set them on the table. Then he walked to the pit and oversaw Ned gathering sticks for a while. "OK, that's enough," he said eventually. "Now I'll show ya how we cook our meat." Thomas took out his lighter from his pocket, aimed it at the kindling in the fire pit, and flicked it. He flicked the lighter again and again. And again. "Dammit! This is the only one I got with me. Shit!"

Ned squirmed warily, hoping he wasn't going to get slapped or shoved.

Thomas tried over and over again to use the lighter, but it wouldn't work. "Ah, hell!" he yelled at last in complete frustration. He threw the lighter into the woods and banged his fists down hard on the picnic table. The plates piled with meat tottered, and the utensils and empty plates rattled loudly. Thomas paced hotly, muttering profanities.

Ned watched him with wide eyes, expecting his father's anger to keep getting worse, as it usually did. But to his surprise, the opposite seemed to be happening. After a few minutes, his dad appeared to be calming and thinking something over.

Thomas suddenly reached for one of the slabs of raw meat, brought it to his mouth, and took a bite. His face twisted a bit but quickly recovered. "It ain't that bad. In some parts, they don't cook their meat. It's all we got, kid."

Hugely relieved that it looked like he wasn't going to get hit, Ned snatched up a piece of the meat and sunk his teeth into it. As he chewed, his face scrunched a little, too. It tasted sort of tangy. But, like his dad had said, it wasn't that bad. Better than the beer, anyway. "Mmmm," he exaggerated, hoping to impress.

It worked.

"Yeah, yeah, it ain't so bad. Now we're real men a' the woods, eatin' our meat raw," Thomas said, smiling.

Ned smiled back. It was rare for his dad to smile, but he'd also smiled when they'd shared the beers. Plus, his dad had complimented him and given him that pocket knife. Compliments and gifts were even rarer than smiles. Today, his father seemed—dare he think it—kind of *happy?* Slightly—was it possible—*proud?*

Yes, this was definitely Ned's most favorite day.

# CHAPTER ELEVEN

Robert and Brenna had eaten dinner and had just perused the dessert menus when their heavyset waitress returned to the table. "Anything tempting you two tonight? The fudge frenzy torte is to die for."

"It looks like you've had way too many of those," Robert snickered cruelly, eyeing the waitress' protruding belly. "I'll opt for the peach sorbet instead." He patted his stomach and boasted, "You don't get abs like these eating fudge tortes."

The waitress' face turned red and her jaw visibly tensed, yet she forced a weak smile.

Brenna's countenance mirrored the waitress', except for the smile. With disgust, she said to Robert, "You're a creep."

"I was just joking around. Lighten up, will you?" he shot back irritably.

She was done. No second date for Robert. She didn't expect perfection from a potential partner, but kindness was a nonnegotiable requirement. Loneliness could plague her until kingdom come; she still wouldn't latch on to someone heartless.

To the waitress, she said, "I'm leaving now. I'll pay you for my meal. Hold on." She fished in her purse.

In truth, she preferred the old fashioned way; it made her feel more like a lady to be treated by a man. Right now, though, she was so repulsed by Robert that being receptive toward him in any form was out of the question.

His hot glare was burning into her. "Did you forget I drove you here?" he sneered.

She had. Her breath caught in her chest. Robert was her neighbor's cousin. She'd thought it would be fine to ride with him, that it would add a chivalrous flair to their date to be picked up and dropped off at her doorstep.

"There's a bus stop on the corner if you take a right out the front door," her instant ally offered.

Brenna and the waitress shared a look of mutual gratitude.

"Sounds good. Thank you." She handed the woman enough cash to cover her meal, the tax, and a generous tip. Getting up from her chair, Brenna curtly said, "Robert," as her only departing word to him.

"Safe home, dear," said the waitress.

"Thank you. Have a good night," Brenna replied. Making her way out the door and to the bus stop, she wondered if she would ever find her Mr. Right. The adage, "Nice guys finish last," was totally untrue for her. She'd had a wonderfully sweet high school beau, and an equally great college boyfriend. Both had been attentive and caring. Both had deservedly won her love. Coincidentally and very unfortunately, neither had wanted children. And to Brenna, motherhood was a dream she couldn't forfeit. So neither of her school-day loves could become her husband.

Now, at twenty-five years old, she seemed to attract only insensitive, arrogant clods. It was as if she'd been wearing a Mr. Obnoxious magnet around her neck ever since college graduation. She knew there were good men here in Perth, Australia, so why wasn't she meeting them anymore? Discouraged, she gazed ahead vaguely at the passing cars on the street.

Minutes later, a bus pulled up. It was east bound, and she needed to go west. Thankfully, a second bus followed shortly thereafter, and its route had a stop near her home. As she boarded and settled into a window seat, she was reminded of one of her mother's comforting sayings: "Men are like buses. If you miss one, there's always another one coming."

# CHAPTER TWELVE

It had been almost a month since their camping trip, and Ned thought his dad was still being nicer to him these days. The pain in his head from the bike fall this summer had been easing up too, so Ned felt content as he sat in the grass in his backyard, playing his new game.

Since observing the way his dad had hunted and skinned the fox, Ned had been practicing the techniques on squirrels. He would seek them out and shoot them as many times as it took with his pellet gun. Then he'd use his pocket knife to do the skinning.

To keep the game a secret, he'd been burying them along with the bloody paper towels he used to wipe the knife and his hands. Ned could hardly wait to surprise his father with his skills this weekend, on their second camping and hunting adventure.

Ned was about to bury that day's squirrel when he heard his mother scream from inside the house. He dropped the squirrel into the hole he'd already dug, quickly wiped his hands and the knife on the paper towel he'd brought out with him, put the crumpled towel on top of the squirrel, and hastily pushed the adjacent pile of loose dirt over everything. Closing his knife and stuffing it into his back pocket, he sprinted inside to find his mom.

She was in the den on the phone, her back toward him. She muttered something he couldn't hear, hung up, and called someone else right away.

"Cora, come over now. I really need ya. I'll tell ya when ya get here." Her voice sounded shaky and sad.

"What's wrong?" Ned asked nervously once she'd hung up.

She turned around and looked at him with red, glassy eyes. She was barely able to speak. "Yer gonna hafta find out…Oh God." She sniffled and sighed. "It's yer dad, Neddy." She sniffled again. "The hospital called. Yer dad was drinkin', an' he was comin' home from the bar, an' an'." She grabbed a tissue from the box on the end table and blew her nose. "He crashed the car. Hit a pole…Doctors think he must've swerved away from somethin' or dozed asleep for a sec…" Her voice cracked. Sobbing, she fell to her knees and pulled Ned to her chest.

They hugged for a long while. His mother's sadness transferred through to him, and Ned cried too. But a large part of him could not believe this was real.

The doorbell rang, startling both of them.

"Lemme get that, Neddy," Delia said, getting up. She walked to the foyer, peered through the peephole, and opened the front door. "Oh, Cora," she wailed, flinging her arms around her sister.

"Whatever it is, I'm here," Cora assured soothingly.

Breathing in gasps, Delia led Cora to the den and tearfully told her what had happened. Cora listened with tears running down her cheeks. She offered to help in any way she could, including driving Delia and Ned anywhere, anytime, until their family's one and only car was repaired.

As Ned listened to the two of them going on about his dad being dead, Lacy entered the room and lazily wandered past him. He glared at her. His world was coming apart, and here was the cat, perfectly happy-go-lucky. Suddenly overcome with rage, Ned lunged forward and clutched Lacy's neck. For a fraction of a second, a small inner voice said, "No, don't," but he didn't listen. He squeezed with both hands until he'd strangled her to death. Momentarily, his hot anger lessened, and a strange feeling of release replaced it. Ned stood there holding his dead pet, trying to absorb the new sensation.

Cora screamed, pointing at him.

Delia whirled around to see what her sister was reacting to. Initially, she gaped and gasped, but the look in her eyes changed quickly. It became—if Ned had to describe it—tough. Marching over, she scooped the lifeless cat from his hands and took it into the kitchen.

Ned and Cora followed her. Delia dropped Lacy's body into the garbage can like it was any other piece of trash. Without a word, she returned to the den, with Cora and Ned still following.

Cora stared at her, open-mouthed. "What he just did…Don't you care?"

"His dad died! Don't look at neither of us like that! His daddy died today, Cora!"

Cora turned to Ned. "I need to speak privately with your mother. Please go up to your room."

Still half dazed from everything that was going on, Ned did as he was told, but he sat right near his doorway, so he could hear their conversation. And when he leaned forward and poked his head out, he could peek down the stairs at them.

"Delia, you can't ignore this. He strangled Lacy! I know he's totally upset right now, but that's not a normal way for a child to express…"

"Ain't nothin' normal today!" Delia sharply cut in.

"I know; I know," Cora said. She hugged Delia for a moment and then stepped back, looking at her sister closely, face to face. "I'm bringing this up because I'm really worried about Ned. I wasn't sure if the fights at school meant anything, but now, seeing him kill Lacy, I think he must have suffered some brain damage with that fall this summer. We're seeing violence! We need to take him to the doctor. Somehow, we'll find a way to pay for it."

"What about the chromosome thing?" Delia asked. "When Ned was first born, the doctors said he might get rough growin' up 'cause of the chromosome thing."

"No. Even though XYY syndrome can make him more prone to aggression…"

"Ya see!" Delia interrupted triumphantly.

"Not this much aggression!"

"Y'ain't no doctor! Stop actin' like y'are!"

Cora bit her lower lip, put her hands on her hips, and was quiet for a couple of seconds before speaking again more calmly. "You're right. I'm no doctor. All I'm saying is you have Ned checked. Together, we'll figure out how to get the money for it. Please."

"Money, money, money. Always needin' more money." Delia made a low, whimpering sound. "I don't even know how I'm gonna afford ta b-bury T-Tom," she stammered, bursting into tears.

Cora hugged her again. "Shhh. I'm so sorry. Shhh."

Still sitting by his doorway, Ned wondered what it meant to have some kroomsoom thing. He knew nothing about kroomsooms. He'd also heard Aunt Cora say she thought he might have damaged his brain when he'd hit his head that summer, and that it might have been why he'd killed the cat. But wasn't brain damage drooling, and not talking right, and sometimes not being able to move? Aunt Cora must have gotten things wrong. Like Mom said, Aunt Cora was no doctor.

But why was Aunt Cora so bothered that he'd killed the cat anyway? Why was killing a cat so different than hunting? He and his dad had hunted and killed a fox together, and it was manly. Ned's eyes filled with tears. Hunting. Camping. With his dad. There would be no more of that. Ever. Just when his dad was starting to love him...

Overwhelmed at the unfairness, Ned bawled, hugging his knees to his chest. Before long, he was punching his mattress. Once he'd winded himself from that, he prayed to God to erase this day and let him wake up in the morning with his dad still alive.

His prayer caused something unexpected: a memory of church. Though his family had only been there a handful of times, he just now remembered the pastor saying, "God takes those that die to be with Him." But why would God take away his dad so soon? Why did God need his father when both Ned and his mom still really needed him? Ned was confused and enraged.

Days later, at the conclusion of the funeral service, Ned stormed over to Pastor Jensen and demanded, "Why did God take my dad away from me?"

The pastor said a lot in response, but to Ned, the main message was, "God has Masterful Plans. Our minds are no match for His. We are not able to understand His Grand Plans."

Then and there Ned decided to become the very first person to figure out God's Plans, even if it took him his entire life to do it.

# Spring, 2030

# CHAPTER THIRTEEN

"I can't wait!" Stanlin whispered.

"Me either!" Corimo replied.

"You should all be very proud of yourselves for passing your intergalactic exams," said Bewexin, their teacher for Travel Excursions. "I know how much you've all been looking forward to this day, finally seeing a planet beyond Andromeda."

The ten Rampont students in the class were agog and grinning.

"A special honor will go to the student with the highest mark on his exam. Corimo, you get to choose which planet we'll visit today."

Stanlin inwardly cringed. Corimo was his best friend, but it was frustrating that he got the best grades all the time. No matter how many hours Stanlin studied, he could never get the marks Corimo got. Worse yet, Corimo barely studied.

"I want to go to Earth in the Milky Way Galaxy!" Corimo announced.

The other students cheered excitedly.

Stanlin exclaimed, "Superbly super!" Even if Corimo was almost sickeningly smart, he was also totally cool. From their class readings, Earth sounded wonderfully complicated. So many kinds of plants and animals, and those wild-looking humans with all their different hair, eye, and skin colors. This was going to be outrageous!

"What special, small things must be brought along with us and used on Earth?" Bewexin quizzed.

Corimo and two other students raised their hands.

"You must give an explanation with your answer," Bewexin qualified.

The other two hands slinked downward, and Bewexin nodded at Corimo.

"We need to bring along and insert plugs into our auditory openings. The Non-Interaction Law says that the humans aren't very morally evolved, so we're not allowed to hear them talking to each other; it could be a bad influence on us," Corimo answered.

"Correct. And it is wise to travel with your auditory plugs in your pocket. In the off chance something unusual happens during transport, you'll want to be able to hear," Bewexin explained.

Everyone was wearing the Capton fashion standard: a one-piece, smock-like, black unisex garment with a front pocket centered at the chest. Bewexin weaved between his students, verifying that their plugs were all properly stowed. "Very good," he murmured, satisfied with his check. "Now, what else must be done when visiting Earth that is specified in the Non-Interaction Law?"

Again, Corimo's hand shot up, but Liron raised her hand nearly as fast, and she was called upon.

"We need to hide ourselves by going invisibly. The humans don't communicate with the rest of the universe, so they get all freaked out by seeing what they call 'aliens.' And we don't want to cause any upsets or problems with our travels," Liron said confidently.

"Right, you are!" Bewexin praised.

"Is Earth the only planet where we have to be invisible?" Remsando asked.

Bewexin pointed approvingly at him. "A fine question, Remsando, with a complex answer. First off, there's a difference if we go anywhere as a group versus if you were to go alone, when you're of age. For all of our class trips so far, we've gone visibly to specific planets where the Governmental Council had previously received permission from the planetary leaders. For Earth, and for any other planets where we don't have such express permission, our class will need to go invisibly, so we don't unintentionally threaten the inhabitants. Just imagine a group of strange beings we'd never seen before, showing up on Capton out of nowhere!"

Some of the students chuckled.

"However, when you're old enough for solo trips, as long as you approach only one being privately, you may travel visibly, anywhere. Planet Earth is the one exception. Even when you go there alone, you'll need to be invisible because of the Non-Interaction Law. Liron and Corimo explained the reasoning very well."

Corimo and Liron smiled shyly at each other for a moment before snapping their eyes back to Bewexin.

"OK. One more quiz before we go. What is the best way for me to teach you on Earth that won't disturb any of the life there, meaning plants, insects, animals, or the humans?"

Corimo raised his hand, but so did Stanlin. The teacher called on Stanlin.

"You can talk to us with telepathy speech."

"Good! Briefly review for the class how that works."

Stanlin hesitated. He knew exactly what telepathy speech was, but trying to describe it succinctly was stumping him. He was quiet for several long seconds, and he felt everyone's eyes staring at him. This was just the kind of thing that happened to him during oral examinations and prevented him from excelling.

With a concerned expression, Corimo glanced at Stanlin. Turning to Bewexin, he said, "If we focus our minds and think, 'I'm listening, Bewexin,' we'll tune into your thoughts about the lesson, just like tuning into a radio station, but it'll play in our heads. It works if our auditory plugs are in or not, and the humans and animals and everything won't hear you."

"Precisely," acknowledged Bewexin.

Stanlin felt relieved that Corimo had rescued him from the embarrassing silence. Yet he was irritated at himself for having fallen into a braindead stupor and was annoyed that Corimo, as always, could explain things so effortlessly.

"Other than going invisibly, we will be transporting to Earth in the same way we have to the planets within Andromeda: crossing our arms over our chests while focusing on a particular destination on the planet," Bewexin instructed. "As you all know from your studies, Earth has spectacular plant life. One of the prettiest bushes I've found so far is behind the Secard Elementary-Middle School. You'll hardly believe how lovely the forsythia flowers are! In just a moment, each of you will be focusing on planet Earth and the grounds behind the Secard Elementary-Middle School. Are there any last questions?"

There were none. Everyone was eager to go.

"Alright then. Become invisible, cross your arms over your chests, and think of our destination."

The students did as their teacher instructed, and they all transported to Earth.

# CHAPTER FOURTEEN

Bewexin and the ten students arrived safely behind the school, as planned. They stood just outside a fence enclosing the recess yard. A large forsythia bush lined the outside of the fence, and a few flowerless shrubs lined the inside. In the distance, within the yard and closer to the school building, children played.

The Capton Governmental Council permitted scholastic instructors to bend the rules occasionally for heightened education, if the students' safety was assured, and Bewexin capitalized on the privilege.

Telepathically, he said to the class, "Since the human children are too far away for us to hear their discourse, it's safe to wait to insert our auditory plugs. I'll let you know if or when we'll need to put them in. The reason I'm doing this is to give you all a special treat. Now you'll be able to hear the sounds of animals, insects, and the wind while we learn about this gorgeous specimen." Bewexin walked over to his favorite plant and touched one of the flowers. "Gather in closely now, so you can see these vibrantly yellow blossoms."

His instructions were not easy for the students to follow. While light touches or rubs against one another felt fine, if their semi-solid forms actually overlapped, an intense, uncomfortable pressure resulted. As they tried to crowd in closer to the blooming bush, the students began colliding, inadvertently overlapping their forms. They maneuvered impatiently for a while, each attempting to stake out a prime viewing spot without encroaching on anyone else.

The combined movements of Stanlin's peers shifted him to the outermost border of the group. He was irked, until he saw someone who was only visible from his unique, outlying position. A human girl sat in the grass behind one of the bushes just inside the fence, secluding herself from the other human children. She was crying—and she was breathtakingly beautiful.

Stanlin stared at her, captivated; he simply couldn't help it. Her tearful eyes were a deep green, her nose was slender, and she had thick, fluffy, long auburn hair. There was an air of kindness about her, too. He'd never seen anyone look as sweet and as stunningly attractive as this sad little human girl.

As he stood there, watching her weep, Stanlin thought, "I wonder why you're crying. I wish I could listen to *your* thoughts."

Immediately, a young female voice came into his mind: "Sherry's so mean. Who cares if I'm bad in gym? Why does she have to make fun of me all the time? I wish I didn't have to come to school."

Stanlin's eyes all but popped from their sockets. Were those *her* thoughts?

"Ohhh!" Liron, standing next to him, was impressed with something about the bush. Stanlin realized he'd been missing the teacher's lesson while he was focusing on the girl. He forced himself to tune back in with the rest of the class. "I'm listening, Bewexin," he thought.

In his head, he heard Bewexin's voice: "The forsythia bush is similar in cellular makeup to the..."

Testing things out, he thought, "I'm listening, pretty girl."

The young female voice returned: "Karen's my only real friend," he heard. "She still talks to me, even though the other girls are afraid to. They all think Sherry will make fun of them too if they hang out with me. I'm so glad I've got Karen."

"Wow," Stanlin unwittingly murmured.

He'd proven it. He could telepathically tune into this girl's thoughts! She was a thousand times more fascinating than the horticulture lesson.

Unfortunately, he knew he could not ignore the class, though, or else he might miss the joint transportation back to Capton. Focusing again on Bewexin, he heard, "As the final part of the lesson, we'll examine the bumblebees here in the flowers."

Darn, darn, darn! With the lesson coming to a close, he would have to keep paying attention to the teacher from now on. Maybe the class would visit Earth again. Maybe he could get Corimo and the other kids to help him persuade Bewexin to take them back to learn more about "the lovely forsythia bush."

It was tough being only twelve, always at the mercy of the teachers' decisions. In two years, when he turned fourteen, he could register to travel freely on his own, to any planets he wanted, to continue his studies. But not now. Now, he'd have to somehow finagle another class visit to the Secard Elementary-Middle School, to see the beautiful girl again.

# CHAPTER FIFTEEN

The day after their class trip to Earth, Corimo and Stanlin walked to school together.

"Wasn't yesterday's trip awesome?" Corimo asked.

"It was superbly super!" Stanlin heartily concurred.

"Those flowers were nice looking and smelled good, like Bewexin said, but my favorite part was when that spider thing crawled so fast in and out of that one flower."

Stanlin had completely missed that but faked his agreement. "Oh, yeah! Yeah, that was cool."

"I also liked hearing those bumblebees buzzing, but that spider was the best. I wish our class could go back to Earth again, but I know we can't."

Stanlin's heart skipped a beat. "Whadaya mean?" he asked anxiously.

"Didn't you read the syllabus?"

Stanlin shook his head.

"It says that every week, we'll go to a *different* planet."

"Oh," Stanlin muttered, crestfallen. He did not want to wait two more years to see that girl again. It had only been one day, and already he'd been thinking about her more than he'd thought about any girl before. But what could he do, given that he wasn't allowed to transport alone until he was fourteen? He wondered if he should try to do it anyway. He knew perfectly well how to get to Earth. That rule to be fourteen didn't make much sense. What would be the harm in going alone sooner? And, if he did go, how would anyone find out?

Stanlin decided he would attempt it, right after school. Naturally, from that point forward, the day dragged on—and on. Finally, when his last class finished, he ran out of the school building and all the way home. He breezed into the house and into his room, put his scholastic cylinders on the floor near his Rampont Reader, and called, "I'm going outside to play, Mom. I'll be in by dinner time."

"Alright," Karilu answered. She was preparing food in the gathering room, which, on Capton, was a kitchen blended with a living room.

Stanlin dashed into the backyard to his favorite spot by the garden. He became invisible, crossed his arms over his chest, and concentrated on planet Earth, behind the Secard Elementary-Middle School. A moment later, he arrived by the familiar forsythia bush.

Just like Bewexin had held off on having them insert the auditory plugs yesterday, Stanlin deferred inserting them now, leaving them in his front pocket. An inner feeling told him he might hear something important.

The children were not in the recess yard. He started contemplating how he might get inside the building to search for the girl. He could see one very large door, but he knew from his studies that he wasn't as physically dense as the humans, so he might not be strong enough to open it. And even if he could open it, he wouldn't want to frighten any humans who might see the door appearing to open all by itself. Maybe he'd be better off transporting himself again, this time focusing on the inside of the school building as his destination.

His thoughts were interrupted by a very loud ringing sound. Then he heard children's voices in the distance that sounded like they were coming from the front of the school. He went around to investigate and saw children streaming out of the building. School was obviously letting out for the day.

While scanning the exiting girls, looking for the one with the fluffy auburn hair and green eyes, he thought, "I'm listening, pretty girl from yesterday."

In his head, he heard, "'Sylvia sucks; Sylvia sucks.' She keeps saying that! If I say something back, what if she just gets mad and says it more?"

"Her name must be Sylvia," Stanlin thought triumphantly, and he remembered from her thoughts yesterday that someone named Karen was her only friend. He continued scanning the faces of the girls leaving the school building and also started listening for the names Sylvia and Karen.

Seconds later, he heard a girl's voice call, "Sylvia, wait up!" and he figured it had to be Karen. He looked in the direction of the voice. A girl with dark, curly hair was running toward the beautiful girl...*Sylvia.*

They greeted each other, and Karen asked, "Can you come over today? We got a new cat this weekend. His name's Simon. He's so cute and fun to play with. You wanna come an' meet him?"

"Yeah, that'd be great!"

Stanlin noticed Sylvia smiling and her posture straightening up as she replied.

"Cool. Just walk home with me. We'll call your mom from my place."

Sylvia and Karen continued walking together, with Stanlin invisibly following. When they arrived at Karen's home, the girls were barely inside for a minute. They tossed their backpacks onto the couch, and Karen scooped up a furry little animal who had been sprawled on the couch's armrest.

"Mom, we're taking Simon outside," Karen whispered.

Her mother nodded. Although she had let the girls in and waved hello to them, she wore a headset and was talking into it.

The girls brought Simon into the backyard and began petting and playing with him in the grass. Stanlin stood next to them, observing everything. There was a lot to take in. He found the cat creature highly interesting, with its whiskers, full-body hair, four legs, retractable claws, and agile maneuvering. Plus, he thoroughly enjoyed seeing the smiles and laughter the cat elicited from the girls. They stroked his fur, rolled rocks for him to chase, and complimented his cuteness. When they picked him up to cuddle him, Simon made a low, rumbling sound.

Stanlin alternated between listening to the sounds of the scene and periodically tuning into Sylvia's thoughts. With each dip into her consciousness, he found her mind was very focused on the cat. He mused that Simon was quite the lucky little fellow.

He watched as Karen's mom walked outside and over to girls. She was an attractive woman with dark, curly hair, just like her daughter's. While she was still wearing the headset, she wasn't talking into it anymore. She commented that Simon seemed to be having a marvelous time with his two new girlfriends.

They giggled.

"Does your mom know you're here, Sylvia?" Karen's mom asked.

"Oh, no! I forgot to call!" Sylvia answered anxiously.

"Not to worry. I can easily call now," Karen's mom said, tapping her headset.

"Thanks, Mrs. Delany." Sylvia breathed a sigh of relief.

Standing next to the girls, Mrs. Delany called Sylvia's home. "Hi, Rebecca, it's Rinalda. Sylvia's here with Karen." She paused. "Yeah, I'm in the yard with them. They're playing with our new cat, Simon." She paused again. "You were right. It was only a matter of time before I adopted one of them. You can't be the director of a shelter for too long without getting smitten." She laughed. After a spell of listening, she responded, "Thanks for asking. The project is going really well. We took some dogs and cats to the Sanguinar Nursing Home yesterday. The manager said that residents who'd been depressed for months really perked up and smiled. He's considering adopting a few pets to live there with the residents permanently." She listened again for a while, interjecting a few yeahs and uh-huhs. She ended with, "Sure. Karen and I will walk with her so she'll be back by five-thirty. I'll bring that cake recipe with me. See ya soon."

Just as Rinalda hung up, Sylvia said wistfully, "I wish our family could adopt a cat or a dog from your shelter."

Squatting down next to Sylvia, Rinalda said, "Your mom wishes that too, honey. If only she didn't have those horrible allergies." She laid a hand on Sylvia's upper back, and her eyebrows rose thoughtfully. "Sylvia, since you're not able to have pets at home, why don't you come down to the shelter to volunteer once in a while?"

"I could show you around!" Karen piped up enthusiastically.

"That'd be super!" Sylvia exclaimed.

Awestruck by the way Sylvia's eyes lit up, Stanlin tuned into her thoughts. What had ignited that extra glow? He heard, "I really love animals. Helping them out and playing with them will be fun. And, I think I'll worry less, too. I wasn't worrying about Sherry at all while I was playing with Simon. Yes, volunteering at the shelter will be great!"

Automatically, Stanlin sensed Sylvia's decision could have very far-reaching effects, though he had no idea what those effects might be. He wished he understood the strange hunch, and wished he could stay for a longer visit. But he wasn't sure exactly how much time had passed, and he'd said he would be home for dinner. Besides, since he'd gotten away with this sneaked solo visit to Earth, he could just come again tomorrow.

Feeling sly, and a smidgen prideful, he crossed his arms over his chest, envisioned his backyard, and transported home.

# CHAPTER SIXTEEN

The alarm sounded in the Capton Governmental Council Headquarters control room, indicating that an unauthorized individual had just materialized on Capton. Renito, who was on duty watching the monitors, noted the location identified by the transport detection system and flipped on the orbital cameras in that region to view the entity clearly.

He laughed when he saw the image on the screen and turned toward Munin, who was sitting next to him taking care of some Council record keeping. "I had a scare there for a minute," Renito said, "but look at who the cameras picked up as our unauthorized being."

Munin was already looking at the young Rampont boy depicted on the screen. "The system must've gone off because he's probably under fourteen, not registered yet for solo travel. The little rebel," he said with amusement.

"Indeed." Renito smirked. "I doubt the Rampont militia would appreciate it if I alerted them for this infraction," he said, chortling. Growing more serious, he added, "But I can't let this go, either. The boy needs a warning he won't forget. Would you watch the monitors while I'm gone?"

"If it's all the same to you, I don't mind going to talk to the kid," Munin offered. He had grown up with four siblings, and his parents' disciplinary style had been stern yet calm and compassionate. As an adult, he emulated that style with his own children. He was confident he could teach the errant boy what was necessary while staying even tempered.

"Thanks. Go right ahead," Renito said, saluting gratuitously.

Munin verified the precise location coordinates in the system and crossed his arms over his chest. "Be back in a few, Reni," he said, and disappeared from Headquarters.

He materialized in Stanlin's backyard, right in front of Stanlin, who had just manifested a moment earlier.

Seeing Munin, Stanlin gasped.

"Don't be scared. I'm Munin, here on behalf of the Governmental Council. I've come to give you a very, very important warning."

"Yes, sir?" Stanlin asked nervously.

"At Council Headquarters, we have some pretty neat tracking devices. They can detect when *anyone* materializes on the planet."

"Oh," Stanlin said, mortified.

"Do have anything you'd like to tell me?"

"Yes. I went to Earth by myself," Stanlin confessed. "We went with my class yesterday, and I just didn't want to wait until I was fourteen to go back again."

Munin suppressed a smile as his mind travelled many years back to his friend Nixar's love of Earth. Nixar's love had been more about his infatuation with a particular redheaded female on Earth than the planet itself, but that was beside the point. Returning his focus to the boy, he said, "I like your enthusiasm, but we have rules for your safety, and they need to be obeyed. This will be your one warning. Wait until you are of age, and registered, to travel on your own. If we detect you transgressing this law again, you'll be permanently expelled from school. After that, your career options will be, shall we say, quite limited."

Stanlin's face contorted in horror.

"But if you behave according to the rules, none of that will happen."

"Yes, s-sir. Thank you, s-sir," Stanlin stammered. "I'm really, really sorry," he added earnestly.

"OK. Now be good, kiddo," Munin said with a smile. He waved good-bye and transported back to Council Headquarters.

Panting as he stood alone in his backyard, allowing his lungs to recover their regular breathing pattern, Stanlin thought, "See you in two years, Sylvia."

# CHAPTER SEVENTEEN

Brenna appraised her reflection in the mirror. Her hair did not look as she'd hoped it would today. The hairdresser had put way too much spray in it, so it wasn't natural looking. She looked at all the stiff, dark blond curls swept up on top of her head and the small tiara stuffed amid them.

Her makeup wasn't much better than her hair. The mascara highlighted her large brown eyes but had smudged slightly into her eye shadow, though not enough to justify redoing it, because that would probably create more of a mess. The skin of her small nose was dry and flaked, in spite of the layers of moisturizer she'd applied. She was glad that her red lipstick and lip liner filled out her thin lips, at least.

Brenna had always been told by family and friends that she was very pretty, and was her own worst critic. But, appearances aside, the important thing about today was that she was marrying Anthony Tormeni in just a few minutes.

Her father knocked on her door, which was half open. Peering in, he enthusiastically updated her. "The guests are taking their seats!"

"Great! I'm almost ready," she replied.

Her parents had flown into the US from Perth for the special occasion, and Anthony's had flown in from Hobart. With their home towns so far apart, thank heavens she and Anthony had both vacationed with the Aussie Singles Tour of the US a year earlier, or they probably never would have met. On that fateful trip, they had fallen in love with each other, and with the States, so becoming Americans and settling down in the US together was the natural aftermath for them. Anthony's career prospects had drawn them to the Northeast, which was fine with Brenna, who knew she could write her novels from any location.

As she applied gloss over her lipstick, she reflected upon her groom to be. He wasn't perfect, but who was? He was chronically five to fifteen minutes late, got very irritable if he was hungry or stressed, and was not particularly friendly to those he didn't know well. On the other hand, he treated her like a queen, and she never doubted his love for her. He listened whenever she needed a sounding board and was her biggest advocate in both the good times and the bad. Anthony also gave her the sweetest cards on holidays and special occasions and regularly planned fun ways for them to spend their weekends together. She loved him dearly. He was a wonderful man, her Mr. Right, at last.

Eight months earlier, the time of their engagement, had been one of the happiest and one of the saddest eras of her life. Anthony had proposed to her on a romantic dinner cruise. They were walking out on the deck after their meal when he suddenly got down on one knee. The boat rocked at that precise moment, so his knee smashed against the hard floorboard, and he yelped. She thought he fell and concernedly asked if he was hurt. He started laughing, then retrieved the ring from his pocket and belted out, "I love you, Brenna! Will you marry me?" She laughed and cried, kissed him, and said yes. It was a perfect night.

The next day, however, she received dreadful news at her follow-up gynecologist's appointment. When Dr. Cohen entered the room and said, "I have your results," the look on her face and the tone of her voice scared Brenna. Dr. Cohen sat down across from her and said, "The biopsy was positive. I'm afraid you have endometrial cancer."

Less than a week earlier, the doctor had conducted a thorough examination along with an endometrial biopsy, because Brenna had complained of some irregular menstrual symptoms. Brenna hadn't felt like it was anything serious, though, so she was stunned hearing the news. "Oh…my… God," was all she could choke out.

"We caught this very early on, which is good," Dr. Cohen assured her. "We can schedule surgery as soon as possible. We'll need to remove the uterus, and also, as a precaution, the fallopian tubes and ovaries, because the cancer tends to spread there."

Brenna nodded, half present.

"Your prognosis is excellent, Brenna, really. Not only are we treating it early, but, at thirty-four, you're much younger than the typical case, which should speed your recovery. This type of cancer is usually slow growing, and generally doesn't spread until it hits the later stages. We will remove and test the regional lymph nodes to verify that it hasn't metastasized. As long as it hasn't, you won't need radiation or chemotherapy. The surgery will be enough."

Although relieved at the good prognosis, and substantially more relieved when the surgery was successful, Brenna was devastated about losing her ability to conceive. Following her release from the hospital, she had cried for three days straight. Anthony had held her tenderly, listening sympathetically while she grieved. He had coaxed her into a small walk each day, saying that the fresh air and warm sun would be good for her. He'd also insisted that she eat at least a little something with him for each meal, even though she hadn't felt hungry at all.

On the fourth day, Brenna was finally brave enough to say what had been frightening and plaguing her the most. "Anthony, I know you want a family, but now we know I can't give that to you. I really would understand if you wanted to marry someone else—someone who could bear your children."

She would always remember the look on his face and his words at that moment. His blue eyes, brimming with tears, looked so deeply and lovingly into her own, and his broad jaw, shaded with sand-colored stubble, fell slightly open before he spoke. "You're the one for me. I don't want anyone else, ever," he said, and kissed her. Then, holding both of her hands and looking into her eyes again, he softly and tentatively suggested they could adopt a child. From that day forward, Brenna's sadness began lifting, and her already profound love for Anthony intensified even more.

Brenna's father peered into her room again. "Sweetheart, they're all ready for you now!"

"I'm ready too, Dad," Brenna said. She got up from her seat at the vanity and walked toward her father. He opened her door fully and, donning a caring, sentimental smile and holding one arm out, stood ready to escort her. She was completely aflutter. Anthony was about to become her husband! As a devoted team, they were tackling new adventures, relishing America the beautiful. And soon, their glorious life together would also include an adopted child. She felt happier than ever before. It was almost like living in a fairy tale.

As she stepped into the doorway, she sneaked a quick knock on the wooden doorframe before taking her father's arm.

# Spring, 2031

# CHAPTER EIGHTEEN

Madeline Conely was a petite, blond, spunky forty-six-year-old social worker from the Rima Adoption Agency. She was in Brenna and Anthony's home for the second time, and they were extremely nervous.

They could not afford to make mistakes or screw things up, especially not at this stage. They were so close to becoming parents. They had already filled out the mountains of paperwork, provided multiple character references, had their fingerprints taken, and had been investigated by the FBI for criminal activity, drug usage, and any stains in their personal histories. So far, so good, it seemed. As they understood it, this meeting was likely to be the last step prior to having a judge review all of their information and determine whether they could receive certification to adopt a child.

"Do you have a preference for the child's race?" Madeline asked.

Brenna and Anthony looked at one another. Race was irrelevant to them, but would being raised by Caucasian parents matter to a child of another race? That was where they had been uncertain in their previous, private discussions.

"We don't," Anthony said after the momentary pause. He took Brenna's hand, interlacing his fingers with hers.

Brenna didn't dispute his call.

"Is there an age preference?" Madeline inquired as she jotted notes on her pad.

"No older than three," Brenna replied.

"OK. Why is that?"

"We've heard it can take a long time if we insist on getting an infant, but we want the child to be young. We also feel sad that toddlers are over-looked most of the time," Brenna said, holding Anthony's warm hand a little more tightly.

Madeline took a few more notes. "Is there a gender you want most?"

"No preference," said Anthony matter-of-factly, and Brenna nodded.

"Does it matter to you if the adoption is open or closed?"

No one spoke right away, so Madeline reviewed the difference for them. "In an open adoption, the adoptive parents and child communicate with the birth mother; in a closed adoption, there's no contact."

Anthony and Brenna had mulled this over together in the past few weeks. Brenna explained their conclusion. "We think the child will feel more loved and less abandoned in the open format, but we also don't want to exclude adopting in the closed format, especially if the child feels like the right fit for us. So we'll consider either option."

After a few more questions, Madeline packed her notepad and pen into her briefcase and shook hands with Brenna and Anthony. "Thank you both for your time and cooperation."

"When will we know if we're certified?" Anthony asked eagerly.

"The judge is set to review your file later this week. I should be able to call you with his decision on Friday."

"Great!" Anthony exclaimed.

"Yes!" Brenna agreed breathlessly.

They led Madeline out and thanked her for her help.

After closing the front door, Brenna turned to face Anthony. "I can't believe it's finally happening! We're creating a family!"

Anthony hugged her tenderly. "You'll be the most wonderful mother."

"And he couldn't ask for a better father than you."

*"He?"* Anthony's brows lifted.

Brenna's eyes widened. "Oh my gosh! I did say *he*, didn't I?"

"Sure did!"

They both laughed.

Anthony's eyes twinkled. "Hopefully, we'll find out really soon if you're psychic."

# CHAPTER NINETEEN

Madeline did call that Friday, and the news was what Brenna and Anthony had wanted to hear, and more. Not only were they certified to adopt, but the agency had already found a potential match for them. Together they drove to the agency for a meeting with Madeline—and possibly, they hoped, with the child. In her moist hands, Brenna held a colorful toy boat. If they were lucky enough to meet the child today, they thought the small gift would be a good icebreaker.

When they arrived, Madeline brought them into her office and invited them to sit in the two chairs in front of her desk. Madeline sat down and leaned forward, looking at them intently. "We have an emergent situation on our hands this week. The Guyton Women's Shelter contacted us. They're caring for a single mother who's on the run from an abusive ex-boyfriend. They're helping her find safety with a changed name, appearance, and residence. But they called us because she wants to give her boy up for adoption.

"The mother is saying that her ex was threatening to kill the child, she's positive he'll find a way to do it, and she'll never forgive herself if her son dies when she could have saved him. The woman's parents and her sister each live in the town she just left, but she says she can't have either raise her son, because Ron, the ex, has been to both places, so he would find and capture the boy.

"When we suggested she get a restraining order, she refused, saying it wouldn't scare or deter Ron. She said she knew in her gut that her son's best hope was to be raised by another loving family, far away from her. She traveled over seventy miles to get to the Guyton shelter and plans to settle down much farther away, to throw Ron off track."

"Oh," Brenna said softly, and Anthony shook his head slowly as they digested the grievous situation.

"The circumstances are obviously horrible, but the boy does need a home." Madeline paused, assessing their expressions, which were concerned and interested. She continued. "The mother is requesting an open adoption. Once she has her new residence and is working, she's going to contact us with a P.O. box address. Then, we'll become the go-between; any letters and photos can be sent to us, and we'll forward those to the adoptive parents' home or to the mother's P.O. box. She plans to communicate with her own parents and her sister in this way, too. It will ensure privacy for all the involved households but will allow the mother to keep in touch with everyone.

"After a few years, she's planning to begin meeting up with her parents and sister in neutral places. If everything goes well, and she feels it's safe, when her son turns eighteen, she'd like to begin visiting with him, too. She hopes to form a relationship with him and his adoptive parents. Though some people might feel threatened by the level of involvement she wants to have, it only proves that she is a loving mother, which is actually one of the best aspects about this case. It's a well-researched fact that children who were nurtured in their earliest years are most likely to become affectionate themselves, and to develop normal social skills. It's the children who were neglected as infants who are more apt to become socially withdrawn, or even antisocial."

"That makes sense. I'm glad the boy isn't just being thrown away by someone who doesn't care," Anthony said.

"Those kinds of stories wrench your heart," Brenna accorded. "It's great that this boy's mother loves him so much, and wants to stay in touch."

"Yes." Madeline shifted slightly in her chair and glanced down at some notes on her desk. "The boy's name is Cedric. He's African American. From what we can tell, he seems very sweet. He'll turn three in a few months. His height, weight, and IQ are all in the normal ranges. Our medical evaluations didn't reveal any illnesses, but, unfortunately, there were signs of physical abuse: wounds and bruises in different stages of healing, mainly on his chest, back, and upper arms. The mother said that Ron had abused both her and the boy, and similar signs of abuse were apparent on the mother's body. Thankfully, neither of their injuries will cause any permanent physical damage."

Brenna exhaled slowly, and Anthony said, "Good."

"I can step out for a few minutes, give you two some time to consider things, maybe come up with some questions?" Madeline offered.

Brenna and Anthony exchanged a look of knowing. They were so ready to give their love to a child. And this boy needed a home desperately—a new family would literally protect his life—so there was no reason whatsoever to delay meeting him.

Anthony said, "We're ready to meet him as soon as possible. Today, if we can."

"Absolutely," Brenna agreed.

"We brought him over from the Guyton Shelter for the afternoon, just in case you felt that way." Madeline smiled broadly. "We'll start with a brief meeting, so you can get a general impression. If you would like additional meetings set up before making a final decision, that can easily be arranged."

Anthony and Brenna nodded readily.

"Good then." Madeline nearly jumped up from her seat. "I'll be back in a minute, and I'll bring him in." She swiftly left the room.

Brenna and Anthony looked at each other with hopeful anticipation.

Moments later, Madeline returned with the toddler and introduced everyone. Cedric looked tentatively up at Brenna and Anthony with wide-set brown eyes framed by dark eyelashes. His full lips were slightly parted. A few small, dark freckles dotted his nose and cheeks, and his ears poked slightly outward. He was adorable.

"Hello there," Brenna said.

"Pleased to meet you," said Anthony.

The boy shyly looked away, and his eyes found a ceramic dog on Madeline's desk. He walked over, picked up the figurine, and glanced at each of the adults, as though gauging whether what he was doing was alright. When there was no reproving reaction from any of them, he gazed at the ceramic animal, rolling it in his hands and examining it from different angles. Eventually, he settled into stillness, and held the pup close to his chest, with the pup's face facing his own. It appeared that the miniature canine gave him a bit of comfort in this strange place with strange people.

"That's a cute doggie," Anthony said.

Cedric nodded, still looking at the figurine.

"We like dogs, too," said Brenna.

Cedric looked up at her with the faintest hint of a smile before his eyes shifted back to the trinket.

Leaning forward, Brenna held out the toy boat they had brought. "Have you ever seen a boat like this before?" she asked.

Cedric didn't speak but looked at the boat with interest.

"Boats like this go sailing in the water," Anthony explained. "People steer them through the waves. Some people even take their doggies on the boats with them. Do you think that little doggie might like to sit in the sailboat?"

That idea evidently intrigued Cedric, because he placed the ceramic dog inside the boat right away. Brenna and Anthony got down on their knees as Brenna lowered the boat to the floor. "You can make it go, like this," she said, gliding it along the carpet. "You can try now, if you like." She let go and waited.

There was only a brief hesitation before Cedric started moving the boat.

"I think a big gust of wind is coming..." Anthony took a deep breath and blew outward. Carefully, not touching Cedric's hands, he touched the tip of the boat and tilted it from side to side. "Just look at how that wind rocks the boat!" he exclaimed animatedly.

Cedric removed his hands but cupped them over his mouth and let out a small giggle.

When Anthony let go of the boat, Cedric took charge of it more confidently than before. Brenna and Anthony stayed on the floor near him, watching as he rocked the boat and its canine passenger, making his own breathy gusts of wind.

A few minutes later, Madeline squatted down near them and said, "That was fun," which told Brenna and Anthony the meeting was ending. They all stood up.

"It was nice meeting you, Cedric." Brenna smiled at him warmly.

"Yes, and keep that boat, buddy," said Anthony.

Though Cedric was quiet, he looked at both of them with his eyes saying, "I think I like you."

"Cedric, you can keep the doggie, too," said Madeline. "Now bring the toys with you, and come along with me."

Madeline began guiding Cedric out of the room. Holding his boat and pup close to his chest, Cedric glanced back at Anthony and Brenna as if to say, "I wasn't ready to go yet."

Once Cedric was out of sight and hearing range, Brenna turned to face Anthony. "What does your gut tell you?"

"It's all happening fast, but my instincts say this'll work—that he'll be right for us. You?" he asked.

"The same," Brenna said, her heart soaring. "And I think taking him home as soon as we can and getting him adjusted there would be better than dragging things out with more sessions here. I think that would be the safest thing for Cedric also."

"Definitely," Anthony agreed.

Madeline returned to the room and began explaining that, if they'd like, she could set up more meetings, or, if they weren't comfortable for any reason, there would be other opportunities. They let her know that more sessions weren't necessary, and the other opportunities could go to her other clients, because they would like to adopt Cedric. Madeline was delighted, and promised to complete the new paperwork ASAP.

As promised, Madeline worked rapidly. The following week, Brenna and Anthony expressed their immense gratitude to her—when they picked up little Cedric to take him to his new home.

# Summer, 2031

# CHAPTER TWENTY

It was the summer before his senior year, and seventeen-year-old Ned was skinning a possum. He still enjoyed the hunting and skinning game he had invented as a boy, but he'd improved it.

Originally squirrels had been his only targets. Now possums, chipmunks, rabbits, birds, and any neighborhood cats that were stupid enough to enter his yard were all fair game. He used to bury the entire carcass. Now he separated the scraps from the edible meat and buried only the scraps. The edible portion, he'd set behind a particular bush. It never failed that when he checked the spot the next day, the fresh meat would be gone. He was feeding some type of carnivore. An owl? A raccoon? A fox? A buzzard? He had no idea, but the mystery was intriguing.

As he sliced through the day's possum's hide, Ned felt glad to have the summer break from schoolwork. Trying to pay attention to the dull lessons was torturous. Thankfully, after one more year, he'd be done with the books for good and could find a full-time job. Finally, he could make his own money and move into his own place.

Because of his low grades, his mom was only letting him work during the summers, not during the school year. But the pitiful amount he was earning stocking shelves at the local supermarket where she worked as a checker disappeared with her paychecks into their household bills. He wasn't sure what job he would get after graduation, but he needed to find something that paid better and gave more hours than the dumb grocery store.

Ned's family had had money troubles for as long as he could remember. Things were tight enough when his father was alive, but they got worse after he died. His mom's salary barely made ends meet, and her boss never gave her enough hours to qualify for health benefits, no matter how many times she asked.

Even still, she'd planned on taking Ned to a doctor when he was younger, for that head injury from the bike fall. She and Aunt Cora were going to save and pool their money together for the appointment, once she managed to pay off the funeral expenses.

But everything changed when, just weeks after the funeral, Aunt Cora had a stroke. She needed long-term therapy sessions and doctor's checkups because she was partially paralyzed. Eventually, she went back to work part-time, but with all the medical bills, she had no money leftover at the end of the week. Neither did his mother; home or car repairs cropped up any time she came close to having extra cash.

So Ned never went to a doctor. He still had the headaches, but they weren't as bad as when he was a kid. He never complained. What would be the point?

His head hurt now, as he separated the possum's scraps from its edible meat. He tried distracting himself from the pain by thinking of God. His mom had been bringing him along with her to church every week since his father died. She said it helped her cope and go on.

Ned hated God for taking his dad away; yet strangely, God fascinated him, too. He could easily memorize Bible passages and points from the pastor's sermons. Reading the Bible, even for hours at a time, didn't bore him the way schoolbooks did, and he could find deeper meanings than even preachers could, hidden in the scriptures. This was all very good for his goal to figure out God's Master Plans.

He had, over time, devised a plan of his own for this. First, he was staying on God's good side, because God would only share His Secrets and Plans with someone He liked. And as long as he kept a lid on his anger with God, he could impress Him. After all, how many people could rattle off sermons, scripture, and deep insights the way he could?

Second, knowing God through and through to the core was important. If he learned *all* about God, wouldn't his mind become more like God's? And that would get him ready and able to understand The Plans once God explained them. Pastor Jensen had said that people's minds were no match for God's mind, but other people weren't studying like Ned was, unless they were preachers, and they still didn't have Ned's unique Bible talents.

Yes, eventually God would see how special he was and would spill the Master Plans. Finally he'd learn why his dad had died—and something incredible would happen that he hadn't realized when he was younger—he would become the smartest, most powerful person in the world.

Digging the burial hole, his thoughts shifted to the previous weekend's church sermon. Pastor Jensen had talked about the story of Noah's ark. Noah had trusted God completely, following His orders to build the ark and put two of every creature inside it. The pastor had encouraged everyone in the congregation to be like Noah and completely trust in God.

Ned had focused on something different about the story. God was trying to get rid of lots of evil on the Earth with a big flood. Noah and the animals and the people on the ark were supposed to start things fresh and new when the flood was over and all of the evil was destroyed. That meant God could kill if He wanted to make things better later on. This had to be part of the Master Plans—somehow. Ned was sure of it.

He buried the soiled paper towel and the scraps from the possum. Luckily, God would approve of the hunting game. Since the killings were, in fact, providing food for another mystery animal, Ned was participating in the food chain, which was one of God's orderly arrangements.

After taking the possum's edible meat to the feeding spot, he gave his hands a quick rinse with the hose and lay stretched out in the grass on his back, crossing his long, strong legs at the ankles. He pushed back his wavy, shoulder length, dark brown hair from his icy blue eyes. His biceps bulged as he folded his hands under his head. Staring up at the clouds, he took some deep breaths and tried to feel relaxed, which was never easy for him.

That was when it happened. In a flash, three large clouds came together, taking the form of a face framed by long hair and a long beard. Ned stared in wonderment.

The mouth said, "You must listen to me." The incredibly authoritative tone of the voice assured Ned that this was God, talking directly to him. "Many years ago, I sent my son to the world with powerful messages and a most holy sacrifice. This has not been honored. Man has been spreading my word and praying to me less and less as the years have passed, which both saddens and angers me. Therefore, my plans for the future of mankind have changed. All must be renewed. Like Noah helped me ages ago, very soon, Ned, you will be helping me to purify the Earth. I will not cause floods again, but another mission of great cleansing is needed."

Before he could fully absorb or respond to what God had said, Ned couldn't stop himself from explosively blurting out the question that had been burning inside of him for so long. "Why did you let my dad die?"

"Your father drank and crashed his car. It was his own doing."

Ned grimaced in fury. "You could've saved him. Why didn't you save him?"

"I have a purpose for him."

With that, the wind howled, and the face dissolved as the large mass of white divided back into three separate clouds again.

Simultaneously full of rage, sorrow, shock, and bewilderment, Ned was, for some time, immobilized there in the grass.

# CHAPTER TWENTY-ONE

After the church service the following day, Ned told his mom he needed to stay a few minutes to ask the pastor some questions. She agreed to wait for him out front, where she would be chatting with some friends.

Ned approached the pastor.

"Hello, Ned," Pastor Jensen greeted affably. He was a gray-haired, stout, sixty-five-year-old man with a small pot belly and a congenial countenance. He held his Bible, with all of the pages from the sermon bookmarked.

"Morning, sir. Can I ask you some things about today's sermon?"

"Yes, certainly."

"Did you say that God can speak to us sometimes? I thought I heard you say that, but I wasn't sure."

"Yes, Ned, you heard me correctly," the pastor confirmed. "You see, many people feel that God speaks to their hearts when they strongly sense they need to say or do something specific. They'll feel as if they know God wants them to choose that particular path."

"Oh," Ned muttered, noticing that Pastor Jensen had emphasized God speaking to other people's *hearts*. This wasn't what had happened the day before with the clouds. Ned's chest puffed with pride. God had singled him out, had talked to him straight up—not in some weird, roundabout, heart way. Already, he was on God's good side; his plan was working.

The pastor leaned forward. "Any other questions for me?"

"Yeah. Could you repeat what you said about God providing for us and leading us?" Ned asked eagerly.

"Of course," Pastor Jensen said, opening his Bible to one of the bookmarked pages. "John 6:35 says, '...I am the bread of life. He who comes to me will never go hungry, and he who believes in me will never be thirsty.'" The pastor looked up at Ned. "When we place our faith in Him, God provides for our needs, and gives us direction in life." He flipped to a different bookmarked page, and added, "As Proverbs 3:5 says, '...He will make your paths straight.'"

"Hmm," Ned murmured. God would provide for his needs and would give him directions and a straight path to follow. Good. When? *When?* God said He wanted Ned's help with a cleansing mission to purify the Earth. What exactly did God need him to do? He hadn't said, which had been very frustrating. "Could you go over the part about questioning God?" Ned implored.

"Yes, sir," Pastor Jensen piped. Pausing briefly, he cocked his head to one side. "It's great that you are interested in so many points, Ned. And God does answer all of our concerns." He turned a few pages of his Bible, stopped at another bookmark, and said, "Luke 11:10 tells us, 'For everyone who asks receives; he who seeks finds; and to him who knocks, the door will be opened.'" Smiling at Ned, he qualified, "The catch is that we may not get the answer the moment we ask the question. In other words, we'll get our answers on God's timetable, not on ours. Some answers may come quickly; others may come after many years; still others might come in little bits and pieces, over time."

Little bits and pieces was right; the pastor had nailed it. That visit from God the other day was like a bit or a piece. So more bits and pieces about the mission would be coming. That must be how God was handling this.

"Thanks a lot," Ned said, shaking the pastor's hand. As he headed outside to find his mother, he mentally reviewed the biblical verses Pastor Jensen had quoted, committing them to memory.

# CHAPTER TWENTY-TWO

The next few months flew by as Brenna, Anthony, and Cedric adapted to one another. Cedric was having trouble sleeping and was not eating heartily. There were crying fits, by both Cedric and Brenna, though, of course, Brenna never unleashed hers in front of Cedric. Anthony was becoming a master at consoling and encouraging her when they were alone in their bedroom. They knew this wouldn't be easy but kept telling themselves that over time, things would smooth out.

Yet, even at this early, challenging phase, some rewards were surfacing. Little by little, Cedric was opening up to them, stringing words together into sentences, and talking. He climbed in the mini jungle gym they'd set up in the backyard, and he liked kicking around a blow-up ball with them. He'd also made friends with the two neighbor children next door, Scott and Sandy, five-year-old twins. They had a puppy, Rolly, who Cedric fawned over.

When the day arrived to celebrate Cedric's third birthday, Brenna let him help as she measured the flour and sugar for his cake. She felt tears of joy tingle in her eyes when she set three candles in the center, which would be lit as soon as Daddy was there with them.

Anthony arrived home early from work, bringing in a pizza for dinner and a wrapped gift for later. All three of them dug into their pizza slices and their generous pieces of birthday cake. Cedric wasn't finicky that night.

"Maybe we need to eat pizza and cake more often," Brenna chuckled.

After the meal, Anthony handed Cedric his present. "This is for you—the special birthday boy!"

Cedric held the package in front of him and sat perfectly still as he looked at the colorful paper and ribbons with wonder. Brenna and Anthony laughed.

"We can save the paper and ribbons for you too, buddy, but there's something inside. Here, open, it," Anthony said, ripping the paper slightly so a hint of what was within showed.

Cedric tore off the rest of the paper and squealed with delight when he saw his new toys: three cute, plush beagle puppies.

"If you take good care of these puppies, then when you're a bit older, we'll get you a real one," Anthony said, beaming.

"Like Rolly?" Cedric asked him with wide eyes.

"Yes, little man, like Rolly," Anthony replied with a wink.

Cedric's face glowed. He started playing with the pups, moving them around and making them bark at each other. He burst into giggles that quickly spread to Anthony and Brenna.

"I also have a surprise for you," Anthony said, turning his gaze to her.

Brenna raised her eyebrows expectantly.

"Today, Leonard said he's preparing to give me an exciting new project—one that'll involve a promotion and a raise!"

She flew into his arms. "That's fantastic!"

"He said he's still ironing out logistics with the new client, and most likely, the project won't start until the spring. So we'll probably have to wait about eight months for the extra money, but at least we know it's coming!"

"Yes! And I think it's great that your boss wants you to know he has something lined up for you."

"Yeah," Anthony said, gripping her waist and lifting her up in the air. They laughed giddily as he lowered her gently to the floor and hugged her.

Cedric looked up at them with a curious smile.

"We can sock away more for somebody's college education," Anthony said.

Brenna imagined Cedric as a young man in a cap and gown with a rolled college diploma in his hand. "I'm always afraid of jinxing things," she said tentatively, "but our dreams really do seem to be coming true."

# Spring, 2032

## CHAPTER TWENTY-THREE

Over the past two years, Stanlin had relished learning about and visiting many different planets with his teachers and classmates. But he'd also been working a private project on the side: figuring out a way to legally interact with Sylvia, once he was permitted to visit Earth again, solo.

When the morning of his fourteenth birthday finally arrived, Stanlin was the first in line outside the Council Headquarters Building for registration. An older Rampont who introduced himself as Bartholith led him inside and into the control room. As they sat down at the far end of a horseshoe-shaped table, Stanlin gawked at its fifty-foot-long surface, covered with buttons, keyboards, levers, and rectangular cubby bins.

"This is the control panel," said Bartholith, "and those are our viewing monitors." He pointed to the seven, ten-by-ten-foot, square screens mounted above the panel.

"Cool," Stanlin muttered incredulously, taking it all in.

"Yes, it is quite a system," Bartholith said, smiling. "Your name and birth date, please."

Stanlin straightened up in his chair and provided the information.

Bartholith entered it into a keyboard on the panel, reached into one of the cubby bins, and retrieved a tiny cube—about a millimeter on all sides. It was faint blue in color, matching Stanlin's body. "This computerized chip contains an identification code number, which I just assigned to you and linked in with your name and birth date in our database," Bartholith explained. "After I insert this into your shoulder, any time you materialize on Capton, it will send out a signal with your code number that our sensors will detect."

"Can the system tell you where I've just traveled in from?" Stanlin asked, wondering if the Council would be keeping track of all the Earth trips on his agenda.

"No," Bartholith chuckled. "It's not that advanced. It simply informs us that you've arrived home. But more importantly, the system alerts us when anyone manifests here without an identification code. Our orbital cameras will transmit the intruder's image onto the monitors. If necessary, we can summon the militias."

"Oh," Stanlin said, filled with chagrin but attempting to sound detached. He realized he must have shown up on those very screens two years earlier, when he had traveled alone without identification. He forced his thoughts to the present. "Will it hurt when the cube gets put in?"

"You'll barely feel it," Bartholith assured him. He delved his hand into another cubby bin on the panel and took out a metal instrument. It resembled a revolver, except that an extremely thin probe existed where the nozzle would have been. He placed Stanlin's identification chip onto the end of the probe, explaining that a weak magnetic charge would temporarily hold it there. He repositioned the instrument, aiming it at Stanlin's shoulder, and pulled the trigger. Within an instant, the probe lengthened and receded, pushing the cube into place.

Bartholith replaced the instrument inside its bin. "Not so bad, right?"

"Right; I felt pressure there, but only for a second," Stanlin said, checking out his newly branded shoulder. "Boy, you really can't see this at all."

"It blends right in," Bartholith agreed. He crossed his legs and folded his hands in his lap. "Now, Stanlin, I'm sure you've learned that with the exception of planet Earth, you may interact with other beings in your travels. So, I'll need to confirm your knowledge of The Highest Authority's Free Will Decree. Please recite it."

Stanlin didn't feel his usual anxiety about the verbal quiz; this subject matter had been etched into his mind when he was a very young Rampont. "The Highest Authority's Free Will Decree states, 'All creatures of the universe are meant to make their own choices in life and must learn from the consequences of those choices. Entities are not to command the course of anyone else's life but their own.'"

"Fantastic. Can you creatively expand upon the decree's application for me?"

Stanlin recalled the discussion he'd had with his parents so many years ago, the first night they had read from *Captonian Wisdom* together. He said, "I not only won't command other beings, but I won't even advise them. I might ask them to consider what they think they should do about a situation, but that's it. Getting too pushy with advice can creep into being controlling. It can be a fine line, and I don't want to take any chances when it comes to obeying The Highest Authority."

Bartholith raised his eyebrows. "That's a more conservative approach than many take, but I like it a lot. Again—fantastic!"

Stanlin grinned. His wise parents had taught him well.

"We're almost done. You'll just need to read through some legalities." From yet another cubby bin, Bartholith got out a Rampont Reader and handed it to Stanlin. "It's already loaded with the cylinder, so go ahead."

Stanlin set it in his lap and began reading. Moments later, he looked up and noticed Munin entering the room and conversing with another Rampont. Mortified at the memory of Munin busting him for underage travel, Stanlin blushed and snapped his gaze back to the hologrammed sentence in front of him. Munin and the other Rampont spoke briefly with Bartholith. Then Stanlin heard the sounds of soft whispering as Munin and his companion exited the room.

Munin allowed the grin that he had just stifled to spread now that he and Nixar had their backs to the boy and were leaving the control room. He asked, "Remember that story I told you a couple of years back, about the young mystery intruder? The twelve-year-old who loved his class's Earth trip so much that he went back there all alone?"

"Yeah," Nixar said. "Was that him with the Reader?"

"Yep."

They laughed lightly as each veered off to his desk.

Munin promptly returned his attentions to the day's business.

Nixar needed a moment of pause. Talking about that lad who loved Earth brought back his own memories of Earth, which, of course, centered around Miss Julie Abler. Oh how smitten he had been, beseeching her to transport to Capton with him! No, it wasn't meant for him to end up with Julie. He knew that now for sure. Sillu, his beloved Rampont wife of twenty years, proved it. Smiling to himself with gratitude, he shifted back to work mode.

# CHAPTER TWENTY-FOUR

It took nearly fifteen minutes for Stanlin to read through the various legalities. When he handed the Reader back to Bartholith, the elder asked, "Make sense?"

"Yes," Stanlin affirmed.

"Good," Bartholith replied, replacing the Reader in the cubby bin. Turning to face Stanlin, he exclaimed, "Congrats! You're allowed to travel wherever you want, to continue your studies!" He shook Stanlin's hand heartily.

"Thank you! Thank you!" Stanlin was absolutely elated.

He could not go to Earth right away, though, because today was a school day. So from Council Headquarters, Stanlin headed to class. Naturally, the day seemed to drag on—just as it had that day two years earlier, when he'd planned to sneak back to Earth and see Sylvia for the second time. When it finally ended, he ran home. He dropped off his scholastic cylinders, let his mom know he'd be home for dinner, and darted into the backyard.

Legal Earth travel AND legal—through his crafty loophole—interaction with Sylvia! BOMBS AWAY!

Stanlin invisibly transported to the Secard Elementary-Middle School. The last time he had run home from his school and immediately gone to Earth, Secard had let out for the day just minutes later. He hoped it would be the same today.

He situated himself in front of the school, where he could easily view the large double doors the students should soon be exiting. Stanlin once again deferred inserting the auditory plugs, which he had tucked into his front pocket. Hearing Karen call Sylvia's name had helped him locate the girls last time, and he wanted every advantage available.

After a few minutes, a loud bell rang and everyone began exiting the building. Stanlin scanned their faces, listening for the names Sylvia and Karen. Unfortunately, a mishmash of children's voices was all he could seem to hear. He thought, "Time to tune in. I'm listening, Sylvia."

That familiar female voice came into his head, though now, it was a bit deeper in tone: "That math lesson really sucked. I was totally lost. How am I going to do the homework?"

As Sylvia thought about some of the equations, Stanlin searched the sea of human faces even more intently. At last, he saw her walking in his direction. She was more beautiful than he remembered, which was saying a lot. She wore her thick, auburn hair styled in a twist on top of her head with a few wispy strands around her face. Her pink, shiny lips and lovely green eyes made his heart beat quickly in his chest.

"Ready, set, go!" he thought. Stanlin shape-shifted himself into a small black cat and became visible. "I'm not breaking the Non-Interaction Law," he said to himself with a sly grin. "I've never heard that Ramponts are forbidden to shape-shift on Earth. *By becoming something else*, I'm not *a visible Rampont* interacting with the human."

Earlier, when devising this plan, Stanlin had considered shape-shifting into a human child to meet Sylvia, but he had opted in favor of becoming a feline for a couple of reasons. First of all, from what he'd learned of the Non-Interaction Law, Ramponts were worried about exposure to human conversation. If he were to become a human, other humans would expect him to converse with them, so he would have to keep his auditory plugs removed, and he might overhear bad things. On the other hand, as a cat, he would not need to talk, and could keep the plugs in—or leave them out, whatever, since it probably wouldn't make much difference without discourse going on, anyway.

The overriding reason Stanlin preferred to be feline, however, was that success would be easier. He wasn't familiar with all the social customs for being a human child, so what if Sylvia found him weird, and awkward, and didn't like him? That would be awful. But he had watched the cat, Simon, playing with the girls, and there wasn't much to it. Sylvia had loved Simon on site. Playing with him had made her smile, and that was the reaction Stanlin wanted, too.

So, as the little black cat, Stanlin excitedly tested out his four legs, taking a few fast paces straight ahead. Initially, he tripped, but he recovered quickly and trotted forward for a bit, ran for several strides, and then walked slowly for a while. After practicing the various speeds, he felt comfortable with his new limbs and looked at them appreciatively. His eyes wandered to the blades of grass around him.

They looked huge! Boy oh boy, was he close to the ground. Peering upward, everything looked gigantic: the school building, the trees, the children. Already, this was an incredible experience, and the best was yet to come!

With bouncy exuberance, Stanlin trotted over to meet Sylvia. He boldly brushed up against her legs as she walked.

"Oh," she said, noticing him. She picked him up and talked to him. "Who're you, little fella? I don't see a collar. Hmmm. Could you be a stray?"

Stanlin recalled Simon making a low rumbling sound when the girls picked him up. He imitated the sound the best he could and tuned in to what she was thinking.

He heard, "He's purring—how sweet he is. I should bring him to the shelter, but I want to play with him first. Yes, I'll take him to the park."

"Let's go, little guy," she said aloud, nuzzling her nose into his and hugging him. She walked ahead briskly for several blocks, cradling him in her arms.

Being cuddled by her was even better than Stanlin had anticipated. She was so pretty up close, it was ridiculous. Those eyes—they were spectacular! Their rich, green color; their warm, accepting gaze...he was helplessly enamored.

They arrived at their destination, and Sylvia's pace slowed. A wooden sign read "Ashbury Park." He looked around, impressed with the well-manicured lawns and the wide variety of playground equipment.

Sylvia brought him under the shade of a large tree, set him down in the grass, and knelt in front of him. From there, it was games galore. Like he'd observed Simon doing, he chased the rocks Sylvia rolled and batted them with his paws, repeatedly pushing out his neato claws and retracting them. He made the purring noise and rubbed his head on her shoulder each time she picked him up, and his small tummy tightened whenever their eyes linked.

Their fun afternoon flew by. When dusk wasn't far off, Sylvia said, "We really should go to the shelter now. I wish I could just take you home." She sighed sadly, scooped him up in her arms, and walked with him again.

Stanlin reasoned that the shelter must be within walking distance. He was right. They arrived a few minutes later. Sylvia's friend Karen was working at the front desk.

Sylvia explained that she'd found this cat by the school, and that she guessed he was a stray. "I played with him in the park for a while before bringing him," she confessed. "I just couldn't come straight here. I really wish I could adopt him."

"Well, why don' cha come by every day an' play with him until he's adopted?" Karen suggested. "You can even take him to the park. Everyone'll be fine with it."

Sylvia looked at her uncertainly. "Cats always stay in here. We don't let anyone take them outside."

"As a volunteer, you can do stuff the customers can't. I'm sure my mom won't care if you pick up and drop off this cat. She's in her office. I'll go double-check with her." Karen scurried off and came back fast with the official approval.

"OK, yeah! I'll be back to see this cutie tomorrow," Sylvia said, giving Stanlin a hug.

The girls took him into a room filled with cats in cages, put him inside one of the empty ones, and gave him a bowl of dry cat food and a bowl of water. As they locked the latch on his cage, the sounds of a dog coughing loudly startled them all. Stanlin cringed reflexively.

"Aww. It's OK, little guy. The doggies are in the other room," Sylvia soothed, reaching her fingers into the cage and rubbing Stanlin's furry ear.

"That's just Pimpy's cough," Karen explained.

"Did the vet check him yet?" Sylvia asked anxiously.

"Yes, and she told my mom that Pimpy's not sick at all. He just laps up his water too fast sometimes and chokes on it for a second."

"Oh, thank goodness. I'm so glad it wasn't that canine influenza. It was so bad last year when it spread around here."

Karen nodded slowly. "Yeah. Hopefully our animals don't catch it this fall." She poked her index finger into the cage and affectionately tapped Stanlin's tiny black nose. "I'll have an admitting specialist get his paperwork going."

"Good," Sylvia said, giving Stanlin's ear one last rub.

She and Karen said their good-byes. Karen returned to the front desk post, and Sylvia left the shelter.

Stanlin knew he couldn't stay, but the bowl of food in front of him smelled interesting. Curiously, he leaned forward, lapped up a nugget with his scratchy tongue, and chewed it. It was crunchy and had an odd menagerie of flavors. He couldn't decide whether he liked it or not. Whatever. He did have to get home.

Stanlin became invisible, transported to his backyard, and shape-shifted back into his visible Rampont self. Well, he was himself too much, really. He was stark naked! Within seconds, he surmised that his clothing must have fallen into a heap on the Earth ground, when his body had transformed into the cat.

"And I bet my garment was under my paws when I first started walking, causing me to trip," he concluded.

His next epiphany was more troubling. "Oh no!" he thought. "No, no, no! My auditory plugs were in my pocket; I have to find that garment!"

He zipped back to Earth and invisibly searched the grounds in front of the school building. He combed the lawns and the pavement there for a long, long while before finally giving up on the fruitless hunt. He reasoned that the wind could have blown the garment far away. Plus, it was probably invisible anyway. Most likely, it had fallen off right at the start of shape-shifting, when his invisible alien body had just shrunken down to feline size. Regardless, the plugs were gone, which was unsettling.

Stanlin contemplated his situation. He hadn't heard anything bad or dangerous on Earth without the plugs so far. Besides, with a nice girl like Sylvia as his playmate, what ominous chatter could possibly come about?

There seemed to be no potential detriment to continuing to go to Earth plugless. The alternative, asking one of his teachers for a new set of plugs, would be embarrassing and would undoubtedly raise questions. Not good. Plugless would be harmless. It was the way to go.

As for the clothing issue, he could not lose a garment with every trip, for crying out loud. From now on, he would take it off and hide it under a garden plant before departing for Earth, so he could easily slip it back on upon his return.

Feeling much better overall, Stanlin transported home.

Usually, he manifested in his favorite spot, alongside the lush, bountiful family garden. Growing up, this was always where he'd felt the most at peace. He'd played near the sweet-smelling, budding fruits, had helped pick the ripe ones, and had read many stories shaded by the large, round, fuchsia-colored leaves. The black stalks of the plants were twice as tall as his father and a little thicker than his two fists put together. Being around the regal-looking plants always gave Stanlin an extra feeling of safety. Traveling in and out of Capton from this special place was most natural and enjoyable for him.

Usually—but not right now. He manifested directly into his bedroom instead. Nakedly waltzing from the yard into and through the house would be about as fun-filled for him to do as it would be for his parents to watch. Tomorrow's Earth visit would be smoother, though. He had learned a lot from today's mistakes.

# CHAPTER TWENTY-FIVE

That evening, Karen called Sylvia. "It was the weirdest thing. The cat you brought in today was gone by the time I closed up. I don't mean he was adopted—he was just gone!"

"Just gone?" Sylvia repeated.

"Yeah! I dunno what happened."

"Did the admitting specialist ever do the paperwork?"

"No. I got real busy with a phone call right after you left. Then my mom needed me to help her out, and by the time we were done, the admitting specialist had left, and the cat's cage was empty, but closed up."

"Hmm," Sylvia murmured thoughtfully.

"The only thing I can think of is maybe one of the newer volunteers played with him but didn't fully close his cage after, and the cat sneaked outside. And later on, a volunteer or maybe a customer noticed the cage dangling open and closed it.

The girls agreed that Karen's theory was probably right, but Sylvia was very sad that the adorable little black cat was gone.

The following day, the weather was beautiful. Sylvia went to the local park after school to enjoy the sunshine. She was gliding back and forth on one of the swings, appreciating the fresh breeze, when she noticed something coming toward her. She slowed down, dismounted the swing, and peered at the approaching animal. Squinting and blinking her eyes, she hardly believed what she was seeing. The cat from yesterday was prancing toward her.

"Why, hello again!" she cooed happily.

The two played together for a long time. At one point, Stanlin was no longer able to restrain himself, and a huge smile, teeth and all, crept its way across his feline mouth. When he saw Sylvia looking a little unnerved, he had to think fast. He faked a sneeze as cover, and she giggled.

Eventually, Sylvia checked her watch, frowned, and said, "OK, little guy; we've gotta go." She picked him up and started walking.

They exited the park and walked down the familiar streets of the previous day. Stanlin could tell they were heading toward the animal shelter again. He did not want to go there each day. His constant appearing and disappearing would cause too much confusion for the staff. He had to communicate to Sylvia that he did not like it there. When they were a few yards from the front door, he stiffened his body, leaped out of her arms onto the ground, and looked up at her intently.

"What's wrong?" she asked. "You'll be safe in there. Don't be afraid." She reached down to pick him up.

Stanlin maintained eye contact, but dodged her grasping hands. He ran back toward the park, glancing over his shoulder to ensure that she saw where he was going.

She chased him and tried picking him up several more times. "I can't do this all night!" she yelled at last, exasperated. Letting out a huge sigh, she gave up and turned around for home.

Stanlin's feline throat tightened up. He hated upsetting her, but he had to avoid that darned shelter. He walked the rest of the way to the park and toward a particular fluffy bush, from behind which he had trotted out to surprise Sylvia earlier. He stepped back inside the bush, transported home, and shape-shifted into himself. As he slipped on his clothing, he fervently hoped that Sylvia would come to the park again the next day. She needed to understand: She didn't have to adopt him or visit him at that shelter to see him each day; she only needed to show up at Ashbury Park, and he would find her.

# CHAPTER TWENTY-SIX

As he drove home from the office, Anthony was not looking forward to what he would have to tell Brenna that evening. The idea of the promotion, involving an exciting new client, had seemed perfect. But now, he knew better. There was a catch. Anthony found it ironic that along with his pay raise came a hidden price tag. The cost wasn't to be in dollars but in lost time with his family.

At least the separation was limited; his overseas assignment was to last for one year. And it was highly purposeful, goal oriented, which was definitely good. But the whole thing seemed almost surreal to him. In his time so far with the global business management consulting firm, he had primarily worked from the local office. Brief trips, typically of four days or less scheduled only every six to eight weeks, were all that had been necessary as computers and phones shouldered the bulk of the company's business. Not so with the new client.

He pulled into the driveway, got out of the car, and stood gazing at his home for a few moments. The colonial-style was handsome, especially with the new, pale yellow siding they'd added. The rose bushes and patches of brown-eyed Susans, tiger lilies, and marigolds they had planted in front of the porch gave the place real curb appeal. Even in the dimness of evening, the beauty of his home was plain to see.

Clearing his throat, Anthony walked up the porch steps and entered the house, pausing again in the foyer. He looked from the spiral staircase ahead of him to the den off to his right and then to the living room on his left, appreciating the many hours he and Brenna had spent on renovation and decorating. They'd redone the wooden floors, painted the walls a light sea green, and upgraded their furniture to well-made Victorian-style pieces. They had aimed to strike a balance between elegant and cozy, and they had succeeded.

"Hi, honey!"

"Hi, Daddy!"

Brenna and Cedric came rushing over to greet him.

"How's my favorite dynamic duo?" Anthony asked, hugging and kissing them both as usual. But today, his heart felt like it weighed fifteen pounds in his chest. The depth of his love for them, and the reality of being apart from them for so long, was sinking in.

During dinner, and later, while they were watching television, he inwardly grappled with his reeling emotions and thoughts. After they had tucked Cedric into bed, he carefully broached the topic. He wasn't ready to, but then again, he probably never would be. "Honey, I found out that my promotion, well, it has a temporary...drawback." He took a deep breath.

"Oh?" Brenna looked at him attentively.

After another deep breath, he said, "Our firm's new project involves the South African government. They've decided to improve their country's healthcare programs. And, since I have more experience than our other healthcare consultants, Leonard thought I should lead our team." He paused for a second before quickly finishing the blow. "A group of us will be down there for a year, to put streamlined systems into place and make sure their government can maintain those systems long term."

Brenna's eyes widened, and her voice raised in pitch. "What? South Africa? For a *year*? Is Leonard nuts? There's too much violence down there! I don't want you going!"

"And I don't want to leave you and Cedric for a year," Anthony said earnestly. He pursed his lips together. The idea of leaving them was horrible, but at the same time, he believed he would make a real difference in the world by going. Softly, he said, "Our technology and organization over there will save thousands of lives. It will stabilize the whole country more, too, and who knows what positive ripples could come from that?"

There was a long silence before Brenna asked, "What about protection? Did Leonard think about that?"

"Part of his arrangement with their government is that they're setting us up with armed bodyguards, and our hotel and office buildings will have super tight security. I'll be safe," Anthony said, trying to convince himself as much as her.

Brenna stood staring at the floor with her jaw tensed and her arms folded across her chest. Disregarding her sullen posture, Anthony wrapped his arms around her and held her, rocking her slowly. The rigidity in her body slackened, and she returned his embrace, resting her forehead on his shoulder.

"It's hard to explain, but I feel like I need to do this. I know that must sound crazy."

She sniffled.

His throat burned. He had to be strong, and help her to be strong also. "I'll be alright, and so will you," he assured her. "Just keep busy with Cedric and with our neighbors like you've been. The bills are automated, and my salary will still directly deposit into our account, so you won't have any worries about money. Leonard's giving me a company cell to call you on; I'll call you every day. A year will be over before we know it." He hugged and kissed her lovingly.

Two weeks later, Anthony was already overseas, beginning his new assignment.

\* \* \*

As time trickled onward, Brenna did her best to maintain her routines with Cedric and the neighbors, as Anthony had recommended. She continued arranging frequent play dates next door. Cedric would race around with Scott, Sandy, and Rolly, and Brenna would chat and chaperone with Mary, the twins' mother.

Brenna also kept her weekly luncheon date with her other friendly neighbors, Rebecca and Rinalda. Every Thursday, the three women met up at the Candlewood Diner while Sylvia and Karen were in school and Cedric was in his weekly art class at the community center.

In the late afternoons, Brenna often walked with Cedric to Ashbury Park. She knew the walk was good for both of them; plus, Cedric absolutely loved the playground and the other children. One boy in particular, James, had become Cedric's regular playmate. The two toddlers got along swimmingly. James was an albino, who most of the other children teased or shunned. Brenna was extremely proud that Cedric was receptive toward him, in spite of James' unique appearance.

Cedric seemed to naturally possess acceptance—a trait she and Anthony valued very much. In their adolescent years, Brenna had blossomed earlier than her peers, and Anthony had terrible acne. Each had endured hurtful scoffs and jeering. While they hadn't known each other back then, as adults, they had commiserated about those trying times, and both had become empathetic toward others who were, in some way, different. Now, seeing their little Cedric being inclusive and nonjudgmental moved Brenna and warmed her heart.

Brenna was also enchanted by Cedric's love of animals. Not only did he adore Rolly next door, but at the park, his first order of business was always saying hi to Sylvia and petting Melvin, the small black cat she played with there.

Brenna's activities helped in keeping her spirits up, but talking with Anthony each day was her greatest comfort. He usually called around 2:00 p.m., which was her and Cedric's after-lunch treat. With the time difference, it was 10:30 p.m. for Anthony. He said that hearing their voices just before going to sleep ensured a happy ending to each day for him. Brenna looked forward to swapping stories with him, and putting the phone on speaker for a while to let Cedric tell Daddy whatever was on his blossoming young mind. Cedric was speaking very well and was even learning the art of persuasion. Anthony had barely been gone three weeks when Cedric convinced him to agree to take the whole family puppy shopping the very day he returned home.

Initially, the phone calls were always uplifting. The first alarming conversation wasn't until Anthony's sixth week on the job. As Brenna listened to Anthony talking with Cedric, she could tell something was amiss. Typically, Anthony was engrossed, his voice inflected and animated. Now, he sounded monotone and preoccupied. When Anthony said his good-bye to Cedric, Brenna got on and said, "Let me find a nice TV show for Cedric to watch, and you can tell me what's going on today."

"That would be...good," Anthony agreed.

"Yeah!" Cedric cheered.

She put her headset on, grabbed the remote, and flipped the channels until she found a cartoon. Cedric climbed on the couch and pulled a pillow into his lap.

"You cozy?" she asked.

He nodded, eyes fixed on the TV.

She walked to the far side of the room and kept her voice hushed. "What's wrong?"

"I'm not sure how to say this, but first of all, don't panic, because I'm fine."

"'Don't panic' makes me want to panic," she thought. But, with effort, she slowed and steadied her voice. "OK. What happened?"

"Early this morning, terrorists infiltrated the capital building."

Brenna gasped.

"It was the capital building," he repeated, "so I was far away from the whole mess. And they didn't succeed in killing anyone."

"Thank God," she breathed. "But it's still scary, because they got in! How did they get in?"

"That's the big question. Nobody knows," he replied warily. "Thankfully, they were detected in time, but the government's in an uproar now, trying to find the security leaks. They just put the whole country in a lockdown mode. No one can enter or leave. They're investigating and revamping all the security systems nationwide. It'll take months and months." He paused a moment before speaking again in a brighter tone. "But the good news is, they estimate the lockdown will be over by early spring at the latest, which is right around the time my job here ends. I should be able to come home as planned, regardless of all this."

"OK," Brenna said tenuously, fearing more was coming.

"They're checking all the land lines and cell towers," Anthony continued, "and they just confiscated our cell phones. But we're allowed to make outgoing calls from land lines to preauthorized numbers, and your number is preauthorized. I'm calling you from the land line in my hotel room. All incoming calls will be blocked, though, until further notice, so you can't call me. But since I was always calling you anyway, this really won't affect us either."

"As always, your glass is half full," she remarked with awe.

"Maybe three-quarters full," Anthony jested.

"I'm afraid for you." It was blunt and pessimistic, and she hadn't wanted to say it. Yet, not saying it would have felt disingenuous.

"Remember, we've got personal, armed bodyguards, and with the lockdown, and all the revamping going on, the country's security will be tighter every day."

"I hope you're right," Brenna said, knowing it was impossible for her to be as confident as her habitually optimistic husband.

# CHAPTER TWENTY-SEVEN

He crouched inside the fluffy bush, waiting for her to arrive. Fortunately, Sylvia had caught on that she could play with Melvin—the name she'd given his feline self—by going to the park directly after school each day. And she'd long since given up on the maddening, failing efforts to carry him to the shelter.

Over the past weeks, Stanlin had grown very fond of her. Yes, she was still beautiful from head to toe, but it had become so much more than that. Around her, he felt really alive; her presence energized him and buoyed his heart. Even between visits, the thought of her kind smile and caring touch inspired him to be a better Rampont—the best that he could be.

It wasn't a one-way street, either. He had consistently intuited her mood boosting as she played with him, and he had confirmed this by tuning into her thoughts. On most days, she came to the park fretting about school assignments, exams, and things her classmates did and said. Gradually, though, her thoughts would transform into musings about Melvin's cuteness and sweetness, and then, quite amazingly, her original worries would return to her mind with more calm, balanced perspectives. It was wonderful how they uplifted each other. They'd become true blue friends.

Happily huddled, he continued peering out from the bush until she arrived. He trotted over to greet her, she picked him up, and he tuned into her thoughts.

"Little Melvin," he heard. "Seeing you here, it's almost like you're my cat. With Mom's allergies, it's probably the closest I can ever get. But what am I going to do with you when the weather gets colder? For now, you being an outside cat is OK, but when it's cold, you'll have to go to the shelter or you'll freeze! But how in the world will I take you there without you running off first? And what if I get you there and someone adopts you?"

Sylvia's concerns didn't distress Stanlin yet. From what he'd learned about Earth's seasons, summer would arrive before the colder autumn and winter, and the summer was what worried him. Now, they had an after-school park routine. But what would happen when school was out? What if she and he were always arriving there at different times? He would have to rethink his strategy—and soon. Summer was around the corner. He'd already heard Sylvia cheerfully thinking that school would be done in just a few weeks.

Stanlin didn't know how to ease either of their concerns at the moment, so he made some purring sounds and rubbed his head on her shoulder to help her smile.

"Awww," she said, petting him. "Are you ready for your lunch?" She gripped his torso and lowered him to the ground. Sifting through her backpack, she found the small container. She pulled it out, opened it, and set it down in front of him. "Here you go, Melvin. Eat your tuna fish."

The taste of the stuff wasn't too bad, and Sylvia always seemed gratified when he finished it, so face first into the fish he went. The first day she'd brought it for him, she'd told him it was her parents' idea. They'd heard her go on and on about Melvin, and since they weren't able to adopt him, they felt the least they could do was give him some good food. Stanlin thought it was a very nice sentiment.

Before long, he'd eaten the last morsel of the tuna.

"All done?" Sylvia asked. She closed the container and stowed it.

Stanlin noticed a familiar mother and toddler approaching. The two stopped by to see Sylvia and Melvin nearly every day.

The mother, Mrs. Tormeni, and Sylvia greeted one another.

The toddler, Cedric, chimed in. "Hi, Sivia," he said, looking up at Sylvia.

"Hi, Cedric," Sylvia said, waving at him.

Cedric turned toward Stanlin. "Mewven!" he exclaimed before lunging clumsily at him.

Stanlin could tell the toddler had the best of intentions, but truth be told, he was nervous around the lumbering child. From his observations at the park, Stanlin had learned that very young humans weren't so steady on their legs, so he feared being squashed by Cedric accidentally toppling over onto him. And although Cedric was small relative to adult humans, he wasn't small relative to Melvin.

Fortunately, as in prior days, the boy's legs held firm as he petted Melvin spiritedly. A short while later, Mrs. Tormeni and Cedric said good-bye and walked hand in hand toward the monkey bars.

Sylvia and Melvin played a bit longer, until she inevitably checked her watch and hugged him farewell. "See ya tomorrow, Melvin," she said.

As she walked out of the park, he pranced into the fluffy bush, became invisible, and followed her. Because his affection had taken on a hint of protectiveness, for the last week or so, he'd been ensuring that she reached her postpark destinations unharmed. Only after her safe arrival, either at the shelter for a shift of volunteer work or at home, would he feel ready to return to Capton.

While shadowing her on this particular day, he was struck with a fabulous idea.

To this point, he hadn't paid much attention to the location of her house; there had been no need. But when she walked up her driveway this time, he looked at the number on the door and then at the street sign, memorizing them: house number seventeen on Holloway Drive.

He darted behind a tree, became visible Melvin again, and ran to the garbage can in front of her house. Leaning his front paws on it, he pushed with all his might. Thank goodness it was empty. The can toppled over and caught Sylvia's attention, just like he wanted.

"Melvin! What are you doing all the way over here?" she asked.

He bolted in the direction of the park, leaving her to stare after him quizzically. With a laugh and a shake of her head, she erected the fallen garbage can.

Once Stanlin saw her tending to the can, he gleefully leapt into the nearest bush and transported home.

He realized Sylvia must be thinking Melvin was one heck of an odd cat, but that was OK. He had accomplished what he'd intended. Sylvia now knew that Melvin had followed her and seen her house, so if he happened to show up on her front or back lawn in the summer time, she would not be shocked or confused. Although she wouldn't always be home, it would probably be the easiest place to catch her for impromptu visits when school days were over.

Smiling with pleasure, Stanlin transformed into himself and slipped on his garment. But all at once, out of nowhere, he felt an inexplicable wave of trepidation. He sensed that their summer wouldn't be lighthearted, that danger loomed ahead of them.

Desperate to erase the unsettling impression, Stanlin chastised himself. "Who do you think you are? A prophet? Everyone gets weird ideas in their heads that are sometimes right and sometimes wrong. This one is clearly wrong. Dropping by at Sylvia's house for some visits is not exactly risky business. Oh, the hazards of playing together in the yard! So treacherous!" he thought, chuckling.

He almost had himself convinced.

# PART II

STRIVING TO AVERT DOOM

# Summer, 2032

# CHAPTER TWENTY-EIGHT

Ned had graduated high school a month earlier, and had started looking for a full-time job so he could make money and move out of his mother's house. He also imagined it would be easier to learn of and carry out God's instructions from within his own private space.

Deep in thought, he walked alongside the neighborhood creek. God had spoken to him lots of times, always from within the clouds. But He had only mentioned having "a purpose" for Ned's father in the very first conversation. Since then, He had refused to discuss it, despite Ned's repeated asking. For a whole year, God had said the same stuff: Ned was to help Him in purifying the Earth, and more details would be coming soon.

Soon. Ned's patience was wearing thin. Pretty much the only thing that kept him from going bonkers was remembering what Pastor Jensen had said. Answers would come according to God's timetable. Information could come in bits and pieces. Eventually, God would fill him in.

He tossed a twig into the creek and looked out across the water to where a boy, maybe eight years old, swam. The kid looked kind of familiar, yet Ned couldn't place where he'd seen the young face before.

A sudden rustling in the bushes behind him redirected his attention. Following the sounds, Ned came across another boy, who looked about ten or eleven years old. He held clothing, shoes, and socks in his hands, but he was fully dressed. The boy was grinning, and seemed to be sneaking off with the clothes—clothes that surely belonged to the boy in the creek.

Hot fury boiled inside Ned as memories of his own, similar childhood humiliation came flooding back. His face reddened, his hands rolled into fists, and, for a few seconds, his right ear tingled.

It was when the tingling stopped that he heard it, the voice he knew to be God's, resounding inside his right ear. And the message was more specific than ever before: "The cleansing can begin now. This boy is evil. I don't need people like him. Get rid of him."

Ned's heart raced. It was his first command! A small, inner voice said, "Don't," but he ignored it, knowing God's instructions totally outranked any of his own stray thoughts. Pouncing upon the evil one, Ned wrapped his hands tightly around the slender, young neck. The boy squirmed and clawed, but his fight didn't last long.

As the youth died, Ned's anger vanished. He felt relief and lightness, almost weightlessness. He also felt very powerful. After strangling the cat as a child, he'd experienced a similar feeling, but it hadn't been as intense as this was now.

Completely absorbed in the moment, Ned didn't hear the other boy come out of the water and into the bushy area to look for his clothing. The dripping wet little child gaped at the sight of a big teenager holding a blue-faced boy around the neck, and he screamed.

Jolted out of his haze, Ned whipped around and faced the screaming boy. In panic, he dropped the dead child and ran home.

\* \* \*

While Ned hadn't recognized his observer, the boy certainly knew Ned. Two months earlier, Ned had been at the young boy's home receiving math tutelage from the boy's older brother, Frank, who was Ned's classmate. Ned had said Frank was talking down to him and punched him in the face. Frank's loud yell brought his mother and little brother rushing into the room. Seeing blood gushing from her son's nose, Frank's mother fiercely ousted Ned from the house, grabbing him by the collar. "Ned Chambers, you are a bully! Get out of here, and never come back!" she'd hollered. The bloody scene was burned into both her sons' memories.

The eight-year-old boy at the creek would have been scared simply by seeing Ned Chambers again; watching Ned commit a murder absolutely terrified him. Somehow, he was able to do what was necessary. The boy had been trained well by his parents. He had a cell phone in the pocket of his shorts, which had fallen to the ground when Ned seized the older child. The boy pulled on the shorts, took out the phone, and called the police. He described the event, the location, and Ned's appearance. He also mentioned that this was the same bully who'd punched his big brother.

"What was the bully's name, son? Do you remember?" the dispatcher asked.

"Ned Chambers," the little boy replied.

Police swiftly arrived at both the crime scene and the Chambers residence, and Ned was arrested.

As policemen escorted him to the station, Ned's lips curled impishly. So what if he went to prison? He was sure his work for God could be carried out from there as well as from anywhere else. What really mattered was that God had finally specifically instructed him, and He had delivered a new piece of information.

At last, the mission had begun.

# CHAPTER TWENTY-NINE

Claire Evans was his soul mate. Ron Camm knew this in his core. They had so much in common. Both had grown up with mothers who were addicted to pain killers and fathers who weren't around. When Ron was only five years old, his father had walked out. No warning; he just up and left the family one day. Claire's father had been away on business trips so much that he was hardly ever home, and whenever he did show up, he'd beat her. Ron's stepfather used to beat him up, too.

So Ron and Claire understood each other. He loved her more than he had ever loved anyone, and she loved him. She'd said so. Although she had left him over a year ago, he knew she still cared and would take him back, again. But this time around, it was requiring a lot more scheming on his part.

When she'd left last spring, he could tell it was different. Her old pattern had been threatening to break up, moving in with her sister for a few weeks, realizing her mistake, and running back to him, saying she'd try harder to make things work out. Last spring, though, she did not threaten anything or go to her sister's at all. She sneaked away to a women's shelter, which was protected by police, so it was too risky for him to go there. Little did she know, he'd been having her followed since the day she left.

Ron sat at his kitchen table, scotch glass in hand, waiting for a special delivery. He ran his other hand over the top of his shaved head as he recalled the events of that fateful day last spring. He had woken up lying on the floor a few feet from the foyer, hung over, exhausted, and aching everywhere. His eyes were mostly closed, but the lids were separated just enough to see Claire slip out the front door with a bag of stuff and the lousy kid. Hardly able to move, through willpower alone, he had managed to crawl across the floor to the nearest phone.

He'd called his friend Larry, told him Claire had just left the apartment, and instructed him to tail her and report back to him. Because she had sneaked out, he'd instinctively known she must be followed, and he hadn't had the strength to do it himself. He soon realized it was more efficient for Larry to do it anyway, at least until Claire was on her own, away from those shelters. Of course, Larry wanted good pay to stick with the job, but that wasn't a problem. Ron had arranged to get him the money, and the tailing and reporting continued. Both Claire and Larry were now over twenty-five hundred miles away.

Ron mused over how thankful he was to be able to afford the essentials. Dealing drugs raked in cash and hooked him up with lots of contacts. In his world, whatever special favors one wanted, there was always someone who could help out, for the right price. Friends knew people, and those friends had friends who also knew people. Since Claire had gone, some very special favors were needed to bring her back home—especially in light of her unnerving behaviors.

Last spring, Larry had informed him that Claire had checked into the Guyton Women's Shelter with Cedric, but several weeks later, she'd left the shelter alone and then checked in alone at the Secoya Women's Shelter, about twenty-eight hundred miles further west. Immediately, Ron had personally spied on Claire's sister and mother, whose homes were somewhat close to his own, to see if they'd picked up Cedric from the Guyton Shelter. But no, neither one had him.

Ron was sure his clashes with Cedric had played a big part in Claire's decision to run away. He knew in his gut that getting along better with the little runt would be a necessary evil in getting Claire back. But he needed more information. Where in the hell was the kid sent off to? Had he gotten sick or hurt? To find answers, a special favor was required, and Ron found the needed friend: a brilliant computer hacker. But when Ron described what he wanted—Claire's records from the Guyton system, which would have notes on what had happened with Cedric—the hacker demanded a price that shocked even Ron. Pissed off but determined, Ron noted the computer hacker's cell number and said he'd call again once he'd saved up enough cash.

That day had finally arrived yesterday. Ron was able to pay the hacker, and the ally agreed to retrieve, print, and deliver Claire's Guyton Shelter file sometime today. Ron had been waiting since he woke up at 8:52 a.m.

He looked at the clock: 4:37 p.m. He sighed, gulped down the rest of his scotch, and lowered the empty glass to the table with a thud. He began thinking of some of the updates he'd received from Larry. Claire had changed her hairstyle again. The first change had been to cut her long, dark hair to shoulder length and dye it with red streaks. Last month, she had cut it shorter still, and she'd changed the red streaks to blond. But so what? He would get her to grow it all out again.

The more important news was that a few weeks ago, she had found a job in a town not far from the Secoya Shelter. She had moved into her own apartment, minutes away from the new job. Better still, Larry had seen Claire hiding a spare key on top of the molding above her front door, and he had already complied with Ron's instructions to steal, duplicate, and return it while Claire was at work. Ron then had Larry FedEx him the duplicate, which had arrived last week. Once Ron reached Claire's place, it would be easy access.

At last, she was in one spot—alone. Not surrounded by lousy cops. All he needed to do now was find out what had happened with Cedric and use that to his advantage. The boy was key; he could feel it in his bones. He would find a way to use the little runt as leverage; then Claire would definitely come back.

A loud knocking interrupted his thoughts, and Ron quickly rose from his chair to answer the door. When he swung it open, no one was there, but a manila envelope was on the doormat. "This has to be it," Ron thought, snatching up the envelope. He brought it to the kitchen table and hastily opened it.

There was a lot to read through. Impatiently, his eyes darted over the pages, taking in the new information:

Claire had changed her name to Mona Banks. The Guyton Shelter had referred her to the Secoya Shelter because Claire had said she wanted to move far out west, and the Secoya Shelter was the best in the region. It had a staff of counselors to teach her job skills and help her find employment. Also, both group and individualized therapy sessions were available, so the progress she had made at Guyton could be continued.

"Yeah, yeah," Ron thought petulantly. "Progress. What a load of crap." He read about Claire's history:

Claire's mother was a narcotics addict. Her father was rarely home, yet verbally and physically abused her when he was present. Loneliness led her into promiscuity, followed by teen pregnancy. She never learned the paternity of her son, Cedric. She habitually formed relationships with verbally and/or physically abusive partners. Her most recent partner, Ron Camm, had been the most violent.

Ron seethed at seeing his own name in print, but he read what the therapist had written about him:

Early in the relationship, Ron had started with verbal put-downs, calling Claire a slut, stupid, worthless, etc. He was highly critical in general, of both her and her son. Over time, his verbal abuse had expanded to threats to harm her physically. He followed through and began hitting her, primarily in the torso and upper arm regions, where the bruises were concealed by clothing. Abuse further expanded to threats to hit Cedric, who he then began hitting in the same manner. Periodically, Ron would try to offset his demoralizing behaviors with gifts, romantic gestures, and compliments. Claire had tried to leave Ron a few times, staying with her sister, Joline. But Ron always begged her to come back, with apologies and declarations of undying love, and she gave in, hoping things would be better. January of 2031 had been a turning point. Claire's mother began counseling for her narcotics addiction and was informed of a local chapter of Adult Children of Alcoholics/Addicts (ACOA). She convinced Claire and Joline to attend the weekly meetings together.

"Damn!" Ron yelled aloud, banging his fist on the table. He thought, "She said she was going to Joline's for *lunch* every week. Lunch my ass." Furiously, he read on:

In the group sessions, Claire had discussed issues both from her childhood and her current, adult life. Gradually, she stopped denying Ron's abusiveness, and her confidence grew. Ron, likely sensing that Claire was becoming more secure in herself, had escalated his threats by saying he would kill Cedric if she misbehaved or tried to leave again. After Claire divulged this to the group, she realized her son's life was in danger, no matter what. Ron's violence was getting worse. He had followed through with his other threats in the past, and he had always resented Cedric, saying he was a bastard child and a leach who took up all of Claire's attention. Talking things out with the others, Claire had determined she needed to leave Ron and find a way to protect Cedric. Petrified that Ron would hunt down and kill Cedric if she raised him herself, or if her mother or sister raised him, Claire had asked for assistance in finding Cedric a safe home with adoptive parents. She was referred to the Rima Adoption Agency, where an adoption was arranged.

Ron's jaw dropped. He could not believe she had given up Cedric.

The notes also included a report sent by the Rima Agency. Ron brightened up when he saw that it contained the adoptive couple's address.

# CHAPTER THIRTY

After contemplating all that he had read, Ron took action. He owned a red Corvette, and had recently received a gray Toyota sedan as payment from one of his customers. Since the sedan was much more practical for what he had in mind, he stocked it up with some needed items, purchased from Wal-Mart and a local friend: a child's car seat, a baby's blanket, ropes, thin plastic gloves, a razor, and a supply of chloroformed rags in an airtight bag.

He packed a suitcase full of clothes and the daily toiletries. In a separate satchel, he stashed stacks of bills. Cash was important; it wasn't traceable. Neither was his prepay cell, which he tucked into the front pocket of his jean shorts. He knew he'd be on the road for a while, but it was hard at this point to tell for exactly how long.

He got in the car and drove seventy-four miles, arriving in the Tormeni's neighborhood very late at night. While navigating the streets, he could tell even in the darkness that the homes were well kept. "Yuppie types," he muttered contemptuously.

He found the Tormeni's home, parked diagonally across the street, and walked over to survey the house, first from the front, and then from the back.

When standing on the back patio, he saw a very dim light shining from one of the windows on the second floor. The rest of the home was unlit. A smile spread across Ron's face. Cedric had always slept with a night light. White curtains, gently lit by the night light, ruffled slightly with the breeze. The window was open. Yes, Cedric had always liked the fresh air. The new parents probably thought letting in some cooler air at night would be perfectly safe. After all, the bedrooms were on the second floor, and they lived in a good section of town. They were in for a real surprise.

Satisfied with what he had seen, Ron stayed in a local motel that night. The next morning, he purchased a collapsible ladder that could fit into his trunk. That afternoon, he called Larry to confirm the directions to Claire's new apartment. He waited until nearly midnight to drive back to the Tormeni's house.

Wearing the plastic gloves to avoid leaving any fingerprints behind, he carefully set up the ladder under Cedric's window, and climbed up. He cut the screen with the razor and slithered inside. Grabbing the chloroformed rag he'd planted in his shirt pocket, he covered Cedric's nose and mouth. Cedric awakened, squirmed, and tried to scream. Ron pressed the rag down hard, muffling the sounds, and the chloroform did its job.

Ron had also worn a five-foot-long rope, draped in loose circles around his neck. With the razor, he cut two small sections from the rope and bound up Cedric's wrists and ankles. He used more rope to tie Cedric's torso to his own, so the kid was pressed to his back as he climbed out the window and down the ladder.

Moving with the utmost efficiency, Ron took down the collapsible ladder, stowed it in the trunk, and tied Cedric up in the child's seat in the back of the car. He spread the baby blanket across Cedric's body, concealing the ropes. The little runt was out cold. Anyone catching a glimpse back there would assume the kid was fast asleep. Ron was extremely grateful for that chloroform. The doused rags would also quiet all of the brat's attempts at screaming and crying for the whole trip. They had some long days of driving ahead.

As he started the engine and pulled away from the curb, Ron thought about seeing his sweetheart again. It had been way too long—with her two shelter stays and his saving for the hacker's fees—but the wait was almost over, and now he had his special bargaining chip. Maybe scaring Claire into staying with him hadn't worked before, but once she saw the kid with him, she would realize how powerful Ron really was. *He could track down both her and her son, in spite of all of her best efforts to hide, in spite of the shelters, in spite of the adoption, in spite of the police.* She would give in to him. He could calm her by promising to get along better with her and Cedric.

Already, he felt victorious. He would have his Claire back very soon. And if, for whatever reasons, Plan A failed, there was always Plan B. If she refused him in this life, he would take her with him into the next.

Either way, Cedric would be history before long.

# CHAPTER THIRTY-ONE

Sillu, this week's orator, had just transitioned the Capton Governmental Council meeting to its next topic—news in other galaxies. "As most of you know, my intergalactic committee speaks with planetary leaders in the Milky Way. This week, the king's scientists on planet Ignaturia told us of an upsetting dilemma.

"About two months ago, their king sent out scouts to find unique-looking creatures, and transmit the creatures' images to his personal viewing monitor. He became enthralled with the look of the giraffes on Earth, and had his scouts capture five and transport them to Ignaturia's Primary Genetics Laboratory Complex. He ordered his scientists there to produce five new animals by blending the genetics of the giraffes with the genetics of five ringeos, which are common pets on Ignaturia. The offspring turned out to be affectionate and docile; they look like two-foot-tall giraffes.

"At first, the king was ecstatic, and publicized images with himself and his new pets. Of course, then everyone on the planet wanted little giraffes of their own. To capitalize on the demand, the king instructed the scientists to breed hundreds of the animals. But, very sadly, after a couple of weeks, the king grew bored and ordered his personal deputy to care for his pets. Word leaked out to the public, and the demand for the newly bred animals sank.

"Now, there are hundreds of these domesticated, miniature giraffes on Ignaturia who need homes. I propose that we allow our citizens to adopt them. My committee has calculated that we can fit about fifty at a time on board our traveler ship, and from Ignaturia's central tarmac to ours here at Headquarters, the flight should take less than two hours."

"It's a great idea for us to help out," Cadence piped up. "My only concern is how we're going to get momentum with it. There's always fear with the unknown, and our citizens won't know what to expect with these pets. They might hesitate to get involved."

"What if we can come up with some type of incentive to get the first ones adopted?" Renito suggested. "Then word of mouth about their affectionate personalities will spread, and it will be easier to adopt out more."

"Yes, yes," Sillu agreed.

"I have an idea," Nixar said, donning a boyish grin of admiration at his wife commanding the stage. "The office complex across the way might be a good place to start. We could offer the rest of the day off of work to anyone who walks over here and picks up a pet."

Munin, seated next to Nixar, patted his shoulder. "Yeah; that'd be perfect!"

Similar comments flooded the room.

"This is wonderful! I'll contact the king's scientists right after the meeting. I bet we can have the first fifty animals sent over and adopted today!" Sillu projected enthusiastically.

Everyone cheered.

"Is it possible that the giraffes from Earth were hurt at all when the genetics blending work was being conducted?" Sequentor asked, causing his colleagues to quiet themselves.

"Hmmm. The scientists only mentioned returning the original five giraffes to Earth, nothing more. It wouldn't hurt to check on them," Sillu resolved.

The meeting room had a Probability Sphere set up on its stage to the left of the orator's podium. An apparatus similar to a video camera was positioned so it could project images from the Sphere onto five large, mounted screens for all of the Council members to see. Spontaneous questions such as Sequentor's could thus be investigated by everyone.

Sillu approached the Sphere, looked into its center, and focused her thoughts to: "Giraffes on Earth that had been utilized on Ignaturia."

The depiction totally silenced the room. The five giraffes were lying splayed on a grassy field; three of them were obviously dead, and the other two were fitfully coughing. When the picture faded, it was replaced by the words "Six months from now, with 95 percent certainty."

"How could this be? They seem sick, don't they?" Sillu spewed frantically, half to herself, and half to her peers. "This doesn't look like something that could arise out of genetic sampling, does it?"

"Check if the ringeo-giraffes on Ignaturia are going to be sick. Maybe the Earth giraffes caught the sickness in Ignaturia and brought it with them to Earth," Munin conjectured.

"Good thinking," Sillu said. She engaged the Sphere appropriately, and the ringeo-giraffes on Ignaturia appeared perfectly robust in the foreseeable future.

Bartholith raised his hand. "It definitely looked like those five giraffes contracted a disease, but if that's true, wouldn't the disease also affect other giraffes, and maybe different animal species, too? How about assessing the future for animals on Earth, and we'll see what comes up?"

Sillu complied with the recommendation, and everyone stared at the screens. In rapid succession, one species after the next was shown; the creatures were either lying dead or coughing violently. The final frames depicted the humans.

It was almost unbearable for the Council members to view. Wails, gasps, and stilted screams of their shock and fright were all that could be heard. When the devastating visuals ended, the ominous words appeared: "Six months from now, with 95 percent certainty."

Sillu looked around the room, seeing her own grief and terror reflected in everyone's eyes. "How can we help?" she asked desperately.

"Check the influencing factors—in case!" Lithantor called out.

Sillu nodded and heeded him. She focused her gaze toward the top of the Sphere while concentrating on Earth's desolate forecast. An image of three puppies in an animal shelter flashed across the screens, followed by a picture of an inmate in a maximum security prison.

"The influencing factors are indeed Earthbound," Sillu confirmed dejectedly. She pressed her fingertips to the bridge of her nose and closed her eyes, drawing in a deep breath. Exhaling slowly, she opened her eyes. "I don't see how we can intervene without breaking the Non-Interaction Law, and we absolutely can't violate the Free Will Decree. Even if we could somehow intercede lawfully, what if this disease could infect *us?* Are there any ideas? Is there anything we can do?"

A mournful silence was the only reply.

"Please, please ruminate on this," she urged. "Hopefully we can come up with *something* that will help. But in the meanwhile, for our planet's safety, I will announce to the public that Earth visitation is banned and that a breach of the ban will be punishable by imprisonment, for a term as long as the Council deems fit. Is this reasonable and acceptable to everyone?"

No one even considered contesting her.

# CHAPTER THIRTY-TWO

Stanlin sprightly walked home, relieved at having just finished his very last final examination. For the next eight weeks, he and his fellow students would be on the annual "meditation and recreation break" from school. On Capton, they believed replenishing time was vital, so even the adults in all fields of work got their eight weeks off every year. Only theirs weren't taken in one big clump like the students'.

During the eight weeks the students were off, the teachers formulated lesson plans and observed and noted any astronomical changes. Capton's orbit was very close to its nearest sun at this time of the year, so their space viewing units produced very clear images. Consequently, Captonian coursework was always up to date and very thoroughly detailed.

As Stanlin had anticipated, his exams were extremely challenging. He'd prepared rigorously by studying almost nonstop for weeks, staying up late and getting up early. He hadn't been able to visit Sylvia at all since the day of his shenanigans with the garbage can. From listening to her thoughts previously, he knew she was already enjoying her summer break. Now, his school year was done, too!

With a spring in his step, he entered the house, eager to transport to Sylvia's yard for an impromptu visit. To his surprise, both of his parents were waiting for him, looking distraught. They sat in the gathering room, and an animal Stanlin hadn't seen before sat on the floor between their chairs. Although smaller, it looked very much like the pictures he had seen of giraffes on Earth.

"Stanlin, please sit with us. We need to speak with you right away." His father's voice sounded strained, and he was almost never home this early from work.

Feeling apprehensive, Stanlin sat with them. "Is everything alright? And what's that creature?"

"Yes, let's start with the animal; that's the better news," Andrigon said, looking down at it as if he'd almost forgotten it was there. "The Governmental Council made an announcement that there are hundreds of these animals in need of homes. They're domesticated pets from Ignaturia. The Council gave our office access first. We were given the rest of the day off if we adopted one." A tiny smile came across his otherwise troubled expression. He lightly ran his hand over the animal's back. "I've named our friend here 'Mini-G.'"

In response to Andrigon's touch, Mini-G's tail moved back and forth and her head bobbed up and down.

Karilu stroked Mini-G's neck and said to Stanlin, "Go ahead, honey. She's such a lovable little girl."

Stanlin softly petted the miniature giraffe on her head, neck, and back. Looking at her and touching her smooth fur was soothing. "Hey there, girl," he murmured.

Again, Mini-G's head bobbed and her tail wagged in gratitude.

Knowing that aside from the sweet new pet, something dismal was going on, Stanlin steeled himself. "So, what's the other news?"

"Yes, there is something more difficult to tell you." Andrigon rubbed his temples, and then rested his hands on his knees. "In a radio alert this morning, the Governmental Council announced that from now on, all Ramponts are forbidden from traveling to Earth."

"What? Forbidden? Why? I don't want to stop going to Earth!" Stanlin protested.

"A horrible incident is coming, and we must stay away to protect ourselves. I know you really enjoy visiting there, Stanlin, but safety comes first," Andrigon insisted gravely.

Karilu nodded emphatically.

Stanlin could not believe what he was hearing. "What horrible incident?" he choked out.

Andrigon and Karilu looked at one another somberly. After a woeful sigh, Karilu explained. "According to the Governmental Council's Probability Sphere, in approximately six months' time, a highly contagious disease will be spreading rampantly across planet Earth, killing animals and humans alike."

Stanlin was shocked into silence. When he was finally able to speak, the words tumbled out rapidly, and his voice raised and cracked. "Maybe something can be done to stop this disease before it starts! If I did some detective work, by going to Earth without my auditory plugs, I could see and hear everything. I'd catch wind of something that would help us figure out how to help—I just know it! And I'm the perfect Rampont for the job. You know how I really love Earth!"

Stanlin had previously told his parents that Earth was his favorite planet, so he knew his proposition to sleuth there wouldn't seem incongruous to them. He also knew that Governmental Council members could not physically prevent their fellow Ramponts from engaging in interplanetary transport. Sure, they could make an announcement forbidding travel to attempt to protect their citizens, but if he were to go to Earth at his own risk, searching for answers and solutions, were they really going to enforce a harsh punishment? He was willing to take his chances.

Fear crept into Karilu's eyes. "You can't do that, Stanlin," she whispered hoarsely.

"You'd like to volunteer for imprisonment, would you?" Andrigon challenged.

"Imprisonment?" Stanlin echoed lamely.

"Yes. Breaking the law is a *crime,* and *crimes* are punishable by *imprisonment,*" Andrigon patronized. "Omitting the auditory plugs like you suggested breaks the Non-Interaction Law, which has a consequence of one year in jail. And now, ignoring this ban and traveling to Earth is punishable by imprisonment for a term as long as the Council decides."

The harsh truth of his father's words impaled the wall of denial Stanlin had been shielding himself behind. At long last, he considered his recent actions realistically. Bewexin had, for educational purposes, permitted them to go plugless their first day on Earth, and Stanlin had latched onto that as an excuse to minimize the importance of the Non-Interaction Law in total. His rationalization that, as "Melvin," he hadn't actually been a visible Rampont interacting with the humans, was, well, shady. Yes, he had broken the law every time he had visited Sylvia on Earth.

But what about the dire circumstances now? He was in turmoil. Could he abide by this Earth ban and the Non-Interaction Law when Sylvia's life was on the line?

# CHAPTER THIRTY-THREE

Desolate, Stanlin ran to his bedroom. When his mother came in a moment later, carrying Mini-G, he suppressed his brewing tears.

Karilu walked over and lowered Mini-G onto the bed next to him. "I think you could use her company right now."

"Thanks, Ma." Stanlin slowly rubbed the animal's long neck; she had already lain down.

"Hearing about a beautiful planet's demise is upsetting for all of us, and I know you were especially fond of Earth."

"You don't know the half of it," Stanlin thought, but he muttered, "Yeah."

"I'll give you some quiet." Karilu cupped Stanlin's cheek in her palm before leaving his room and closing the door behind her.

Mini-G looked up at him and blinked. Innocence shone in her bright eyes. His mother's compassion, the little pet's soft countenance, his sweet

Earth friend at death's door…How could life have such purity and still in-flict such pain? Unable to hold off any longer, Stanlin let the tears gush. He stroked Mini-G's fur and gazed at her through a blurry, watery haze. "What am I gonna do?" he moaned.

Stanlin's head spun with questions. Was absolutely everyone on Earth going to die from the terrible disease? Was it possible that Sylvia might be spared? If only there were a way he could find out if she would be alright, without breaking the laws and traveling to Earth to check on her…

And suddenly, it dawned on him: If a Probability Sphere could show Earth's future, it should be able to show Sylvia's future. Stanlin knew just where he could find one, too! His Universe course instructor, Ramaway, was one of a select group of teachers who were also members of the Governmental Council, so he had a Probability Sphere right inside his of-fice. And, most likely, Ramaway would still be there now, grading exams. Stanlin had never used a Probability Sphere before, but maybe, hopefully, Ramaway would teach him.

"Come on, girl," he said to Mini-G as he hopped to his feet. She leaped off the bed, followed him to the gathering room, and curled up on the floor between where his mom and dad sat. Stanlin told his parents he needed to go ask a teacher some questions, and he'd be home in time for dinner.

He left the house and sprinted to school; running always helped him release some pent up energy. Once he reached Ramaway's office, he peered through the open door. Ramaway sat at his desk grading tests, just as Stanlin had anticipated.

"Hello, R." The abbreviated title had become Ramaway's nickname among the students. "Do you have a minute? I'd really like to ask you about something," Stanlin said, breathing a little heavily from his run.

"Sure, Stanlin; come on in. Must be a burning question for you to come back to school after just finishing your exams!"

"Yeah," Stanlin confirmed, walking in. "I want to learn about the Governmental Council's Probability Spheres." He stopped in front of R's desk and peered at him imploringly. "Can they predict the future about anything—or anyone?"

"Come on, this way," R instructed. He got up and led Stanlin toward the corner of his office, where his cream-colored Sphere lay nestled into its stand of coiled, transparent wire. "Yes, Probability Spheres, like this one, can reveal predictions of the near future—meaning a few days, to several months out—for any topic, most typically a situation, a place, or a being." R stood with his arms folded across his chest, looking at the Sphere with obvious respect.

"That sure is an incredible invention," Stanlin said, simultaneously awestruck and nervous. "Is it tough to use? Could I, um, try it out?" Asking for this special permission, combined with his fears of what he might find out if granted the permission, made his palms shaky and sweaty.

"I'll tell you the basics of how it works, and if you grasp the main concepts, then I'll let you use it," R consented.

"Thank you, sir," Stanlin replied graciously, subtly wiping his palms on his garment.

R rubbed his chin thoughtfully. "You know how radios work, right?"

"I know that different stations are broadcasted at different frequencies, and whatever frequency you tune your radio to, it'll play the station that transmits with that same frequency. Is that what you mean, sir?"

"Yes," R affirmed. "Now, going beyond that, each station plays its own type of music. You listen to frequency 10, and you hear soft music; you listen to frequency 12, and you hear upbeat music, etc."

"Uh-huh," said Stanlin.

"Well, every thought has a unique frequency too, and the Sphere receives thought frequencies."

Stanlin nodded slowly.

"When we send the Sphere a specific thought, it picks up that thought frequency and simultaneously emits rays of light within itself, which mimic time travel into the future. The Sphere momentarily holds the specific thought frequency within that simulated future. Remember, any thought we send the Sphere is of a particular subject. So, when held within that new era, the thought frequency will transform, but only enough to correspond with whatever changes have occurred with the thought's subject in the future. The Sphere perceives the subtly changed frequency signaling, and it displays those changes as images of the future for us to view."

"Incredible," Stanlin said, turning this over in his mind. "I think I've got an analogy. In a way, the Sphere is like a forecasting radio: Our present thought about, let's say, 'song X' initially sets the tuning dial, but the radio receives frequencies about 'song X' in the future—maybe from a future era radio station broadcast—so it plays back the 'future X' song for us."

"Why, yes! Excellent!" R patted Stanlin's shoulder.

"But how does the Sphere decide how far into the future to look?" Stanlin delved.

"I love your thoroughness," R extolled. "The Sphere shows us only the most potent near future images of the thought's subject. For example, if you checked up on Capton's future and learned that an attack from planet Nupon was coming in two months, that would be the most potent near future image it could show you. Capton might also experience a rain storm in three weeks, but the Sphere wouldn't show you inconsequential things like that. In fact, the Sphere can't even sense the minor things. It only detects strong signals, and potent data emits strong signals."

"Hmmm, strong signals," Stanlin muttered as he mentally linked in with the radio analogy again. "Then, could we say that potent data is like a future era radio station that has a super strong broadcasting signal, which the forecasting radio easily picks up and plays?"

"Yes," R said, clasping his hands together and rocking back and forth from his heals to his toes.

"And things like a rain storm would be like weak broadcasting signals that the radio can't clearly tune in."

"Uh-huh." R smiled at Stanlin and rocked some more. "Now, put it all together in sum for me, without the radio analogy."

Trying his best to rehash the salient points, Stanlin said, "The Sphere picks up a thought frequency that we send, and suspends it in a simulated future environment. Whatever most potently relates to that thought's subject in the near future will alter its frequency. The Sphere then shows us the images from this new frequency, so we see the most relevant near future of our subject."

"You've grasped the concepts very well," R praised. "You've definitely earned yourself the opportunity to try the Sphere out."

"Good," Stanlin replied shakily. He could feel his body temperature rising.

R jovially patted Stanlin on the back. "Ahhh, to be young...It'll be fun for you to have a heads up on next week's sporting events, or maybe you'll see a summer romance on the horizon," he teased, laughing congenially.

"If only my questions were carefree like that," Stanlin thought sadly, but he pushed a polite smile.

"To put it to use, first, completely focus your mind on your topic while peering directly into the Sphere's center," R instructed. "In an instant, you'll see pictures of the future, followed by an estimated time frame. Which reminds me—there's one small caveat we haven't touched on yet: No future prediction is 100 percent guaranteed. For this reason, the Sphere also gives a numerical probability of likelihood for the scenarios it shows."

Stanlin nodded.

"Alright. Go for it! As for me, exams are beckoning." Giving Stanlin privacy, R winked and headed back to his desk.

Stanlin pictured Sylvia in his mind while looking into the Sphere's center. An image emerged of a small brown casket being closed and sealed—with Sylvia inside. The following image showed that little casket being lowered into the ground. Then words arose: "Three months from now, with 95 percent certainty." The words blurred, and the Sphere slowly returned to its cream coloring.

Stanlin was trembling. The Sphere had not only confirmed his worst fear, but it had predicted a time frame of only three months! The rampant spreading wasn't projected until six months out, so apparently, Sylvia would be catching the disease early on. There was so little time! Feeling frantic, he quickly thanked R and rushed out. He had *a lot* of thinking to do.

# CHAPTER THIRTY-FOUR

Stanlin was very quiet all through dinner. He was trying to come up with a lawful way to intervene, to save Sylvia. His deliberations continued deep into the night as he lay awake in his room, becoming progressively more frustrated. He didn't know the first thing about stopping some crazy disease from spreading, but Sylvia deserved to live! He knew that.

All of the time he'd spent with her had confirmed the initial impression he'd had—that she was kindhearted. Shouldn't that count for something? Shouldn't at least one good representative of the human race be salvaged from Earth's disaster? If only he could rescue her before that disease struck, so she could live safely somewhere else...like on Capton.

He considered that, in a technical sense, he *could* bring Sylvia to Capton. By embracing another being, he could transport that being along with him; all Ramponts possessed that ability. And if, theoretically, he were to transport her, he had read in a scientific journal that a human's physiology should be adaptable to Capton's atmosphere. No humans had ever been physically brought to Capton before, but the mathematical calculations showed they could be.

This train of thought recycled in Stanlin's mind, and the more he thought about it, the more convinced he became. Transporting Sylvia to Capton with him was her best chance for survival.

Yes, but then there were the laws. He had broken the Non-Interaction Law repeatedly. He had certainly been wrong. However, he'd had no malicious intentions; his reason, friendship—and, OK, attraction too—had been good natured. So maybe now, with saving a life as his reason, it wasn't terribly outlandish to break the Non-Interaction Law again, and breach the ban on traveling to Earth.

On the other hand, he must unequivocally obey The Highest Authority's Free Will Decree. He could not tamper with Sylvia's free will. While he could offer to rescue her, she would have to choose whether or not to be saved.

The only option was simple and direct: He would manifest at her home in the morning as his true Rampont self, tell her the atrocious news, and give her the opportunity to escape death by transporting with him to Capton.

If she opted not to go with him, he would be grief stricken, but he would know he'd done all he could do to try to save her. Empty handed, he'd return to Capton, and no one would ever need to know about his brief Earth excursion. The Council's monitors couldn't detect where one traveled in from, so as long as he wasn't questioned by the Rampont police, a sly trip was feasible. And since the police only questioned citizens randomly and infrequently, the risk was minimal.

If she chose to go with him, as he was praying she would, when they materialized together on Capton, the Council's monitoring system would detect her—a being with no identification chip. The Council members, along with the Rampont police, would probably detain the two of them for intense questioning before rendering punishment. He could only hope that once the authorities met Sylvia, they would see she was a good person and would grant her citizenship. And, Highest Authority willing, they would also understand why he had broken the two laws to rescue her and would be merciful with his punishments. Yet, even if he was imprisoned for years, he could be proud that he had saved the life of a very, very special girl.

Stanlin stretched, yawned, and closed his eyes. He knew what to do. He didn't like breaking more laws, but he saw no other way. At least now, Sylvia had a chance to live, which, in turn, granted him just enough peace of mind to finally fall asleep.

# A Look Ahead to Autumn, 2032

# CHAPTER THIRTY-FIVE

Following his summer arrest, Ned's attorney advised him to plead guilty. He explained that a jury would be vicious, given the age of Ned's victim and the evidence stacked against him: an eyewitness, traces of Ned's skin under the victim's fingernails, scratch marks on Ned's face, bruises consistent with the size of Ned's hands around the victim's neck. Ned heeded the counsel and was incarcerated at Jungilo Maximum Security Prison.

Having been in for nearly two months, Ned's most valuable lesson learned so far was to always be on guard. Lots of fights broke out, especially in the rec yard. His favorite outdoor spot had become a bench up against the building, where no one could sneak up behind him.

On this crisp autumn afternoon, he sat on his bench, feeling the sun warming his brow. He reflected on the words he'd heard in his right ear the first night in his cell—and almost every night since. "I'll show you a way to escape. I know you would follow my orders in here, but the mission will move faster with you on the outside. Soon, Ned, you will see. I will show you."

Two loud, arguing voices interrupted his thoughts. Standing up to get a look, Ned saw the two men off toward the left outermost border of the yard. In seconds, punches were flying, and a crowd was gathering. He stepped on top of the bench to see above the others' heads.

The brawl was getting brutal. One guy was turning the other into a bloody mess. The guards struggled to push their way through. They found the loser lying face down on the ground when they finally got to him. They started shaking him to get up, but his body was limp. They rolled him onto his side. One guard stayed with him and used his radio to make a call, while the other guards broke up the crowd.

Ned found it interesting that the guard with the radio kept looking at the sky. Minutes later, Ned understood why; a helicopter with a big red cross painted on it arrived. The guard waved and signaled the pilot. As the copter started lowering, that guard joined the rest in keeping the other inmates back to leave the medical crew room to work.

Ned watched as the team put the man in a stretcher and hoisted it into the aircraft. "If only I could somehow get onboard, that would be a clear ticket out of here," he thought.

He stepped off the bench and walked toward the helicopter, as close as the guards were tolerating. He wasn't expecting to hear it right then; it came as a wonderful surprise. The voice whispered into his right ear, "The underside. When the helicopter starts liftoff, grasp onto one of the underside legs. When you're outside the gate, let go before it gets up too high."

Ned loved the idea, but there was a flaw. He whispered back, "But, God, how can I get close enough to it with the guards there?"

Rather than hearing a reply in words, Ned received his answer through an instant opportunity. A second, much larger brawl erupted, distracting and occupying the guards and prisoners. Simultaneously, the hospital-bound copter began its liftoff. Seizing the moment, Ned, with remarkable speed, sprinted, leaped, and grasped onto one of the copter's legs. He wrapped himself tightly about the thin metal and, lying horizontally, pressed his whole body up against it.

The prison personnel inside the building barely glanced at the monitor showing the rising helicopter. Their focus was drawn to the altercation. And Ned's flattened, slender frame wasn't obvious upon an inattentive glimpse.

By the time the guards in the recreation yard had begun settling down the tumult, the helicopter had cleared the security walls, and Ned had just released his grip. To his advantage, the craft's altitude was barely forty feet, so when he landed in some thick, soft bushes, he suffered no more than a few bruises and scrapes.

He got up, brushed himself off, and started running, fast, distancing himself from Jungilo. He knew that his disappearance wouldn't go unnoticed for long, so he would need to keep running through these woods for as long as he could manage, getting farther and farther away. They would be out searching for him, a wanted criminal on the loose. Definitely, he would need to lay low. He should make himself look different too; not shaving his face could be an easy first step.

As he ran on, Ned felt grateful for how well God had arranged for his escape. Everything had come together perfectly, and he'd been led toward the right actions.

Feeling triumphant, he thought, "He will make your paths straight."

# CHAPTER THIRTY-SIX

Hours later, Ned was still running. He needed short breaks once in a while to catch his breath, but his stamina was excellent. He'd worked out every day in prison, and it was paying off.

These woods seemed to go on forever, though. He couldn't see any signs of civilization any way he looked, so he simply pressed on forward. Finally, at dusk, he saw a teenager some distance ahead, which was good, because it meant homes couldn't be all that far away. Yet he didn't want to be seen, and he wondered warily if the other guy had noticed him.

"Damn!" Ned thought, when the teen broke into a run, straight toward him.

"Hey, Mister! I was takin' a jog, and got lost out here. Could you direct me back to Ashbury Park?" he yelled.

Acrimoniously, Ned hollered, "Can't help you! Lemme alone!" He hoped the guy wouldn't come any closer. Trying to hide his face, he squatted down and pretended to investigate a small plant.

Undeterred by the surly response, the teen kept running until he was beside Ned. He stopped, knelt down, and looked at the plant, too. "What kind is it?" he asked, shifting his gaze toward Ned. His face went ashen as his eyes wandered up and down the length of Ned's body. In some sort of fearful recognition, his eyes bulged and his mouth opened. He sprang to his feet and started running away.

"He knows who you are! He mustn't interfere with your duties. Get him!" urged the voice in Ned's right ear.

Loyally obeying, Ned pursued the teen, but he was bothered that the guy had recognized him. Had the prison guards already picked up that Ned was gone? Could they have put up his mug shot on TV so soon?

All at once, he was angry with himself. "Stop thinking about it! Who cares?" he inwardly chided. "You're lying low, no matter what. Follow the instructions and get the guy!"

Ned sprinted faster, gaining on his target. When he was close enough for contact, he jumped, kicked, and forced the sole of his shoe hard into the teenager's lower back, slamming him forward onto the ground. Following up with a heavy stomp on the back of his victim's neck, Ned heard the crunch of the small bones breaking.

It was done. A mild high coursed through him, not as intense as after either of the stranglings, but he'd made the right decision in how to kill the teen. When he'd strangled the boy at the river, the kid had scratched and gotten Ned's skin under his nails. Killing this way didn't leave behind evidence like that.

For a minute, Ned stood still, looking down, admiring his Godly work. A chilly wind whipped through his clothes. He shivered, and then realized why he was so cold, and what had sparked the recognition in the teen's eyes. Ned was in his prison uniform—not a good idea for warmth or for being in hiding.

The dead guy wore loose-fitting sweats and a windbreaker. Ned removed the clothing carefully, without touching the body. There would be no fingerprints and no hand bruising of any kind this time. He slipped into his new outfit, which was almost his size. It wasn't eye-catching, either. The windbreaker was solid black, and the sweats, gray.

"God really does provide," he thought thankfully.

He balled up his prison uniform and stored it by his abdomen, inside the zipped-up jacket. He had a feeling he'd find it useful in the future.

The wind kicked up again, and Ned stuffed his hands into the jacket's side pockets.

"What's this?" he muttered in surprise.

He could hardly believe his luck: There were things inside the pockets!

As excitedly as a child opening a present, he pulled out the treasure from the right pocket: $50 in cash, folded in a money clip. "Alright! Money's always good," he thought.

Practically panting with anticipation, he delved into the left pocket: a house key, and a pocket knife much like the one his dad had given him so many years ago, which had been taken from him at Jungilo. Looking at the sky, he thought, "Dad, are you watching over me?" And with renewed vigor, he took off running again.

# CHAPTER THIRTY-SEVEN

It was very early in the morning on their third day of running. Apparently, fate had been quite the helper this particular week. Two days earlier, they had escaped, and although they did not know it, later this afternoon, hours from now, Ned Chambers would be finding his freedom by grasping a helicopter leg.

As fortunate as they had been to break out, however, they were proportionally unlucky in finding food in the woods while they fled. Some wild berries had barely sustained them so far, and now, they were so weakened from hunger that running had morphed into a slow wandering. Feeling on the brink of starvation, they needed real food. *Protein. Meat.* So it seemed fabulous when one of them spotted a wild turkey, just a few feet ahead of him.

He crept up close, and lunged at it with all of the strength he could muster.

The startled bird attempted to fly away, but a mere second after lifting off, it was yanked by its foot back to the ground with a crash.

The hunter's companions joined him in killing the bird and devouring it raw. Proper food preparation was not on their minds, and uncooked meat was new for all of them. But in that moment, they didn't care.

Even taste wasn't relevant, given the severity of their hunger and their limited senses of smell, which all but eliminated their ability to taste, anyway. Each of them was still congested from being on the tail end of an influenza virus that had been widespread among their fellow inmates.

They felt revitalized after finishing their meal and began journeying on. Their vim was short-lived, though, for not three hours later, they were each feeling dreadful. Granted, they hadn't been in perfect health when they'd escaped, but their postinfluenza congestion had been only mildly uncomfortable.

The symptoms they experienced now were infinitely worse. Intense, ultrasharp pains shot like bolts of lightning throughout their overheating bodies. They coughed violently, forcing out purulent sputum. Their muscles were extraordinarily sore and devoid of strength.

Exhausted, they collapsed on the forest floor, where they lay in agony for another three hours, until the leaf-covered autumn ground became their final resting place.

Only minutes after their passing, a hungry, injured fox came across their bodies. Their flesh was not the customary diet of the fox, but it was too good to resist, especially since there was no pursuit required. Chasing prey was very challenging for this unfortunate fox. A storm the night before had caused a large tree limb to fall onto its snout, breaking it and clogging it with blood. At the same time, one of the smaller branches attached to the limb had scratched the fox's cornea, compromising its vision.

The fox ravaged its easy meal, feasting some from each of the corpses. It ate beyond its normal satiety, as instinct warned that it might be a while before it found more food. When finished, the overly full fox meandered away from the remains and found a spot to lie down. Within two hours, it began experiencing the same symptoms as the former captives. Less than four hours after the first taste of its meal, the fox also succumbed to the lethal sickness.

\* \* \*

Since killing the teenager, Ned had been running for over an hour. His hunger was becoming overwhelming, and his energy was waning.

He slowed down to a walk and mumbled, "I need to eat." Wearily, he realized that in the dark, it would be very hard to hunt. And though he thought he could see the faint glow of street lamps way out ahead, it was too far for him to go before needing food and rest. Shaking his head in irritation, he happened to glimpse something out of the corner of his eye, a few yards away. He walked toward it. It was some kind of animal, either dead or severely injured.

"He who comes to me will never go hungry," he thought and grinned.

He stepped closer to the animal, seeing it clearly at last. He froze. He gaped. His heart leaped.

The animal was a fox.

The ideas flooded in. Everything was beginning to make sense. God had said He had a purpose for Ned's dad, but had not divulged that purpose—until now. It couldn't be coincidence that *both a pocketknife and a fox* had turned up today. His dad had to be watching over him, helping him. And, because that help was furthering God's mission, his dad must be working with God, too. Yes. The three of them were purifying the world, together.

He looked at the sky. He and his dad were tackling another adventure. His mind flashed back to his dad shooting that fox and them carrying the heavy thing to their campsite.

He peered down at the fox in front of him. No shooting or lifting was needed for this sucker. With its bloody, broken snout, it'd probably been killed in a rough fight.

Ned flicked out his knife blade. As he skinned and separated, he reminisced about watching his dad carve up their hunted fox. And as Ned ate, he thought about eating the raw fox meat with his father, who was smiling and had seemed proud. Ned's eyes stung with tears. He blinked them back. As he finished up the last raw slab, he mused that this meat tasted more tangy and pungent than he'd remembered. But he shrugged it off; that camping trip was so long ago. He wiped his hands and the knife with his prison uniform. Stuffing the bloodied outfit deep into the thick of a bush, he was ready to search for a place to sleep. He was totally wiped out.

It wasn't long before he came across two older men, asleep on a large makeshift mattress of piled leaves. Their dirty, ripped clothes and lack of camping gear led him to assume they were homeless. But their spot looked comfortable, and there was room enough for him to lie down there. So he did.

Soon afterward, he was feeling miserable—terribly hot, achy, and weak. He started coughing and spitting out phlegm that gathered in the back of his throat.

Throughout his life, his body had usually resisted the bugs that infected other people. The couple of times he had gotten sick, he was better in a day or two. His mother always said, "Neddy, you're as strong as an ox."

These symptoms now were so much worse than anything he'd ever felt. Every inch of him was in pain. It was infuriating.

He cursed under his breath as he tossed and turned in the bedding of leaves. He slept fitfully, awakening throughout the night with coughing and searing shooting pains.

# Return to Summer, 2032

# CHAPTER THIRTY-EIGHT

"Aaahhh! No! No!" Hoarse, horrified screams spewed from Brenna. Her heart hammered in her chest, and she was gasping for air. Her eyes darted back and forth from the empty bed to the adjacent cut window screen in disbelief.

Hardly able to maintain her balance, she shuffled on weak legs toward the window. It was higher than Cedric was tall, so she could not fathom him cutting the screen himself and climbing out. Nevertheless, she peered outside to make sure there wasn't a toddler lying on the ground below.

There wasn't. Which left only one other bloodcurdling explanation.

She ambled down the hallway, holding onto the walls for support, made her way to the phone in her bedroom, and dialed 911. Her speech choppy and her breathing labored, she forced out the words, "My son...my son is m-missing. His screen window was cut open, and he's g-gone!"

The police said they needed to investigate the crime scene and not to touch anything; they would ask additional questions when they arrived. She gave them her address and they assured her they would be there soon.

When she hung up, Brenna looked at the clock on her nightstand through tear-filled eyes. It was 7:36 a.m. Feeling so drained that any movement was onerous, she compelled herself to get dressed before plodding downstairs to wait. She stood looking out the window weeping until the police cars pulled up in her driveway.

Wiping her wet cheeks with the backs of her hands, she let the uniformed men and women inside. Most of them greeted her and went straight to work upstairs in Cedric's room. But one policewoman, Jane Canton, stayed with Brenna. They sat on the couch together as Jane asked questions and took notes.

The officer's red hair, freckles, and dimples gave her a nonthreatening appearance, which was further enhanced by her calm demeanor. "How old is Cedric?" she queried gently.

Brenna leaned forward and took a tissue from the box on the coffee table in front of them. "Almost four. He'll turn four next month," she answered, dabbing her eyes. She prayed she would have her little boy home for his birthday. She reached forward again, this time picking up a framed photo of Cedric to show Jane. When the officer looked surprised, Brenna explained that Cedric had been adopted from the Rima Adoption Agency in the spring of 2031.

Jane raised her eyebrows. "Do you think Cedric's birth mother or father kidnapped him because they wanted him back?"

"I don't think so. His birth mother gave him up because she wanted to protect him. Her ex-boyfriend was threatening to kill him."

"I'm guessing the ex-boyfriend wasn't Cedric's father?"

"No. I don't think the birth mother knew who Cedric's biological father was," Brenna said, recalling the paperwork she and Anthony had signed when finalizing Cedric's adoption. "Hold on a minute."

Brenna went upstairs to her and Anthony's office, found the paperwork, and returned with it. She and Jane looked at the information together. Brenna's memory had been spot on. The documents confirmed that Cedric's paternity was unknown but conjectured that his father was also black, like his birth mother, Claire Evans.

"Claire Evans," Jane repeated aloud, thoughtfully.

"She recently changed her name to Mona Banks. The Rima Agency gave me her new name last week, saying she was in a stable place now and that it'd be a good time to start communicating. I was in the middle of writing my first letter to her about Cedric." After verbalizing that heart-wrenching detail, Brenna couldn't stop herself from sobbing.

"We'll do everything we can." Jane sympathetically touched Brenna's shoulder. "Excuse me a minute. I need to make a call." As she dialed on her cell, Jane mumbled to herself, "Claire Evans...could swear I just heard that name." She stayed on the line with the police station for several minutes, referring to the adoption paperwork and taking down notes. "Bingo. It says 'referred to us from the Guyton Women's Shelter.'"

Hearing Jane's enthusiasm helped Brenna tear away from her grief. It sounded like there was some progress; something helpful was being uncovered. Brenna waited anxiously for the new information.

When she hung up, Jane said, "The Guyton Women's Shelter called us the day before yesterday, because their computer system had been broken into. Guess whose file was the only one opened?"

Brenna couldn't speak.

"Claire Evans." Jane paused for emphasis. "Yeah. That's why I'd just heard that name. And your adoption agency papers here say that Claire Evans and her son Cedric were referred to them from the Guyton Women's Shelter. Anyway, some of our officers started working the Guyton case already, and they said Guyton connected them with this Rima Agency, and with a Secoya Shelter out west, another place Claire stayed at. Her records all say she's running away from her abusive ex, Ron Camm, so he's the top suspect for hacking into her shelter file."

"He's obsessed," Brenna muttered bitterly.

"You got it. We see it all the time. Our guys updated the police out west, near Claire's new address. They gave Claire a heads up about her stolen records, and she gave them Ron's address, which they passed on to officers in Ron's precinct. The place was checked out, but Ron wasn't there. A Corvette registered in his name is parked in the lot, so he's traveling by some other means. There's surveillance at his apartment in case he shows up there, but police are out looking for him as we speak."

"Did the Guyton Shelter file include this address in it?" Brenna asked tenuously, although she already knew the answer.

"Yes," Jane confirmed somberly. "So our current theory is that Ron Camm paid someone to hack into Claire's file for him, and when he found out about the adoption, he kidnapped Cedric. He probably found out her new address, too, and is on his way over, so we've ordered surveillance and protection at her apartment."

"Good. That's good. Is there anything else can we do?" Brenna asked. Another, horrid thought was trying to surface, but she shoved it down. She couldn't entertain it. Absolutely not.

"There is. Turns out, when we ran Ron Camm's name through our system the other day, he was already in our records for drug-related charges. Now that he's suspected of this kidnapping, we can release his mug shot with an AMBER Alert. My friend, you'll not only have the police, but the whole country lookin' out for this perp," Jane said, tapping her hand on Brenna's knee supportively. "And if you give us a picture of Cedric, we can publicize it right along with the mug shot."

"Yes, of course. Can I e-mail it to the police station?"

"Yes. Good idea," Jane agreed.

Brenna led Jane upstairs to the office computer, and they sent out the picture.

"Hello, ladies," one of the investigators said, stepping into the room. He told them that while no fingerprints had been found, there were two muddy, partial sneaker prints near Cedric's bed, and clothing fibers had been recovered from the window screen.

"Great," Jane said to her colleague.

"We'll keep you informed," he replied, and left.

Jane turned to Brenna. "With evidence like that, once we nab this guy, we can put him away quick."

Brenna smiled faintly. She felt a little better, but was still forcing down that most fearsome thought. "Would you mind if we sit outside to get some fresh air?"

"Fine by me," Jane assented.

They situated themselves on the front porch in wicker rocking chairs. After a few minutes of sunshine and gentle breezes, Brenna noticed two people heading toward the house. She squinted slightly and recognized them as her neighbors, Rinalda and Rebecca. It looked as though they were speed walking, but as they drew closer, their pace began to slow. Once their faces became clear, Brenna saw worrisome expressions.

"You know them?" Jane asked, gesturing toward the two ladies.

"Those are my neighbors. They must be wondering what the police cars are doing here. I really want to let them know what's happened, but…" Brenna didn't quite know how to finish the sentence. The idea of speaking the terrible news out loud to her friends was overwhelming.

As if reading her thoughts, Jane said, "If you want, I can run through the basics with them. Would that help?"

"Yes, yes," Brenna said, sighing with relief. "You've been so nice this whole time. Thank you."

"I've worked these kinds of cases a lot over the years. I've seen the toll it can take. And I'm a mother myself. My daughter's about Cedric's age."

"Mmmm." Brenna nodded at her appreciatively before waving to signal her friends to join them.

As promised, Jane told them what had happened. Brenna struggled in vain to remain composed. She couldn't prevent the tears from rolling down her checks as she listened to the tale of her living nightmare.

"The AMBER Alert will be televised starting today. Keep an eye out for it," Jane concluded.

"That will help; I know it," Rinalda said, giving Brenna a hug.

"You've got our support, whatever you need," Rebecca said, and took her turn at hugging Brenna.

"Thank you," Brenna croaked.

She waved good-bye as they left. Soon the police would be leaving too, which she was really dreading. Then, she would be completely alone, in the empty, silent house. Without Cedric. Without Anthony. Completely alone, heavyhearted, and frightened.

# CHAPTER THIRTY-NINE

Stanlin groggily opened his eyes to see two tiny eyes looking back at him. Mini-G was standing next to his bed, seemingly waiting for him to arise. He leaned forward and petted her.

"Yes, I'm getting up," he murmured, rolling out of bed. He changed from his gray pajamas into a typical one-piece, black garment.

He looked over at the Captonian timepiece on the wall and mentally calculated that it was 11:31 a.m. where Sylvia was. Although he knew he'd been up for hours the night before, the current time seemed late. He had a very big day ahead.

"Get some food, get some energy, and get going," he told himself.

With Mini-G trailing at his heels, he walked to the gathering room. Inhaling deeply, he couldn't help but smile; something smelled wonderful.

"Morning, honey. I'll get you some breakfast," Karilu said.

"Thanks, Mom." He sank into a chair at the table.

"I'm glad you were able to rest. Yesterday was so hard," Karilu soothed, placing a cup of hot keechin, an herbal stimulant beverage, in front of him.

"Yeah, it was." Stanlin took a few sips of the bold drink and formed his alibi for the day. "After I'm finished eating, I think I'm gonna take a long walk. That usually helps me feel better about things." He would, in fact, be walking some, and the term "long" was relative; he wasn't really fibbing.

"That would help me, too. Mind if I join you?"

"Errr, ahhh," he stalled. "I'm sorry, Ma, but I think today I need to be alone. But next time, we'll go together," he recovered. "And we'll bring her with us," he added, pointing at Mini-G, who had curled up by his feet.

"I'll look forward to it," Karilu said, serving Stanlin his breakfast plate.

"Oh! Cimatas! My favorite!"

"Yes, honey. I baked a batch earlier, with freshly picked ingredients from the garden. Your father's reaction was about the same. I thought we could all use something uplifting this morning."

"Uh-huh," Stanlin heartily grunted with his mouth full of food. The cimatas were large, round pastries stuffed with nuts, grains, and super-sweet fruits grown exclusively on Capton. After devouring the first, Stanlin gobbled down a second and a third cimata. "Boy, those were good," he said, rising from his chair with one hand on his stomach.

"Wait 'till your father hears you ate one more than he did!" Karilu teased.

"This was a record," Stanlin chuckled, "but it'll keep me going on my long walk. Thanks, Mom. See you later."

He left the house and walked down the black sandy streets for several blocks until he reached a more rural sect. The residences looked like beige domes, with round, cut-out, open-air windows and red, oblong doors. The homes were similar in style to his, but in this part of town, they were spaced farther apart. And here, very few Ramponts were seen on the streets or milling about outdoors.

When he was sure no one at all was in sight, he became invisible. "Planet Earth, seventeen Holloway Drive," he thought.

He arrived invisibly on Sylvia's front lawn. Unfortunately, she was not there. He searched her backyard, but had no luck finding her there, either. "Hopefully she's inside the house," he thought, and invisibly arrived in the foyer. He heard voices and followed them, which led him to the kitchen. Sylvia sat at the table with her mother, Rebecca. Stanlin was amused by the clear family resemblance. Rebecca and Sylvia had the same distinctive, fluffy auburn hair and striking green eyes. He guessed they had just finished eating lunch, because a delicious aroma lingered and plates were piled near the sink.

"Remember, you are never, never to leave your windows open at night, ever again. You understand?" Rebecca was saying.

Stanlin thought it almost sounded like she was scolding, but not quite, because there was fear in her voice.

"I won't," Sylvia answered sadly. "Can I go up to my room now?" She got up from her chair.

"Yes." Rebecca's eyes looked glassy. She reached for Sylvia and hugged her. "I love you so, so much. You know that, right?" Her voice was wavering.

"Yes, Mom, I know. I love you, too."

They were both starting to cry.

"I hope they find Cedric," Sylvia sniffed.

"Me too, sweetie," Rebecca whispered. "The mug shot on TV with the AMBER Alert should help."

"Uh-huh."

They hugged in silence for a minute. Rebecca pulled back, looked at Sylvia concernedly, and wiped a tear from Sylvia's cheek. "You alright?"

"I'll be OK," Sylvia replied softly. They let go of each other, and Sylvia slowly walked upstairs to her room, with Stanlin following behind her. She closed the door, meandered to the bed, and lay down on her side, looking dreary.

He tuned into her thoughts and heard, "I can't believe Cedric was kidnapped. He's such a cute, nice kid. It isn't fair. It just isn't fair."

"No, it's not fair at all," he thought, commiserating.

Stanlin knew the toddler from the park was a sweet boy, undeserving of being stolen away by a mean human. And the pandemic disease that was coming was infinitely more unfair. But he could only do what he could—give her the chance to escape.

"Ready, set, go," he thought. But just before becoming visible, he saw something right outside her window, which spurred on a better, less frightening idea for how to approach her.

Planning for what was to come, he disrobed first, leaving his invisible garment next to her desk chair. Then he transported into a rectangular flower bed that hung outside her windowsill. It was the perfect spot for him to stand and claw at her screen—as Melvin! He transformed into the little cat, became visible, and clawed.

Sylvia jumped out of bed and checked her window, panting. Once she saw Melvin out there, she laughed and caught her breath. "Melvin! My God! You nutty, crazy cat!"

Opening the window, she brought him inside. "You must've climbed up that birch tree to get up here. You clever little guy," she said, setting him on the floor. She rushed over to her stereo and turned on music. Returning to him, she knelt on the floor in front of him. "This is the loudest my parents allow. We need background noise," she explained, petting him. "But you can't stay, because my mom has allergies." She picked him up and hugged him. "We can play for a little, Melvin, but then I'll have to sneak you back outside and totally vacuum my room."

"I'm sorry," he whispered. With his tiny feline vocal cords, his voice sounded sort of like a toddler's.

Sylvia pulled him away, holding him in outstretched arms, her eyes riveted on him. "Huh?" she squawked.

"I'm sorry," he repeated.

"I'm crazy," she murmured.

"No. You're not. I'm not a cat like other cats."

"No kidding," she snorted sardonically. "I'm certifiable," she mumbled.

"Sylvia, I'm not only not a cat, but I'm not even from Earth. I'm here from another galaxy to warn you that Earth is in danger."

"Maybe I'm dreaming," she said softly, gingerly placing him onto the floor.

"No! No, you're not!" he protested. "I'm sure this seems impossible, but it's all true, and I'm here to help you. In a minute, I'll show you how I normally look, on my planet, and then I'll explain everything to you. Just please, please don't scream when you see the real me. I'll be about your size, and blue. Can you promise me you won't scream?" He did not want Sylvia's mother barging in on this.

"OK, I won't scream," she consented hesitantly. Melvin disappeared before her eyes. "Huh?" she gasped.

Stanlin felt around and found his garment near the desk chair. He slipped it on and reappeared as his Rampont self.

Sylvia stood up and backed away from him until her calves collided with the edge of her bed behind her, forcing her to flop down and sit. She was wide-eyed and breathing heavily, but she kept her word and didn't scream. She stared silently at him standing in front of her. "Who are you?" she asked at last, her voice and body quivering.

"My name is Stanlin. I'm from planet Capton, in the Andromeda galaxy. I'm here with very tragic news." His heart was aching emotionally, and pounding physically.

She quietly echoed, "Very tragic news?"

"There's no easy way to say this. I'm so sorry." Stanlin took a deep breath in and let it out. "Billions of people and animals on Earth are going to die in a few months from a terrible disease. Probability Spheres, which are our prediction tools on Capton, have shown us that this is coming."

Sylvia blinked repeatedly and shook her head, saying nothing. He heard her thinking that maybe her eyes and ears were playing tricks on her, and if she could only clear them up, it would erase the blue alien boy with the message of death.

He prayed that his presence and persistent words would penetrate her shock. "I know this is overwhelming. I'll do everything I can to try to help you cope."

Her blinking was slowing down, but she remained speechless. Stanlin could hear her wondering if maybe he could be for real.

Encouraged, he continued. "My people know from The Highest Authority that all beings are meant to have free will. That's why I'm giving you a choice. If I encircle my arms around someone, I can transport them with me to Capton. If you come with me, I can take you where it's safe."

Sylvia's face contorted with confusion and contemplation. "If billions of people and animals are going to die, why are you here to save me? What about everyone else?" she asked.

It was an understandable question, but he couldn't directly answer it the way he knew she wanted him to. She'd end up thinking of him as a stalker. So he chose a dry, technical reply.

"I'm only able to encircle *one person* in my arms for transport. Once I return to Capton with a human, we'll be detected and detained for questioning, so I won't be able to come back to Earth. Actually, my coming here now is forbidden, but I wanted you to have a chance to live." His throat was tightening.

"But, why did you choose *me?*" Sylvia pressed.

He decided to focus on Melvin, and to be as brief as possible. "I've really liked visiting Earth for my schooling. After we met, I found that spending time with you while I was Melvin was the best way for me to keep learning and to have fun, too. I've come to think of you as one of my best friends." His face was roasting.

Sylvia was clearly overloaded, trying to process everything.

He swiftly shifted the topic. This was not the appropriate time to be confessing his huge crush. On the other hand, sharing a broader perspective about the whole atrocity might be useful for her. "I read that, according to The Highest Authority, human spirits live on after the human form has died, just like Rampont spirits, and the spirits of all other sentient beings do, too. That means no one you love will be gone forever. You'll all be reunited as spirits. You can choose to let your human form die with your loved ones very soon, but I really wish you'd choose to live longer, by letting me save you."

He heard her think, "He isn't in my imagination. He's really here, warning me and trying to take me with him."

A flash of inspiration struck him: Hundreds of animals like Mini-G still needed homes. His words poured out. "We're trying to get lots of little creatures, like miniature giraffes, adopted right now! At that shelter, you've helped to adopt out animals, so you'd be the perfect person to help find homes for the little giraffes! We need you on Capton! You see? We need you there! Please, Sylvia, choose to *live*, and come back with me!"

She burst into tears.

Stanlin instantly felt like a helpless fool. This was all too much for her. What other response could he have realistically expected? Her sorrow became his own. His chest felt sore, his eyes watered, and his chin twitched. He couldn't decide whether to bawl with her or stuff it to seem like the strong hero, ready at any moment to whisk her away to Capton. Would she want him to try to console her with a hug, or would that be scary or offensive? He was in anguish. "Is there anything at all that I can say or do?" he asked woefully.

Through sobs, Sylvia responded with her own questions. "Can't the future be changed? Can't something be done differently now that can change what happens later? If your instruments are smart enough to see the future, can't they give ideas about helping things turn out better?"

Stanlin was dumbfounded. He wanted to kick himself for not thinking to ask those very same questions. He'd assumed that things would have to unfold as the Sphere showed, because he didn't know how anyone could halt a spreading disease. But what if she was right? What if the Sphere had more advanced uses that he hadn't learned about? And R had said that no future prediction was guaranteed. It was definitely worth asking if the Sphere could provide guidance for possibly preventing doom.

He looked at Sylvia with deep respect. She was as brilliant as she was beautiful. "I'll ask my Universe course instructor your questions, and I'll return to tell you the answers. Well, if I get caught and in trouble for coming here this time, I won't be able to come back. But I'm hoping that won't happen." He figured it should be OK, as long as no one witnessed his trips.

"OK," she murmured, her voice barely audible. She curled up into a fetal position in her bed and pulled up the covers.

"My teacher might be in his office; I'll go straight there." R had a lot of exams to correct. He could very well be working on some now.

She gave a small nod. She looked dismal. In the big picture, maybe it was best that way. He wanted her to try to prepare for the highly probable future. This new contingency was hopeful, but unlikely.

"The Sphere, it, um, it might not be able to lead us in this," he cautioned. "I mean, we might not find a way to deter the, ah, outcome."

"I don't want anyone to die," Sylvia sobbed.

"I'll find out whatever I can, and do everything in my power to come back and tell you what I learn," Stanlin vowed, and he disappeared.

# CHAPTER FORTY

By midmorning the police had gone, and by lunch time, Brenna's awful solitude was in full swing. Since she didn't feel hungry, she tried distracting herself with reading the newspaper. But the words on the pages wouldn't sink in. Instead, her mind kept cycling through the same themes. The appalling thought would start to arise, and she would cover it with prayers that the police would catch Ron Camm and bring Cedric home. She would blame herself for leaving the windows open. Then, the encompassing quiet, the absence of Cedric's sounds of play, would become overpowering, and her tears would gush. The sadness and worry that Anthony might also be in danger, and was so far away for so long, deepened her grief.

Eventually, she gave up on the futile effort to read and took a long, hot shower. Afterward, as she was wrapping herself in her cozy robe, she was feeling a little less tense. "That was a lot better than the newspaper attempt," she thought, and slipped her feet into her soft, fuzzy slippers.

She walked downstairs and noticed the clock on the wall: 1:45 p.m. Anthony should be calling in about fifteen minutes. Brenna pined to hear his voice. But when she began thinking about discussing Cedric's disappearance with him, the small relief she had felt from the shower whittled away. She started pacing. How was she ever going to broach this? Poor Anthony, having to hear about it over the phone, when he was trapped and stuck over there! It was horrific. And it was her fault.

Brenna's pacing brought her toward the kitchen phone, where something caught her eye. The light on the answering machine was blinking. Someone must have called while she was in the shower. She pressed play.

"Hi, honey. I'm so sorry I missed you. I know it's earlier your time than I usually call, but it's a totally crazy day here. I'm still at work! Can you believe that? At 10:00 p.m.! We ran into some big-time computer glitches that are taking lots of time to fix. I won't get to call again tonight, but I'll call you tomorrow. Hopefully by then all this stuff'll be settled down. I love you, pretty lady! And I love you, little man! Talk to you guys tomorrow."

Brenna sobbed at his message and replayed it twice.

Her day wore on. In the late afternoon, Rebecca called to let her know she'd be picking her up that evening for a special prayer service. Some church members were gathering to pray for Cedric's safe return. It was a thoughtful idea, and Brenna was very grateful. And yet, she was apprehensive about going, because she would have to force congeniality in public, when hiding from the world in her own cocoon of despair was her natural inclination right now.

Not long after Rebecca's call, the phone rang again. This time, it was Madeline from the Rima Adoption Agency. She mentioned that she had consulted with the police about the case and would be happy to assist Brenna in any other way. Brenna listened to the heartfelt message as it was being recorded, instead of picking up. At least until church, she could avoid putting on the façade of being alright.

The next call, which came in around dusk, she picked up right away. Her caller ID indicated it was the police station. Jane Canton, the pleasant officer from that morning, relayed an update. She told Brenna that since the AMBER Alert had broadcasted, they had received two reports of Ron Camm sightings, from clerks at two different motels. Although both times he had signed in under different names, the motel clerks each felt certain they had checked in the man shown in the mug shot.

Desperately, Brenna panted, "Was Cedric there? Did either clerk see Cedric?"

"No; no one saw Cedric," Jane answered softly, "but we figure Ron would probably leave Cedric in the car while he was checking in anyway." Jane went on to explain that the first motel sighting was about three miles from Brenna's home. Ron had checked in there the night before Cedric was kidnapped. The second motel was sixty-six miles west of Brenna's town. "Ron checked in there at around 2:00 this morning," Jane said. The police had confirmed that stop would be consistent with him traveling to Claire's new apartment. Furthermore, that motel was in the opposite direction of Ron's still-patrolled, still-unoccupied apartment.

Technically, the update was good news. The evidence was pointing at one monster: Ron Camm, whom the police were searching for and people were sighting. The prayer service that evening was also a good thing. In her current emotional state, though, the positives were only mildly reassuring. Her guilt about the window was oppressive. And the scary thought lingered and tormented her, even while she kept pushing it down, trying to ignore it. The battle raged on in her mind.

By the middle of the night, when she was totally exhausted but still unable to sleep, she couldn't submerge the petrifying thought any longer. *Claire had given up Cedric because Ron wanted to kill him. Now, Ron had Cedric. What if the police were too late?*

# CHAPTER FORTY-ONE

Stanlin vanished from Sylvia's bedroom and manifested inconspicuously in his school yard, behind a cluster of yellow trees resembling eight-foot-tall spruces on Earth. Thankfully, no one was around. He beelined into the building, straight to R's office. Like yesterday, R's door was open, and he sat working at his desk.

Stanlin peered inside.

"Hello again, Stanlin," R greeted pleasantly.

"I know you're really busy, but if you have a minute, I have another question for you."

"Come on in. I could use a little break." R stood and stretched up his arms with a slight groan.

Stanlin walked toward him. "Sir, you said that the Probability Sphere shows a numerical probability of likelihood for each future it predicts. You also said the future is never 100 percent guaranteed. Knowing these things, is there a way to ask the Sphere how to change a negative future prediction?"

"Marvelous question, Stanlin, marvelous," R praised. "But the Sphere, as incredible as it is, does have limitations. It can't give instructions for altering the future."

Stanlin's heart sank.

"It can do something else, though, that may be helpful." R walked with Stanlin to the Sphere. "Over the years, we Council members have been gradually refining the Sphere's inner technology. Until very recently, the only changes we'd noticed were that the pictures were getting crisper and sharper. However, just two months ago, Lithantor, one of our senior members, discovered that our technological modifications had given the Sphere a new ability."

"A new ability?" Stanlin's eyes lit up.

"Yes. We learned that after the Sphere reveals a prediction, it can also show us images of factors that significantly influence that particular prediction."

"Hmmm," Stanlin murmured, his brows furrowed.

"It's a little tricky. Let me explain. If a particular future prediction is of concern, we can focus on that negative outcome while peering here," R said, pointing to the top of the Sphere. "An image or two will emerge of things that have a strong impact upon that future. If actions are taken to address those things, the adverse future could become less probable. Again, we can't talk in absolutes. Just as we cannot 100 percent guarantee a future prediction, we cannot 100 percent guarantee a future prevention. It all works in probabilities or likelihoods, not in certainties."

"Please, can I try the Sphere out again, R?" Stanlin implored. He felt a glimmer of hope; he might find out something useful to report to Sylvia after all.

"Yes, but only for today, I'm afraid. Unfortunately, we won't be able to use the Sphere together again for a while," R said regretfully. "A few teachers have been reprimanded recently for student favoritism. I'll be next if I continue giving you special access to my Sphere."

"Oh, I understand, sir. I won't ask to use it again. I'd just really like to see more about something now."

Tilting his head slightly, R asked, "Did you see something upsetting in the Sphere the last time you were here?"

Stanlin paused, not knowing how to answer. "Uh...um...sorta," finally found its way out of his mouth.

"Would you like to talk about it?" R offered concernedly.

"No, but thank you," Stanlin replied, looking at the floor.

"Well, I do hope this helps you." R glanced at Stanlin empathetically, and then reiterated the instructions, pointing at the Sphere. "Focus your gaze here, on the top, while concentrating on the disturbing prediction. Good luck." As he'd done yesterday, R went to his desk, giving Stanlin privacy.

Stanlin did as R directed. An image of the SPCA shelter where Sylvia volunteered formed on the top of the Sphere. Then one cage housing three cute puppies appeared. At first, Stanlin only noticed that they seemed to be of the same litter, as their markings were similar. Upon closer scrutiny, though, he saw that each pup had a minor defect: one pup's right eye was permanently shut; another pup's left ear was small and misshapen; and the third pup held up his right rear leg, as if it was lame. Stanlin's eyes narrowed curiously.

The picture of the puppies began to fade, and in its place arose a huge brick and cement building with very few windows. Black lettering above the front doors read "Jungilo Maximum Security Prison." A man inside a prison cell came into focus. He had long, dark hair and a slim, strong-looking physique. He seemed to be in a heated conversation, yet he was alone. It was so eerie, it gave Stanlin the shivers. Seconds later, the Sphere defaulted to its typical cream color.

Stanlin squeaked, "What in the heck?"

"Did you see anything?" R asked, walking over to Stanlin.

"Yes, but I don't know what the pictures mean, and I don't know what to do."

"There's no way to know; that's how it works. As I said before, the Sphere has limitations and can't instruct us. It's showing you important factors that influence the predicted future you had in mind. By taking action, presumably positive action, toward those factors, the probability of your feared future might diminish."

"I think I understand. By doing something good that relates to the images I saw, their part in forming the future might change, and the future might become better," Stanlin ventured.

"Beautifully stated." R beamed with pride.

"But there's no way for me to find out what good things should be done, right?"

"If only there were." R sighed and winked.

Stanlin thanked R and left. As he walked home, he remembered his mother's words of warning about the Free Will Decree and giving others advice: "It can be a fine line, and when it comes to obeying The Highest Authority, we don't want to take any chances....Inspire others to think for themselves, and you'll be abiding by the first decree every time."

He realized that even if he did know exactly what to do about those puppies in the shelter, and that creepy man in Jungilo Maximum Security Prison, giving Sylvia a blueprint for action would not sit well with The Highest Authority. But simply telling Sylvia about the Sphere's images and letting her decide what to do about them, should be on the safe side of that fine line his mother cautioned of.

Stanlin was home in time for dinner.

"Did the walk help?" Karilu asked as they seated themselves around the table.

"Yeah. I'm feeling a little bit better," Stanlin replied in earnest. For now, there was a small ray of hope for Sylvia and for Earth.

After dinner, he told his parents he was going to the library, which was not a lie. He planned to stop off there on his way back from Sylvia's to bring home a cylinder of that scientific journal with the article he'd read about the humans adapting to Capton's atmosphere. It was high time to review it. Sylvia could try to save Earth, fail, and still choose to come to Capton with him.

"I'll be home a little later!" he called, leaving the house.

As he'd done earlier that day, Stanlin walked until the streets were barren of other Ramponts, and then transported invisibly to Sylvia's home. This time, no one was in the front or back yards or inside the house.

"Darn!" he huffed in exasperation, and transported back to Capton. He manifested outside the local library by the most remote corner of the building, ever careful of being seen and questioned. So far, so good on that end. Casually, he walked to the front and inside the building.

Botendil, a senior librarian, helped Stanlin find his journal cylinder and reviewed some of its other articles with him. He was thrilled, telling her he'd relish *The Journal of Intergalactic Theories and Research* through and through. Botendil also showed him a shelf lined with dozens of similarly themed cylinders.

"These must remain in the library, but you're free to come in and read through them any time we're open. They are specially equipped for our hologram-illustrated Rampont Readers. When you view these cylinders, you'll see 3-D pictures above the words to illuminate the concepts," she explained.

"Thanks! I'll definitely be back for them," Stanlin replied.

Journal cylinder in hand, he left the library and walked back to the rural sect of town. When no one was in sight, he transported to Earth to see if Sylvia was home yet. Still, no one was there, and it was starting to get late. He needed to go home or his parents would worry. Unfortunately, he would have to update Sylvia in the morning.

# Another Look Ahead to Autumn, 2032

# CHAPTER FORTY-TWO

Early in the morning, Ned was abruptly awakened by loud coughing from both homeless men. He heard them complaining to each other about being in pain and feeling hot.

"It's his fault," one of them said, pointing at Ned. "I heard him coughin' before. We wasn't coughin' 'till he came along."

"Yeah, this is our turf; get outta here!" the other yelled at Ned, followed by a spit and a fit of coughing.

"Ah, bite me," Ned retorted, rising to stand. Whatever. He wasn't sticking around anyway. He coughed and started walking away. His sore, weak legs moved slowly, although his mind was very active. He was intrigued. The bums seemed to have his symptoms, exactly. Could they all have caught the same sickness out here in the woods? If so, from who? Or from what? The bums were saying they hadn't coughed until he came along, that it was his fault they were sick. But he'd only been there overnight. Could a sickness even be passed on that fast? He didn't think so. Maybe they'd been sick beforehand, but hadn't known it yet? It wasn't clear.

Ned turned around at the sound of footsteps rustling in the fallen leaves behind him.

"You bastard!" one of the bums yelled hoarsely, coughing and hobbling weakly toward him. "We wasn't sick before you got here! Now my friend's dead, and it's your fault!" accused the bum, feebly lunging at Ned.

Stepping to one side, Ned easily dodged the lame attack. The bum landed flat on his stomach. Several moments passed, and he didn't move at all. Highly curious, Ned squatted down and checked for breathing and a pulse. Finding neither, he stood up in amazement, peering down at the lifeless body. This bum was dead, and he'd said the other bum was already dead. *The bums had the same symptoms as he did. Was he going to die, too?*

Feeling panicked, Ned implored out loud, "God, am I going to die? Please talk to me! Please!"

"Everyone dies, Ned," the voice said calmly in his ear.

"I mean now! Soon! You know what I mean!" He was losing his temper even though he knew he shouldn't, not with God.

"I need you around, living, to further the mission for me, Ned."

Ned exhaled loudly with relief. "How? What should I do next?" he asked a little more calmly.

There came no reply. It seemed God was finished discussing the matter for the time being. Still, Ned was comforted that he would live a while longer, to continue helping God rid the world of bad people. He breathed a second sigh of relief and lumbered on.

His symptoms were getting worse. He had nowhere near enough energy to run anymore. It was a huge effort just to walk, but that was probably fine at this point. Civilization couldn't be too far off, since he was moving in the direction of the lights he'd seen the night before.

He walked until he saw a clearing. "Thank you, God," he muttered as he reached the edge of the wooded area and headed into an adjoining park.

Stopping for a moment, he looked around and saw picnic tables, a playground, and a baseball field. A path wound around the grounds. A parking lot was off to his right, where a wooden sign read "Ashbury Park," the park the teenager had been looking for. A few houses stood in the distance to his left, their backyards facing the outer border of the park.

Ned began making his way toward the homes. He would sneak into one or more and take some money. The $50 he'd found wouldn't last him very long. At the monkey bars, he had to pause; a severe coughing spell got a hold of him. Grabbing onto the bars for support, he coughed heavily and spat several times on the acorn-covered ground. Eventually, the coughing subsided, and he was walking again.

When he reached the outer border of the park, he rested, standing with his hands on his hips, his eyes scanning the homes. One in particular stood out; it had a kitchen door accessible from the backyard. He saw the doormat and had an intuitive feeling that there would be a key stashed under it.

He checked on his hunch, and he was right. Ned smirked smugly as he quietly unlocked the door, entered the kitchen, and closed the door behind him. He stowed the key in his jacket pocket, next to the pocketknife, for safekeeping.

A large bowl of grapes on the table caught his attention right away. Because he was so sick, he wasn't as hungry as usual, but he was hungry enough to eat something. He helped himself to two handfuls, eating sloppily. A few grapes fell out of his hands onto the floor. He didn't bother picking them up.

He moved through the wide, open walkway connecting the kitchen with a family room. A couch, chairs, a crate filled with children's toys, a TV set, and a coffee table were neatly arranged. On the coffee table, he spied a woman's purse. Rummaging through it, he found $87, which he clipped into the money clip with his other cash.

Cheerfully, he mused, "He who seeks finds."

He heard stirring from upstairs and ducked behind the couch, trying to keep his coughing as hushed and stifled as possible.

"Come on, James! You can do it!" a young girl's voice goaded.

Ned heard light thumping sounds on the stairs.

"You're almost at the bottom now!" the girl encouraged.

More thumps.

"You did it, James!" she praised.

"I did it!" the boy said proudly.

The two of them giggled.

Ned noticed that the couch he was behind had three sections that were pushed next to one another but were, in fact, separate pieces. He pushed two of them ever so slightly apart so he could see between them and peer across into the kitchen. He coughed quietly.

The children walked into the kitchen. The boy looked very strange to Ned; he had white hair and extremely light eyes and was incredibly pale. The girl looked more normal, with brown hair and a medium skin tone. Ned guessed she was about eight years old, and the weird boy, about three.

The toddler cooed, gazing at something on the floor. He bent forward, getting a closer look. He picked something up and ate it. He picked up a second and a third and ate those, too, before his sister caught him.

"James, no!" she scolded. "If you want grapes, you get them from here," she said, reaching into the bowl on the table. She gave a handful to her brother and took a handful for herself.

When they finished snacking, they went into the family room. She turned on the TV, and they started sifting through the toys in the crate.

Struggling to suppress his coughing, and feeling miserably ill overall, Ned was at a loss for what to do with these stupid kids hanging around right near him.

"You are where you should be. Stay there and wait. Stay and wait for the parents to arise," he heard in his right ear.

"Then what?" he very softly whispered.

Ned listened but got no answer. Trying to control his temper, he thought, "Bits and pieces. God will say more when the parents wake up. Hold on. Hold on and wait."

# CHAPTER FORTY-THREE

Waiting and waiting he was. It had to have been over an hour that the children had been playing while their parents slept upstairs. The kids were shifting from toy to toy while the TV flashed and piped with cartoon shows. The background noise covered up Ned's hushed coughing and spitting, and for that he was grateful.

Eventually, the children decided to sit on the couch to watch one of the shows. The girl sat next to her brother, and he coughed loudly. She asked him, "James, are you OK?" The toddler coughed some more. "I'll get you a cup of water," she said.

The boy continued coughing, and Ned heard a spitting sound.

The girl brought the water and set it down on the coffee table in front of the couch. She saw the spit on the floor and pointed to it. "Eeeww! Yuk! James, why did you do that?"

He didn't answer but coughed even more loudly. She coughed a few times, too.

Ned suddenly remembered that they had both eaten from the same bowl of grapes that he had eaten from earlier that morning. And the boy had eaten the grapes that had fallen from Ned's hands onto the floor.

"You're sick. Lie down," she said, helping to reposition her brother onto his side. "I'll go wake up Mommy and Daddy." She coughed and headed upstairs.

James coughed more heavily and spat again.

Ned slithered behind a high-backed chair in the corner of the room so he would be better hidden from the adults. From here, he couldn't see into the kitchen anymore, but he could carefully peer around the side of the chair to see James on the couch, which was where all the action was going to be.

He reflected with fascination. These children started coughing an hour or so after eating grapes that he had touched. And the boy was spitting in the same way that Ned felt compelled to. When they had first come down the stairs, and until just recently, they hadn't been coughing at all. Were they sick now because of his germs? The bums had blamed him when they'd gotten sick. Was it possible that the bums and these kids had actually caught his illness so incredibly fast? Also, the parents would be down any minute, and God had instructed him to wait for them. Surely more directions would be coming. He felt a thrill, like he was in the middle of a suspense movie, only better.

The stairs creaked. A moment later, he heard the girl and her mother walking through the kitchen, the girl coughing a little along the way. At the entryway into the family room, the mother stopped and felt her daughter's forehead. "Jillian! You're hot! Maybe you and James both picked up the same bug," she said. They came into the family room together, and upon seeing her son, the mother cried, "Dave! James is bright red! Call the doctor!"

Ned heard the husband running down the stairs and fumbling with the kitchen phone. The girl was starting to cough more deeply now. The mother felt the boy's head and swiftly picked him up in her arms. "Dave, he's way too hot. We need to go to the hospital!" the mother urged.

The husband didn't argue. He got off the phone immediately, and they took both children out to the car and drove off.

Ned stood up slowly, using the chair as support. He'd gotten stiff from crouching for such a long time. To get some fresh air and think, he dragged himself out the kitchen door and walked back into the park. God hadn't given him directions when the parents had come downstairs, but things had happened so quickly. The mother said both children were hot. She wanted to go to the hospital, so she must have thought the boy's life was in danger. He was coughing really hard. The girl's coughing had started out lightly, but was quickly getting worse.

As Ned wandered along speculating, he neared the monkey bars and saw something there on the ground. He walked closer to investigate and found a squirrel lying dead, right near where he had coughed and spat earlier. There were fewer acorns in that spot now, too. "Hmmm," Ned murmured.

It definitely seemed like the squirrel had died from eating the acorns he'd germed up. And if his germs really were deadly, then the bums were right to blame him. But, if the bums and the squirrel had died from his germs, what about the children? Would they die, too? To find out, Ned went back into their home to wait for the family to come back from the hospital.

He was a little hungry again, and helped himself to the refrigerator. He drank some milk from the carton and ate a sandwich with lunchmeat and cheese. Content, he lounged on the couch to watch some TV—at a low volume, of course, so he would hear when their car pulled up the driveway.

Almost three hours later, he heard the engine. He didn't know how much longer he'd want to stay in the house or what was going to happen, so he hid near his exit. Ned spotted a freestanding pantry a few feet from the kitchen door. With a small push forward, he created just enough space between it and the wall for him to fit in.

He heard the parents enter the house from the front door.

"How could this have happened? They were both *fine* last night!" the mother cried, and then coughed.

"I don't know," the father said hoarsely through sobs; he started coughing, too.

"Now, there's funerals!" she wailed.

Ned heard them shuffle into the family room. Their loud bawling, talking, and coughing covered up the sound of him slinking out the kitchen door.

# CHAPTER FORTY-FOUR

Ned walked back into the park, found a picnic bench, and sat while he mulled things over. This crazy sickness looked like it could be spread shockingly fast. And whatever it was, though it made him feel like hell, it seemed to be killing others within hours. The old bums, the squirrel, the children, and now the parents were coughing. Would the sickness be able to kill them? Middle-aged adults? He would have to peek in on them one more time. But first, a nap; the weakness was taking over. He coughed profusely, spat, and then lay down on the bench.

When he awakened, the sun was strong, and the park was filling in with people. It had to be mid to late afternoon. He must have slept a good two hours at least.

He walked back to the house and crept in through the kitchen door. It was quiet, except for a faint beeping. He cautiously entered the family room. A cordless phone on the floor turned out to be the source of the sound. On the couch, the parents sat slumped and still. He felt both of their necks. They were dead.

Ned waltzed out of the house. Old men, squirrels, children, and healthy, middle-aged adults: None of them could withstand this disease. But he could. He was stronger than all of them! But was it possible that someone other than himself could survive it, too? Or, was it that no one could survive it, and in time, he would die from it also? Ned couldn't answer those questions, so he posed them to God.

"Many around you have been dying recently," the voice stated flatly in his ear, bypassing Ned's specific questions.

"Yes," Ned acknowledged.

"You have managed to live with the sickness, yet, by exposing the others, you have been causing them to die."

"Yes," Ned agreed petulantly. This was not helping. God was only stating the blaringly obvious.

"Did you know that the dead all deserved to die and were part of the mission?"

Now Ned saw where God was leading him, and he was excited. "You mean this is how we do it? I spread this sickness all around, and the bad people die from it? Is this how the world gets cleansed?"

"Highly efficient, don't you think?"

"Yes! Yes!"

"Spread it far and wide," the voice instructed.

"Far and wide," Ned repeated.

It was a real challenge. How could he spread his disease to the most people? After some consideration, he decided that touching, coughing, and spitting on frequently touched surfaces in public places was his best tactic. He settled on a few favorites: supermarkets, where he could contaminate the produce; train stations and airports, where he could germ up seats, tabletops, phones, door handles, sink knobs, and water fountain buttons; and school yards, where he could infect the playground equipment.

No doubt his photo was circulating in the press by now. To look different, he'd keep growing his beard and would dye his hair and wear some nonprescription glasses. Most of the time, people looked at each other less in mobbed places, anyway.

Smiling insolently, he thought, "Finally, I can shift this mission into high gear."

\* \* \*

Nearly a week slipped by, and Ned contaminated as many supermarkets, airports, train stations, and school yards as he could, whenever he was awake. He had to sleep sometimes, because of his weakness and pain. He didn't know how much longer he'd live, but he couldn't imagine it would be more than another day or two. It amazed him that he'd held on for as long as he already had.

But with all of this hard work, he had to know: How many people were actually dying? The media would be reporting about this. He needed a TV break.

He found a car dealership and sauntered into the waiting area. He took a donut, poured himself a cup of coffee, and sat down by the television. The newscast that followed thrilled him. The disease was killing millions. Infected people traveling by train and air were spreading it to every state and to countries throughout the globe. Animals were dying in droves, too. Ominously, and with terror, the news anchor concluded, "The incubation time and potency of this influenza strain are unlike anything doctors have seen before. I'm sorry to say, everyone is at risk."

Feeling vindicated, Ned got up, walked outside, and looked up at the sky. Now he knew, undeniably, that both his father and God were proud of him. This mission was truly his calling; he would continue on with it until his final breath.

# Return to Summer, 2032

## CHAPTER FORTY-FIVE

Stanlin woke up, got dressed, and joined his parents for breakfast. They were enjoying cimatas and cups of hot keechin.

"I'll have the same, please," Stanlin requested. He thought the cimatas were almost as delicious on the second day.

"Or do you mean three of what we're having?" Andrigon joked. "Having two yesterday was overdoing it for me!"

"Yeah, I was pretty stuffed after the third. Today I'll have only two." Stanlin really wanted to have three again, but knew it wouldn't be fair to hog the majority of the batch.

Andrigon was amused. "Only two. There are some benefits to being in your growing years."

"Yes, there are," Karilu chimed, placing a cup of hot keechin and a plate with two large cimatas in front of Stanlin.

"So, what are your plans for the day?" Andrigon asked Stanlin.

Since he was returning to Sylvia's, he needed an alibi again. "That journal cylinder I checked out last night is awesome. I'm gonna go back to the library today and look at some similar journals that the librarian showed me. Those cylinders can't be checked out, though, because you view them on the library's special 3-D Readers." This was not false, because, once again, he planned to stop off at the library on his way home from Earth.

His parents seemed pleased.

"Let us know what you learn," Karilu said.

"Mm hmm," Andrigon said as he finished the last bite of his cimata and gulped the rest of his keechin.

"Sure," Stanlin agreed.

Andrigon got up, kissed Karilu, and rubbed Stanlin's shoulder. He reached under the table and stroked Mini-G's back. "See you all tonight," he said, and left for work.

Mini-G followed him to the front door and lowered her head when it closed, moaning softly. Karilu and Stanlin heard the sad sound, and played with her once they'd finished eating. A few times, Mini-G bucked her front legs with delight, and they chuckled. It was the first they'd seen of this little antic.

Stanlin was also subtly keeping an eye on the Captonian timepiece on the wall near the front door. When it seemed late enough in the morning for Sylvia to have awakened, dressed, and eaten her breakfast, he was ready to take off. Saying his good-byes to his mother and to Mini-G, he left the house. He took his customary walk into ruralville and transported to Earth. Invisibly, he arrived in Sylvia's bedroom, where he found her sitting at her desk, busy on her computer.

"It's Stanlin. I'm here again," he said, becoming visible next to her. "Is it an OK time to talk?"

She started a little, but recovered quickly. "Yeah! Wait." She got up, ran over to the stereo, turned up the music, and hurried back to him. "Did you get to talk to your teacher? Can the Sphere help us change the future?" she panted.

"Yes and maybe. It's kinda hard to explain." Stanlin did his best imparting what R had told him, and describing what he had seen in the Probability Sphere.

The second he finished, Sylvia said, "I've heard of Jungilo Maximum Security Prison. It's not that far away." Her brows furrowed. "That prisoner there sure sounds freaky. I don't know who it could be." Her brows lifted. "But I do know of the three puppies! You're right—they're all from the same litter. They're really close-knit too, so we've been hoping to adopt them out together." She paused and some sadness crept into her eyes. "It's been hard. People are saying that three puppies are too much to handle. No one has wanted to adopt them separately either, and I think it's because of their little quirks."

"That's a shame," Stanlin said quietly.

Sylvia nodded. She appeared pensive for a moment before speaking again. "Let me make sure I get the big picture of what R told you: If I do something good, something positive, for the three puppies and for the man in Jungilo Prison, because they matter to the future, the future might change?"

"Yes, you've got it," Stanlin affirmed. He hastily reminded himself that supporting her endeavors was fine, but he had to be extremely careful not to direct her in what to do. All choices and actions had to be hers alone.

Sylvia put her hands on her hips and stared vaguely at the floor for several seconds as she thought. At last, she said, "I wonder if doing something positive for the pups and for that prisoner could be getting the Jungilo Prison to adopt the puppies?"

"That sounds positive to me," Stanlin encouraged.

"We've had animals adopted to nursing homes, so I'm sure we could do the same at a prison."

"I don't see why not," Stanlin chimed.

"Come to think of it, it's probably been done at some other prisons already. I'll look it up." Sylvia sat down at her desk. Stanlin stood beside her. She performed an online search for "animals and prisons." Many articles came up, and she took her time going through them. Eventually, she said, "Listen to this, 'When prisoners and pets come together, everyone fares better. Prisoners who meet the required behavioral standards can learn compassion and responsibility by grooming, feeding, and exercising the animals. The animals chosen for these programs are often from shelters and need homes. It is truly a win-win arrangement.'"

She skipped over to another article. "And it says here, 'Violence analyses have shown that after incorporating pet programs, prisons have less fighting among the inmates.' I could show these articles to the Jungilo warden, and then ask him about bringing in the three puppies—and maybe even more of the SPCA animals!"

"Sounds great!" Stanlin grinned widely.

Sylvia printed the two articles she'd read from. "I'll also show these to my parents when I ask them to drive me to Jungilo." Sylvia's voice faltered at the end of the sentence. She gazed down at the computer keyboard and suddenly drew quiet, her lips forming a slight grimace.

"Is something wrong?" Stanlin asked.

"I dunno. I need to think a minute."

Stanlin tuned into her thoughts. "What's bugging me about this?" he heard. "Animals helping prisoners is really positive. And the puppies will finally have a home." In his mind's eye, Stanlin then saw men pointing at the three puppies, derisively laughing at their oddities. He heard, "That would be awful! I used to hate it when Sherry made fun of me. The puppies might not understand everything, but they would sense the meanness—I know it!"

Aloud, Sylvia said, "I still want to help the one prisoner in the Sphere, and lots of other prisoners, by adopting some animals to Jungilo. But I'm thinking I need to find a different home for the three puppies."

"Oh," said Stanlin.

"I don't want the prisoners laughing at them because they look different. Does that sound sorta crazy?" Her face flushed and scrunched self-consciously.

"Not at all." Stanlin respected her view entirely, and it showed in his eyes even more than in his words.

Sylvia's expression immediately relaxed. "The prisoners need to learn compassion, but those puppies need to go to someone who already has it," she expounded confidently. "Now who do I know who has compassion and might like to adopt the three puppies?" She grabbed a pen and a pad. "I like to write by hand when I'm getting ideas. In school, we call it brainstorming."

Stanlin nodded.

Sylvia wrote down some notes. Before long, she let out a small sound, almost like a whine. It didn't seem intentional. Putting down her pen and looking up sorrowfully, she said, "I keep thinking about my neighbors, Mr. and Mrs. Tormeni and their son, Cedric. Remember Mrs. Tormeni and Cedric, who'd come over and play with Melvin at the park?"

"Yes, I remember them."

"They are so nice. They would be a perfect family to adopt the three puppies. But the horrible thing is, Cedric was just kidnapped. Mrs. Tormeni woke up yesterday morning, and he was gone."

"That *is* horrible," Stanlin commiserated. He didn't wish to divulge that he'd invisibly listened to Sylvia and her mom discussing this news already.

"We went to a service at church for her last night. She is all alone now, because Mr. Tormeni is away for work. We prayed that the police will find Cedric and bring him home soon."

"So that's where you and your family were last night," Stanlin thought, but he said, "I really hope everything turns out OK for them."

"Me too." Sylvia shook her head somberly. "At the service, Mrs. Tormeni looked so, so depressed." She paused. Suddenly her eyes widened. "Depressed," she repeated. "'Everyone is less depressed with furry friends around.' That's what Mrs. Delany always says." She hesitated for a second, then touted happily, "I bet if Mrs. Tormeni adopted those puppies, it would help her be a little less sad right now!"

"That makes sense," Stanlin concurred.

"I want to read up on it for a sec." Sylvia searched online for "depression and animals," and skimmed some articles. She read aloud from one. "It says here, 'Positive psychological studies indicate that helping or giving to others is very beneficial for those suffering with depressive episodes. It has been found that caring for animals, in particular, promotes both purpose and joy that might otherwise remain untapped.'" Her cheeks flushed with color. "Adopting the puppies really should help her! And, of course, it will help the puppies!"

"That sounds really good!" Stanlin exclaimed.

Sylvia contemplated for a minute. "Telling her about the puppies wouldn't work as well as if she saw them and picked them up. They're so cuddly. They lick us a lot and snuggle with us whenever we go in the cage to play with them or feed them." She thought a bit more. "But what if she doesn't want to go to the shelter with me when I ask her to?"

"Hmmm. That'd be tough," Stanlin speculated.

She gasped, and then blurted out, "I'll bring them to her! I can bring the puppies to her house to show her! I'll need some help carrying all three of them over, but I'm sure Karen would help me. Then Mrs. Tormeni will see how sweet those pups are, and that they really need her."

"Boy, you're coming up with lots of ideas," Stanlin praised.

"But there's still more to figure out. I want to pick the right animals at the shelter to bring to the prisoners." Sylvia returned to brainstorming with her pen and paper. A short while later, she fidgeted in her seat zealously, picked up her pad, and pointed to a list of names she'd written down. "Some of the shelter's older dogs and cats would be great for the prison. Benton, Sultie, Roxy, Sunset, Teddy, Puff, Apollo, Buck, Cody, and Jesse have all been waiting to be adopted. They could finally have a home at Jungilo and be helping the prisoners there, too!"

"Fantastic!" Stanlin replied vehemently. He was highly impressed. He also cheerfully noticed that Sylvia was growing more and more at ease and comfortable in his presence.

"Like with Mrs. Tormeni, it'd be more convincing to have at least one animal there with me when I go talk to the warden," Sylvia reasoned. "Since Benton's the calmest, I'll take him."

"Superbly super!" Stanlin exclaimed.

Sylvia smiled and squinted at him curiously.

"It's an expression on Capton," he explained.

"Superbly super," she echoed, and for a few seconds, they grinned silently at each other.

"You've come up with terrific plans," Stanlin said at last. "I have no doubt you'll carry them out seamlessly, too."

Instead of broadening, Sylvia's smile began to fade. "I like having you here," she said. "I wish you could come with me to Mrs. Tormeni's and to the prison." Her voice had a sentimental edge to it.

Stanlin felt jubilant. "I like having you here," he repeated in his mind. "I *can* come with you! I can go invisibly, or, I can go as Melvin!" he proposed aloud.

"Really?" She sprang up from her chair.

"Really!" He loved the prospect of staying by her side even longer.

"Oh, that'd be great!" She clapped her hands together. "How about you come along as Melvin? That way, if I talk to you out loud, it'll look less weird." She chortled.

"Alright; Melvin I'll be," he said with a chuckle.

"Time for lunch!" Rebecca's voice called up from the kitchen.

"I hafta go down and eat. I can bring you back up some tuna, or something else. What do you want?"

"Fruit is kinda similar on Earth and on Capton. That would be fine."

"OK. And after lunch, I'll call Karen to see about getting the puppies and taking them to Mrs. Tormeni's house. See you in a few." She waved to him and went down to the kitchen.

He invisibly accompanied her at the table, appreciating the opportunity to stare at her freely, without embarrassing either of them. At the end of the meal, Sylvia selected a peach and a plum from the fruit basket on the counter. "Snacks for later," she said to her mom and scurried up the stairs.

Stanlin materialized in her room just before she stepped in.

"Here you go," she said, handing him the fruit.

While Stanlin ate, Sylvia called Karen, who was, as she had anticipated, completely on board with the idea. "Great! I'll see you there in fifteen minutes," Sylvia said, and hung up. "Stanlin, can you go invisibly with me to the shelter and then become Melvin there? You could trot out from behind a bush somewhere in front of the building. I'll act surprised and ask Karen if you can tag along with us."

His heart soared in his chest; she'd said his real name for the first time. "That can be arranged," he said, nearly bursting into song.

"I guess we're ready. Wait—you need to throw away your fruit pits." She looked at his empty hands with confusion. "Where are they?"

Stanlin put a hand on his stomach.

"You ate them?" she asked, looking aghast.

"You *don't* eat them?" he countered and laughed. "You should try it."

"Yuk." Sylvia shuddered.

"On Capton, all our fruits and vegetables have edible cores." He shrugged. "It's what I'm used to."

Sylvia smiled. "Alrighty. If that's what you like, who am I to say anything? Let's get going," she chirped.

Stanlin became invisible and disrobed, leaving his invisible garment next to her desk chair as he had the prior day.

When they arrived at the shelter, Karen was waiting outside the front door. After the girls greeted each other, Karen said, "My mom's working today. I told her about the idea, and she said for us to go talk to her first."

They stopped into the office, and Rinalda handed them some forms. She described where Mrs. Tormeni would need to sign, should she agree to the adoptions, and cautioned, "While these puppies could help lift her spirits, please just be careful not to pressure her. She's going through so, so much right now." The girls agreed, and Rinalda wished them luck. Karen folded and stowed the papers in the back pocket of her shorts.

Sylvia and Karen leashed up the puppies and exited the shelter. As planned, Melvin trotted out from behind a bush and started tagging along at their heels. The puppies were pulling forward on their leashes and didn't seem to notice him behind them.

"Oh, look! It's Melvin!" Sylvia said, feigning surprise. "He's hysterical! Always popping up at the weirdest times. It can't hurt if he comes with us, right?"

"As long as he won't hiss at the puppies," Karen warned, shooting a stern glance down at Melvin.

"Nah, he's been calm whenever people have brought their dogs to the park. I've never seen him hiss or scratch. But you're right to remind him. I'll do it, too." Sylvia eyed Melvin and jested, "Ya hear that, mister? No funny business around the pups."

He peered up at her and winked.

# CHAPTER FORTY-SIX

It was 1:33 p.m., and Brenna was mentally willing Anthony to call her back as she sat at the kitchen table, staring at the phone on the counter. She took a sip of water and reflected upon his earlier call that morning, 11:00 a.m. her time, 7:30 p.m. his. He'd said he couldn't wait until their usual time to talk because he'd missed hearing from her and Cedric so much the night before.

"We managed to fix the anarchy in the computer systems!" he'd joked. "Now I can relax and focus on the good stuff—my favorite dynamic duo. What's doin' over there?" He had sounded so happy; she had hysterically sputtered out the horror story. After a silent pause, Anthony muttered something about needing some time, saying he would call back soon.

Brenna wasn't surprised by the abrupt ending to the call. She knew her Anthony well. Over the course of their relationship, he'd discovered that, initially, he was best off sorting through difficult things alone.

Usually he would go to the gym to blow off steam, gain perspective, and organize his thoughts. He'd come home afterward, ready to talk. By nature, Brenna preferred discussing things right away, but she had learned that giving Anthony his alone time first made their conversations later less heated. And, though she disliked admitting it, she had noticed herself cooling off and becoming more rational during those mini separations, too.

At 1:35 p.m., the phone rang. She picked it up immediately.

"It's me," Anthony said. "I'm sorry. I needed…that time. You know."

"I know. I know. And I'm the one who's sorry. I feel like this is all my fault. I'm a t-terrible mother," she stammered, bursting into tears.

"No, Brenna! No!"

"Yes. I should've kn-known, with you not here, that I shouldn't be leaving windows open at night. I was so st-stupid; so, so stupid."

"Brenna, stop! It wasn't your fault. Do you remember when we first brought Cedric home, how he had so much trouble falling asleep? That one summer night when we first opened his window was when he finally slept well. That's how it started. It helped him; then it became habit. And we never worried about it, because the neighborhood's sa…Well, it *was* one of the safest around."

Brenna moaned and sobbed.

"The truth is, even if I had been home, it probably wouldn't have made a difference. This guy was skilled and quiet, and he had his mind set, like he would've done this thing no matter what," Anthony inferred.

"Oh, I don't know," she mumbled miserably.

"Look, we're dealing with a total lunatic here. Thank God the cops are out looking for him, and we've got that AMBER Alert going."

"Yes, yes," Brenna muttered. She took a napkin from the table, blotted her eyes, and blew her nose. "I saw his mug shot on TV. He's got a shaved head and a big tattoo on the side of his neck. And his eyes, they were so piercing, so cold." She shivered at the recollection.

"OK, enough about him now," Anthony quipped. He cleared his throat. Softening his tone, he asked, "How are you doing? Have you been taking care of yourself? Have you been eating?"

Brenna hesitated. Her glass of water was the only nourishment in front of her, and thinking back, she'd eaten only a few dried apricots, some baby carrot sticks, and a handful of crackers in total since yesterday morning. No doubt Anthony was remembering how he'd all but force fed her for days when she had faced the depressing reality of her sterility.

"So you're forgetting to eat," Anthony inferred from her silence with a frustrated sigh. "Have you left the house at all? Gotten any fresh air or sunlight?"

"I...no," she replied weakly.

"Listen, I can't have you neglecting yourself," he admonished. "I need you! And if...no, *when* Cedric comes home, he'll need you!"

The doorbell rang before she could respond. The sound startled her and she flinched. "Anthony, someone's at the door. Let me go see who it is." She walked over and peered through the peephole. "It's Rebecca and Rinalda's daughters, and they've got some animals with them," she relayed with confusion.

"They're good girls; they must have something going on," Anthony assumed. "Let's see what they want, but stay on with me."

"OK. I'll get the headset." Once she was properly hooked up, Brenna answered the door. "Hi, girls. What's up?"

"Hi, Mrs. Tormeni," Sylvia greeted nervously. "Could we, uh, come in, please, for a few minutes? We'd really like to talk to you about these puppies."

"Umm, alright; come on in," Brenna acquiesced with befuddlement. Gesturing at her headset, she said, "Anthony's on the line from overseas, but it's no problem." She led the girls and their furry entourage into the den.

Melvin was tamely clinging near Sylvia's ankles, but the puppies were pulling forward on their leashes, gasping for air. Karen was struggling with two of the pups and Sylvia with the third.

"You guys are excited, aren't you?" Brenna said affectionately to the puppies. "It's OK," she said to Sylvia and Karen. "You can let them loose in here while we talk." The puppies were too small to hike up her staircase, and her home's lower level was already toddler-proofed, and thereby, should be puppy-safe. "So what's this all about?" she asked.

"Umm," Sylvia's reply stalled, because she and Karen were unleashing the squirming puppies, who, not a moment later, were racing toward Brenna.

Brenna wasn't the least bit intimidated. She sank down to their level, sitting on the floor with her back leaning up against the couch. The puppies climbed into her lap, wagging their tails wildly and licking her hands. They bounced upward, trying to lick her face, too. Brenna was laughing for the first time since Cedric disappeared. "Anthony, there are three puppies in my lap!" she giddily reported.

Sylvia picked up and held Melvin. Finally, she answered Brenna's question, explaining why the pups weren't being adopted and how they really needed a home.

Brenna and Anthony listened together to the story of the puppies' plight; both were deeply touched.

Sylvia ended by asking, "Mrs. Tormeni, do you think that, maybe, you could adopt them all together? You can see that they totally love you already!"

"Yes; tell her yes," Anthony beseeched instantly.

"Excuse me for a minute, girls," Brenna said. She carefully took the pups out of her lap before getting up. She needed a few words with Anthony in private. She went upstairs to her bedroom and closed the door. "Anthony, I'm barely getting along on my own right now, let alone trying to take care of three small and needy pup..."

"That's exactly why you need to do this!" Anthony insisted. "When you feed them, you'll eat; when they need to go outside, you'll go out with them. They need structure in their day, and so do you."

"But...what if I...screw up?" she whispered shakily. The thought of failing again as a caregiver was unbearable.

"You won't screw anything up. Just listen to me. When the girls leave, use Cedric's baby gates to keep the pups in the kitchen. Line the floor with some newspapers. Then go to the pet store and get some leashes, a few toys, some puppy food, and bowls. Feed them and give them water morning, noon, and evening, and you eat while they're eating. Walk them around the block and take them out in the yard a few times every day. Pet them and love them. I know you won't let *them* starve! And you won't deprive *them* of exercise or fresh air! Caring for them will keep *you* on track. You see? You and those puppies need each other. Please, do this. Please," Anthony implored.

Brenna pictured how the puppies had been so sweet in her lap. "They really are adorable. They were wagging their little tails and licking me. It's such a shame that no one has wanted to adopt them."

"Yes, so let's be the ones to save them. We've already talked about getting a puppy when I come home this spring. So we'll get three instead, and sooner. And once our little Cedric is home again, whoa, he'll really be in his glory!"

They shared a moment of teary-eyed, hopeful laughter.

When it quieted, Anthony asked, "Is it time to go tell Sylvia and Karen the good news?"

"Yes. It is," Brenna answered.

# CHAPTER FORTY-SEVEN

When Mrs. Tormeni consented to adopting the pups, Karen pulled out the paperwork from her back pocket and showed her where to sign. They all exchanged smiling thank-yous and good-byes, and Sylvia and Karen practically skipped out of the house.

Karen was holding the papers and the SPCA leashes, and Sylvia was still holding Melvin—but not for long. Once the shelter was in sight, Melvin leaped out of her arms and scrambled away.

"That's what he does every time he sees this place!" Sylvia whined dramatically for Karen's benefit. She wished she could laugh out loud, though, because she finally understood why Melvin would never, and should never, stay there.

The girls returned the leashes and delivered the signed paperwork.

"This is wonderful! You girls are incredible. I'm so proud!" Rinalda exclaimed.

Karen and Sylvia both glowed.

"I hope you'll like my next idea, too." Sylvia shared what she had read about animals benefiting prisoners. She mentioned the SPCA's specific older animals that she thought would be well suited for the program. "I was gonna ask my parents to drive me to Jungilo Prison, so I could talk to the warden there about doing this. Would that be OK with you, Mrs. Delany?"

"Wow, you're one inspired little lady," Rinalda said. She looked at the planner on her desk. "You're welcome to go with your parents as soon as you'd like, but if you want some extra help, my schedule frees up by midweek next week."

Sylvia stiffened. Time was of the essence. She wanted her deeds to have as great a chance as possible for changing the future, and delaying things wouldn't help. It was nice of Mrs. Delany to offer her assistance, though, so Sylvia felt guilty for declining it. "Thank you, but I'm feeling like I should go right away," she said apologetically.

Clearly impressed rather than offended, Rinalda extolled, "You're so committed. It's terrific." She handed Sylvia a couple of her business cards. "Give the warden my card. If he likes the idea, tell him to call me to coordinate the details. In the meantime, I'll look up how some of the most successful programs have been run."

"Oh, thank you!" Sylvia gushed.

"No, thank you," Rinalda replied earnestly.

"Where are you getting all these ideas from all of a sudden?" Karen snapped jealously, glaring at Sylvia, arms folded across her chest.

Feeling bad, Sylvia shrugged. She wished she had some explanation to offer her best friend that didn't involve a blue alien boy, who, minutes earlier, had been with them as Melvin the cat. Not knowing what else to say, she politely excused herself. "I'd better get home. I'll call you soon, Karen. Thanks again, Mrs. Delany."

Tightly grasping the business cards, she rushed out of the shelter.

# CHAPTER FORTY-EIGHT

After running off as Melvin, Stanlin transformed into his invisible Rampont self and went to the shelter. He witnessed the prison program discussion, and followed Sylvia out when she left.

Walking beside her, he looked around to see who else was nearby. Comfortable that they were momentarily alone, he became a visible Melvin and meowed loudly so she would look down at him.

Barely breaking her stride, Sylvia scooped him up in her arms.

"I was in Mrs. Delany's office with you," he said in his toddler-esque Melvin voice. "Don't worry, Karen will be OK."

"I guess so," she said, patting Melvin's head.

"Mrs. Delany really loved your idea to help the prisoners with the older animals. And you did great with Mrs. Tormeni before, the way you explained everything about the puppies, and letting her play with them—she couldn't help but adopt them. It was superbly super!"

Sylvia giggled. "Thanks. I'm really glad it worked. She was smiling so big. We know we did something positive for her, like your teacher said."

"Absolutely! Now, what's our next step?"

"I've gotta ask my parents about driving me to the prison when my dad gets home from work."

To reply, he meowed once with a subtle head bob. Some children on bicycles were passing by, so he dared not risk talking. For the next few streets, there were more people and cars, so Sylvia carried Melvin in silence.

Luckily, the bustle subsided as they turned onto Holloway Drive. Stanlin seized the moment. "Looks like the coast is clear. I'm going to go invisible now, but I'll stay with you," he said, becoming his invisible Rampont self.

"OK," Sylvia acknowledged.

Sylvia's mom greeted her at the door and requested help with preparing dinner. While Sylvia and her mother sliced and chopped, Stanlin was entertained, musing that the humans all but dissected their produce and meat to ready it for consumption. At one point, Rebecca left the kitchen to talk on the phone. Sylvia quickly gathered a few fruits and a bowl with leftover, prepared tuna from the refrigerator. She darted up to her room, and Stanlin followed.

He found his invisible garment near her desk chair and slipped into it.

Sylvia shut her door, put the food down on her desk, and whispered, "Are you here?"

He became visible next to her.

"Would this be alright for your dinner?"

"It'll be great. Thanks." Stanlin grinned. While the food didn't taste as good as on Capton, the ambiance was incomparable. Having special, secret food deliveries from Sylvia was indeed superbly super.

"After you eat, can you come downstairs, invisible, while I talk to my parents about the prison idea?"

"You got it," Stanlin said, and blissfully bit into his peach.

"You can meet me up here again, right after dinner."

"Will do," he agreed.

"OK. Bye for now!" Sylvia waved and zipped back to the kitchen.

About ten minutes later, just as he was finishing his last mouthful of tuna, Stanlin heard Sylvia's father coming in the front door. "Perfect timing," he thought, and invisibly headed to the kitchen.

During dinner, Sylvia discussed her ideas, pointing out that she had printed articles on the subject and that Mrs. Delany had given her business cards to pass on to the warden, so he could call her to coordinate bringing in some of the animals.

Sylvia's father swallowed a sip of wine and said proudly, "Our little Mother Theresa."

"Oh, Charles," Rebecca chortled. "Yes, it is a wonderful idea," she added supportively.

"Can we go after dinner?" Sylvia begged.

Charles laughed. "I love your enthusiasm, but can you settle for tomorrow morning?"

"I guess so," Sylvia conceded reluctantly.

"I still have some personal days. I'll take one tomorrow, and we'll all go," Charles said. "And be sure to bring those articles, Sylvia. The warden will be more likely to bite if he sees it in print that this kind of program has been successful before."

"Yes, definitely," Rebecca agreed.

"OK. And I want to take Benton, too. Can we stop by the shelter and pick him up on the way?" Sylvia asked earnestly. "He's such a good dog. I know if he's there, it'll help convince the warden."

"Sure, honey," Rebecca said to Sylvia. To herself, she mumbled, "I'll need to take my allergy medication in the morning."

"Yes," Charles affirmed, giving Rebecca's hand a squeeze on top of the table. Toggling his gaze between her and Sylvia, he said, "It's settled, then. In the morning, we'll get Sylvia's idea rolling as a family project, with Benton in tow."

After dinner, Sylvia bounded up the stairs to her bedroom, closed the door, and turned on the music.

"That went well," Stanlin remarked, manifesting in front of her.

"Yeah, except that we have to wait until tomorrow morning to go." She bit her lip. "Do you think you can still go with us?" she asked timidly.

Stanlin had begun fiddling with that question on his own. He'd been gone from his home the entire day, and, without forewarning, had skipped out on his family's dinner, which he never did. In the rare instances when he had alternate plans, he always informed his parents. It was nearing 8:00 p.m. here, and knowing the comparable time at home, he was certain his parents were at best upset, worried, or suspicious—and at worst, livid.

When he came home, they would ground him and keep their eyes glued to him; he could not fathom being able to come back to accompany her tomorrow.

He said sadly, "Once I go home, it'll be really hard, probably impossible, for me to come back to Earth. I managed to sneak over the two times, but I honestly don't think I can get away with it again."

"Maybe you could stay overnight, and come with us in the morning to Jungilo?" Sylvia suggested. "Then, you wouldn't have to sneak back here, and you could go home tomorrow, once everything's done!" she piped up. "Oh, I mean, if you want to, and if it doesn't mess up stuff you hafta do at home," she tacked on sheepishly.

He felt giddy, hardly able to believe his auditory openings. She was actually asking him to sleep over!

"Where will she let me sleep?" he wondered hopefully. Aloud, he steadied his voice for a tame, socially acceptable reply. "Staying the night is a good idea. Then I can definitely come with you in the morning and go home after, like you said."

"Cool," she said, smiling.

"Could I borrow a pen and paper to write a quick note to my folks?" He had to at least assure them that he wasn't hurt.

She handed him a tablet with a pen. "How are you going to send it?" she inquired, bewildered.

"Don't you use mailing robots?" he asked reflexively, and then remembered reading that Earth didn't communicate with other planets.

She was squinting and shaking her head. "Mailing robots?"

"Yeah. A bunch of robots from Capton are orbiting all around the universe. They respond to the thought, "Please mail this, Robot." Whenever we want to mail something, we concentrate on those words, and the nearest robot flies over. We give it the letter, tell it where to go, and it delivers the mail."

"Wow!" Sylvia exclaimed in wonderment.

"Lots of other planets use their own versions of mailing robots, too," he added while composing his letter. Intentionally, he was keeping the note short and vague; his parents could not know he was on Earth. He merely wrote that he was safe, was addressing an urgent matter, and would come home as soon as he'd done all he could to help out. He signed it,

"With Love, Stanlin," and folded the paper. "Can I summon a robot to your window?"

"Sure!" Sylvia opened her window, screen and all, in anticipation. They stood by the window together, and Stanlin performed the mental elicitation.

Not five minutes later, a small robot flew toward the window. It was about a foot tall and resembled a tiny Rampont. It hovered in the open air in front of them.

"The robot's chest is a chamber for inserting the letters," Stanlin explained. He opened the small compartment and put his note inside.

"Oh," Sylvia said with awe.

Stanlin told the robot his parents' address. In a digitized voice, it parroted the address for his confirmation. "Correct," Stanlin said.

The robot zoomed off. Within seconds, it was out of sight.

"Can the mailing robots do anything else?" Sylvia asked.

"No. They are pretty simple contraptions. They come when you will them, deliver your note, and go back to their posts. That's it."

"So they're not also spies?" She sounded disappointed.

"Hey, the last thing we need now is spies! I'm not even supposed to be here, remember?" Stanlin chuckled.

"Right; you're right." Sylvia was laughing as she closed her window. "I'm so glad you're staying. Now we'll have lots of time to talk. There's so much I wanna ask you about your life on Capton!"

# CHAPTER FORTY-NINE

"I'll be back in a few. I need to wash up."

"You're not going," Stanlin inwardly chastised himself for his fleeting thought of following her and becoming an invisible peeping Tom. "Alright," he said to her, trying to sound nonchalant.

Sylvia stepped out, taking her nightgown in hand.

Stanlin stayed in her room, listening to the radio. He wasn't too keen on the first few songs he heard, but then a very upbeat, catchy one started playing. He was tapping his foot in appreciation when Sylvia returned.

"I showered and brushed my teeth, so we can talk straight through 'till bedtime." She rotated her desk chair around to face her bed. "Come and sit here."

Stanlin sat. Sylvia hopped into her bed and sat upright with her legs crossed under her.

He couldn't take his eyes off of her and hoped he wasn't gawking. She wore a long emerald nightgown. Her typically fluffy hair was flattened and darker due to wetness, and her cheeks were rosy red. She looked radiant. But would it be appropriate for him to tell her how pretty he thought she was? Uncertain, he played it conservatively. "I like this song a lot. It's one of the best I've ever heard."

"That's so funny! It's one of my favorites, too! This is the band right here, Rocklore," she said, pointing to a poster on her wall above the bed depicting four band members.

Stanlin noticed that one musician was standing in the foreground while the other three stood behind him. "Why's that one person up front?" he asked.

"He's the lead singer," she cooed.

Stanlin didn't like hearing her response; she sounded a little too impressed with that lead singer guy. But when she changed the topic, he became even more ruffled.

"What I'm dying to know is, why were you coming to Earth as a cat to learn? And why were you spending time with me?" she queried intently.

His face grew hot. It was that awful question again that he'd tried to skirt around the last time she'd asked. But divulging everything would be overwhelming for her, and mortifying for him. An abridged, vaguer version would have to do.

He said, "To expand our knowledge, Ramponts travel a lot to other planets. When I was first observing on Earth, I saw, er, *some* humans playing with a cat and smiling. I thought if I became a cat, it would be an easy, nonthreatening way for me to meet and learn about the humans. And then you and I, ya know, bumped into each other, that day in front of your school. You took me to the park, and it was really fun. I felt so happy around you that I wanted to keep visiting you." His face had all but ignited into flame.

Intense interest shone in her eyes. "When you visit Earth, how do you get here? A spaceship?"

Relieved at the new avenue of conversation, Stanlin explained, "I cross my arms over my chest and totally focus my mind on traveling to planet Earth and the particular location, like Ashbury Park or your house. A few seconds later, I'm there. That's all it takes to transport myself."

"Wow! Kinda like on the old Star Trek shows! But they used the space-ship's computerized transporter, and it didn't matter where their arms were. Why do you cross yours over your chest?"

"Our ancestors experimented with connections between the mind and the body and discovered that some postures distracted the mind, but others helped it focus. Of all the postures, they found that crossing the arms over the chest helps the most with concentration."

"Mm, body and mind stuff is sooo cool! Your mind makes your body travel, without spaceships, computers, handheld gadgets, or anything!" She leaned forward curiously. "Do you ever use spaceships?"

"Yes. If we're moving lots of beings or objects all at once, we do."

Sylvia paused briefly before asking, "But you can also move just one being by wrapping your arms around them before transporting, right? Isn't that what you said the first day we talked, as a way to rescue me?"

"That's right," Stanlin confirmed. He was suddenly feeling awkward and embarrassed. It made perfect sense that she hadn't instantly gone with him to Capton. She had been filled with questions about saving Earth. It wasn't rational for him to feel like a loser right now, as he remembered that earlier conversation. Yet his face was feeling prickly, and he began shift-ing in the chair. He changed the subject. "So, what's your favorite class at school?"

Luckily, she seemed oblivious to his unease. "Biology," she answered. "I love learning about animals and plants. What about you?"

"Travel Excursions, of course. That's the class where visiting other plan-ets is our homework!"

She laughed.

"What's your worst class?" he asked.

"Gym," she said, contorting her face with revulsion.

"I could have guessed that," Stanlin thought to himself. The first day he'd seen her, Sylvia was crying because a girl named Sherry had been taunting her in gym class. Stanlin wanted to ask what had happened with that, but he didn't know how. Sylvia would definitely be weirded out if she knew that he listened to some of her thoughts. He said instead, "I actually like my gym classes."

"How come?" she inquired, appearing genuinely mystified.

"I think it's because we have a bunch of activities we can choose from, so you can do whatever you like best, and you can rotate between different things. There are individual activities, like running, acrobatics, and calisthenics; there are game sports, where two teams compete to see who wins; and also, there are contact activities, the really physical stuff, like wrestling or boxing on Earth. For those, we become fully solid, not sorta airy, like I am now.

"Really?" Sylvia's eyebrows raised in surprise.

"Yeah, if we didn't become more dense for those things, then when we punched or tackled each other, our forms would overlap, so it wouldn't work."

"Hmm," she murmured, her brows knitting.

Stanlin knew it must seem odd to her that his density was mutable. He tried clarifying it. "Normally, Ramponts are semisolid in density. That means we're thicker than air, but we're lighter than fully solid matter, like this chair or the bed…"

"Or like humans! Or like Melvin! You became totally solid when you were him!"

"Right, yes. Both humans and animals are completely solid. But, in our usual semisolid density, Ramponts can still touch fully solid matter, or hold it, whatever. I used your pad and pen to write that note to my parents, remember?"

"Uh-huh," she recalled.

"The problem comes in if we make contact while we're moving faster and with more force; that's when our form will overlap with other semisolid or fully solid things." He demonstrated by rapidly bringing his fist down on top of the desk behind him. His fist partially disappeared into the desk. "You see?"

"Far out," she marveled.

He removed his fist from the desk and folded his hands in his lap. "But if we turn solid, for contact activities or whatnot, it's only temporary. Our teachers and doctors say it's physiologically stressful for us to stay solid too long, like for days at a time, I mean. It has to do with the resonant frequency alterations in our atoms."

Sylvia's face scrunched in confusion.

Stanlin wanted to elaborate, but was having trouble finding the words. "It's really hard to explain." He knew the facts cold yet couldn't convey them. He exhaled slowly in frustration.

Sylvia apparently wasn't fixated on the physics anyway. "If it's stressful for your body to turn solid for a long time, maybe it's not that healthy to do it for a short time either," she posed with concern.

Her caring question melted away his irritation. "No, for a short time, it's fine. They wouldn't let us do it otherwise. And boxing is so, so great! We have these huge punching bags to practice on, and we have matches against each other, too."

She winced. "Doesn't it hurt if you get punched?"

"Yeah, but the pain goes away once we turn semisolid again, so it's no big deal," he said, deepening his voice. He had a rugged side and wanted Sylvia to know it.

"Huh." She nodded, taking it all in. "I'd pick the calisthenics class," she said with a smile. "So, what's your worst class?"

"Languages," he drawled emphatically.

"Well, you're great at English!"

"Thanks, but I screw it up sometimes. Like when a word that has more than one meaning is used, I can have a hard time understanding the sentence."

"Uh-huh. I could see that."

"But more than any one language being tough, the amount of work overall is what I hate the most about that class. There's just too much to learn, too many different words and grammar rules. Plus it's boring. Talking like this is fun, but learning about it in school is totally boring."

Sylvia nodded sympathetically.

"I know languages are important though," he admitted, "for visiting, for business and trade, and for helping out when other planets are in trouble. I've got to just suck it up and keep studying." He sighed. "But I wish schoolwork was easy for me, like it is for my friend Corimo. He barely studies and gets perfect grades on practically everything."

Sylvia was quiet. She turned crimson and avoided his eyes.

Stanlin smirked. "Wait a minute. I'll bet you get lots of perfect marks too, don't you?"

"Maybe, but I have to study really hard for it," she said defensively.

"Don't be embarrassed. It's great to be smart. I only wish I could get those kinds of grades."

She looked at him and smiled humbly.

"What's annoying is that a lot of the time, I know the answer to a question, but I have a hard time describing it. That probably sounds crazy, but it's why oral exams always bring down my average, no matter how hard I study," he groused.

"That's a little like Karen. She knows her stuff, but her grades seem stuck in the B's and C's. She gets frustrated, too," Sylvia consoled.

Seeing an opportunity to resolve his still needling curiosity on the matter with Sherry, Stanlin asked, "If a human gets bad grades, do other humans ever, ya know, tease the person?"

"Yeah, some of the meaner kids do that," she affirmed.

"Do they tease for any other reasons, like if someone wears weird clothes, or messes up in gym class, or anything else?" He studied the carpet, hoping his subtle goading would work.

It did.

"Yeah, when I was eleven, this girl Sherry made fun of me all the time for being bad in gym." Sylvia rolled her eyes at the disturbing memory.

"Really? What happened?" Stanlin inquired gently.

"I mostly cried a lot, but when I started working at the animal shelter, I felt a little better. The next year, things kinda faded out, because Sherry wasn't in my class anymore. Then, this year, we started switching classes all day, 'cause we're in the middle school schedule. Sherry wasn't in my gym class. She was only in one of my other classes, but we sat really far apart, so it was OK."

"That's good," Stanlin said.

They heard knocking at the door, and Stanlin became invisible right away.

Her parents opened the door half way, poking their heads inside. "Hit the lights and the music, Miss Night Owl. We've got a big day tomorrow," Charles said.

"We'll see you at breakfast, honey," said Rebecca.

"OK. G'night," Sylvia responded.

They closed her door, and Stanlin became visible again.

Sylvia whispered to him, "You can sleep in there." She pointed to a large crate filled with her stuffed animals. "It'll be soft and cozy."

Well, it certainly fell short of the soft and cozy he was hoping for. "OK," he managed, climbing inside amidst the spongy things. A tiny gorilla was staring at him with plastic eyes. So was a tortoise. And a goose.

And others. They were chipper-looking little Earth animal replicas, in any case. And alright, yes, they were soft. But he would not admit to cozy.

Sylvia got up and turned off the lights and the music. "I have an extra blanket in my closet if the AC feels too cold to you. Want me to get it for you?" she offered.

"Thanks, but I'm not cold." Stanlin stretched out on his back. "I could stand to be warmer from body heat, though," he mused inwardly, but pursed his lips to prevent the ridiculous commentary from slipping out.

"You should probably become invisible now for the whole night, just in case," she advised, getting into her bed.

Stanlin obliged physically, though mentally, he strayed. He could do it, but it would not be polite. He could move from the crate and lie down invisibly next to her in the bed. That would be heavenly. But not polite was understating it. Rude. Yes, it would be downright rude. And, worse yet, disrespectful. Unwittingly, he snorted.

She heard it. "What? Did you say something?"

"Oh, ah, no," he replied sheepishly.

"I'm gonna pray that what we did for Mrs. Tormeni today and what we're gonna do tomorrow at Jungilo Prison will save everyone from dying," she said softly.

Stanlin felt absurd, and totally thankful that *she* never heard *his* thoughts. "That's a really good idea. I'll pray, too." She was right to be focusing on their goals. He had almost forgotten that her life and the lives of countless others were at stake.

"You also pray to God?" she whispered incredulously.

"Yes, but on Capton, we call Him The Highest Authority."

"That's really cool!" she said, rolling over onto her side. "G'night, Stanlin."

Ah, that sweet, lovely sound: her voice speaking his real name.

"Enough, Mr. Sappy!" he inwardly scolded. "Goals! Goals! Focus!"

He said aloud, "G'night, Sylvia. And I'm praying now, too."

# CHAPTER FIFTY

In the middle of the night, Sylvia awakened. The moonlight penetrated her sheer curtains just enough for her to see. She got out of bed and peered over at the crate, noticing that her stuffed animals were disheveled. With cheery amusement, she grinned hugely at her big secret: There was an invisible alien boy in there! And the alien, and Melvin the cat, were one and the same. She whispered, "Superbly super!" and a small giggle escaped her.

Her eyes left the crate and wandered over to her desk, where the printed articles were stacked with Mrs. Delany's business cards. "To be used in a few hours," she thought with anticipation. Nearby, something else on her desk caught her attention: the empty tuna bowl from Stanlin's dinner, which needed cleaning. She picked it up, and padded downstairs to the kitchen.

After washing and drying the bowl, it dawned on her that Stanlin would need breakfast in the morning. She gathered some fruit and a few granola bars for him, and headed upstairs to her room again.

As she set the food atop her desk, she reflected upon her feelings. It was very strange how comfortable she felt with this alien boy, Stanlin. Maybe it was because they had bonded so closely when he was Melvin. But that didn't explain the craziest part of it. She was finding him, somehow, kind of *cute*, and that didn't make any sense at all. *Not at all!* A blue, bald, nonhuman, looking *cute*? Was she losing her marbles?

Climbing back into her bed, she quietly murmured, "I'm a total wacko." But she was smiling from ear to ear.

# CHAPTER FIFTY-ONE

It was 5:30 a.m. when Ron received the motel's wake-up call. He was planning for another all-day drive, just as he'd done for the past two days. His regimen was to get up early, shower, dress, eat a hearty breakfast, and then drive until somewhere between 10:30 p.m. and midnight, stopping only for restrooms, gas, and food. If the roads continued to move today as they had been so far, he expected that tonight would be his last night in a motel, and he'd reach Claire's apartment some time the next day.

As he rummaged through the clothes in his suitcase, he heard whining noises. His skin crawled. "That brat," he mumbled. Cedric was splayed on his back, slowly stretching out his arms and legs. The night before, Ron had chosen the bed next to the bathroom for himself and had plopped Cedric down on the other bed, flat on the bedspread. The kid had slept through the night, but now, evidently, it was chloroform time again. A doused rag in a zip-lock bag already laid in wait beside Cedric. Ron retrieved the precious silencer and gruffly stuffed it into Cedric's face.

He glared at the unconscious toddler. It smelled like poop again. Three nights ago, when he'd first taken Cedric, barely ten minutes into the drive he had to open all the car windows to vent the stench, and later, he had to purchase diapers at a twenty-four-hour convenience store before checking into a motel. Once he'd carried the stinky runt inside the room, he'd had no choice but to bathe the kid and chuck his gross little clothes. He almost hurled.

Ever since, he had been dressing Cedric in a diaper only, still covering him with the baby blanket and roping him into the car seat. Cedric was probably potty trained when he was awake, since he was almost four years old now and wasn't wearing a diaper that first night. But keeping Cedric knocked out was worth it to stop the whining, screaming, and crying.

So Ron commenced with the disgusting task of diaper changing, right there on the bedspread. After that ordeal was over with, he got on with his morning routine. He took a shower, and shaved his blond beard stubble into a goatee shape. For the past few years, he'd been shaving his entire face and head. Now, not only was he growing the goatee, but he was letting the hair on his head grow out, too.

Standing in front of the bathroom mirror, he placed a long blond wig onto his head and secured it down with a tight baseball cap worn backwards. Until his own hair grew in, the false hair was hiding the tattoo on his neck.

He'd bought the hat and wig at a Wal-Mart the day before yesterday, immediately after Larry's tip-off about the AMBER Alert. Larry had called the prepay cell and told him of the media broadcast with the mug shot, showing Ron's bald head and tattooed neck. Ron knew his appearance needed changing, and his plans for getting Claire had to be thought through more carefully. As he continued driving that day, he'd made a slew of calls. By dusk, he'd spoken with over a dozen business contacts, talked six more times with Larry, and formulated a clear vision of what he was going to accomplish, in spite of the police and the general public.

Presently, gazing at his reflection, he mused that he looked like a grungy college kid, no matter that he was twenty-six. Short and skinny, he had always come across as younger than he actually was. Sometimes it came in handy, but he wondered if maybe that was why his luck with girls was never good. Claire had been the first and only one to love him. He thought of having her in his arms again, sometime tomorrow.

Holding that image in mind, he walked across the street to a McDonald's, ordered a takeout breakfast, and brought it back to his room. Sitting behind the small, round table, he put down his cup of coffee and took out his McMuffin sandwiches and hash browns from the paper bag.

While eating, he pondered all that he had devised the day before yesterday. Larry had reported that cop cars were staked out in the lot near Claire's apartment. Two of them faced her front door, and a third faced her back windows. Tomorrow, once Larry confirmed that Claire was home from work, Ron and Larry would ambush all three cars, with some extra help. Between each of their contacts, friends, and friends of those friends, they had located and connected with allies, some of whom lived by Claire's apartment. And they were more than happy to help with taking out the cops.

When the ambush was well underway, Ron was going to enter Claire's apartment with the key Larry had made for him. He would chloroform Claire just enough to weaken her. With her leaning on him, her arm draped over his shoulders, he would half walk, half drag her to his car. He would buckle her into the already-reclined passenger seat and take off. From there, the best parts of the scheme would unfold.

He smirked, crumpling the empty paper wrapping from one of his sandwiches, and glanced over at Cedric. He was stirring again, but his movements looked really weak.

"Shit!" Ron suddenly hissed. He hadn't given the kid any food or water, and this was the start of their third day. The brat needed some nourishment. Cedric getting sick would screw up everything.

Ron maneuvered Cedric into a slouchy sitting position, leaning him up on the headboard. He filled a plastic cup with water and tipped it to Cedric's lips. The barely conscious boy swallowed until he finished the water. Ron refilled the glass a second and a third time, and Cedric drained the refills. Unwilling to share any of his own food, Ron stepped out to the vending machine, got a candy bar, and fed that to Cedric. The groggy toddler ate what was pushed into his mouth until it was gone, and then started drifting off to sleep. By way of an ankle pull, Ron dragged him back to the bed's center, and chloroformed him. He couldn't risk the kid rolling onto the floor and getting hurt. Claire needed to see her son healthy—at first sight, anyway.

Ron sat back down at the table to finish his breakfast and thought of the other key allies he and Larry had unearthed. Three worked for Mexico border patrol by Nogales, and ten were scattered in cities throughout Mexico. These new friends were eager for his arrival. There was plenty of work for him there, lots of supply and demand. And the pay would be good. The drug business was always reliable, so he could easily build a new life for himself and Claire. Naturally, one new friend, to be determined by the lowest offered price, would get the job of "accidentally" killing Cedric.

He finished his food, packed up the car, roped Cedric into the car seat, covered him over with the blanket, and drove. For years now, he'd made it a habit to use a fake name, and pay the bill in cash, up front, when checking in to motels. It was more difficult for him to be tracked, and he could simply leave the place in the morning.

He turned on the radio and looked at the gauges across the dashboard. The sedan was doing alright. What a stroke of luck it was that it wasn't in his name. When his customer had given it to him a few months earlier, they hadn't changed the title. Meanwhile, his red Corvette, registered to him, sat idle, parked in front of his empty apartment. Ron simpered with amusement.

His thoughts transitioned toward something even more comical. His skills in dramatic acting were going to debut soon. He snickered. An Oscar-worthy performance was coming! Ron played out the scene in his mind:

Claire slowly becomes more alert during the car ride to Mexico.

She asks how he found her.

He says that his connections helped him, because he needed to find her to apologize. He says how very sorry he is for hurting her and Cedric in the past, and he realizes now how deeply he loves them both. He says he wants the three of them to be a family and begin a new life together.

Claire tells him Cedric was adopted.

He explains that through his connections, he learned of Cedric's adoption, and found out that the new parents were keeping Cedric locked in a closet, while he screamed and cried.

He tells her that he rescued Cedric and is now driving them all to Mexico, where they can live very richly and happily together.

Claire turns around to see Cedric just starting to stir in the back of the car.

Ron snickered more. Claire would be so blown away, both by his power and by his newfound commitment to her and Cedric. He would gain her trust again. For the few weeks before the "accident," he'd be very nice to her and Cedric, and after it all happened, he would be there with open arms to comfort her. Then, finally, just the two of them would be together, like he had wanted since the day they met.

"Soul mates," he murmured, and pressed his foot down harder on the accelerator.

# CHAPTER FIFTY-TWO

Sylvia woke up just before 8:00 a.m. to the pleasant sounds of her parents preparing breakfast. She perked up, got out of bed, and searched her closet for her favorite sundress. She took the dress into the bathroom to change. When she returned to her room, she stuffed her nightgown under her pillow and noticed Stanlin becoming visible in the crate.

"Good morning," she piped up vibrantly.

"G' morning," he echoed sleepily.

She brought the fruit and granola bars from her desk over to him. "Here's breakfast in bed for you," she chirped.

"Thanks, Sylvia," Stanlin murmured with a content-looking smile, his stomach grumbling.

"After you finish that up, you can just keep following me around invisibly for a while," she instructed. "When my parents take us to the shelter to pick up Benton, let me load him up in the car first, and then you can trot out from behind that bush in front, like you did yesterday for Karen. I'll pretend to be surprised again, and ask my parents if we can take you along."

"Got it," he replied, tearing into one of the granola wrappers.

"See you soon." With a wave she left to join her parents in the kitchen.

After breakfast, Sylvia got the printed articles and the business cards from her desk. Rebecca took a dose of her allergy medication and stowed the bottle in her purse. Charles gathered everyone into the car and drove them to the SPCA.

Sylvia's parents waited in the car while she went inside. As she walked past the front desk, she quietly groaned when she saw that Sara was working. Sara was a stuck-up teenager whose life centered around cell phone calls, ever-changing boyfriends, and her friends' gossip stories. She was only volunteering at the shelter to fulfill a class requirement for community service.

"Hi, Sara," Sylvia half-heartedly greeted as she walked past her toward the cages. "I'm taking Benton out for a few hours," she called over her shoulder. "Hey there, Mister," she said when she reached the serene, gray mutt. "We're goin' on a special trip today." She let Benton sniff and lick her hand through the cage before opening it. She went about her business leashing him up, but out of the corner of her eye, she saw Sara talking on her phone while feeding another dog, Leroy.

"Really? No! Really?" Sara's jaw dropped, and she belted out dramatically, "You're *not* serious!"

A savvy Leroy squirmed out of his cage.

"Get him!" Sylvia yelled urgently.

Sara lunged forward and caught Leroy by the collar. She roughly dragged him back into his cage and fastened the lock.

"You hafta watch what you're doing!" Sylvia reproved.

"I'll call you back," Sara said curtly into her phone and shoved it into her pocket. "I caught him right away, you little twerp. Or didn't you see that? You're such a complete spaz," she sneered.

Both furious and embarrassed, Sylvia's face reddened. "At least I care about the animals," she retorted, and left abruptly.

As she led Benton to the car and loaded him into the back seat, she fought off impending tears. But when she turned around and saw Melvin trotting merrily toward her, her spirits lifted. She replayed her performance from the other day and asked her parents' permission to bring him along. They approved, provided that Melvin and Benton wouldn't scuffle.

"Benton's partly blind and is really calm. He's always good around the other shelter animals. And I've never seen Melvin react badly to any of the dogs at the park," Sylvia assured them. "Here, I'll show you." She climbed into the back seat with Melvin, and held him out a few inches from Benton's snout. The peaceful mutt sniffed, and stuck out a long tongue to lap Melvin's cheek. Melvin remained relaxed.

"Alright, he can come," Charles said.

"How could we say no to that?" Rebecca laughed.

When they arrived at the prison, Charles offered to take Benton's leash so that Sylvia could carry Melvin in with both arms. "This way, if Melvin gets spooked, you've got him, and if Benton does, I've got him," he said, and Sylvia agreed.

Rebecca toted in the articles and the business cards.

Their wait to see the warden was brief. After less than five minutes, a fiftyish, tall, slender gentleman with a crew cut of silvery hair politely greeted them. He introduced himself as Robert Ginley, and led them into his office. He pulled up a third chair to accompany the two already in front of his desk. "Please, sit," he said to them as he seated himself behind the desk. "I don't see children or animals in here very much. To what do I owe this special visit?"

Sylvia enthusiastically explained her idea to let the prison adopt several of the older shelter animals. She described how the inmates could learn compassion and responsibility by grooming, feeding, and exercising the animals, and how violence between the inmates would be reduced. She cited the articles as proof that these results were typical.

Rebecca handed the articles to Mr. Ginley, but otherwise, she and Charles sat back, allowing Sylvia to command the meeting. Sylvia's passion and vision were infused with her youthful innocence, which was clearly charming the warden.

"And Benton here is one of the older dogs who needs a home. He's partly blind and is super gentle. He'd be great for the program. You can pet him," Sylvia said, motioning for her dad to walk Benton closer.

Charles complied, and Mr. Ginley tentatively reached his hand toward the dog's snout. In typical fashion, Benton sniffed and began licking the hand in front of him. The warden chuckled on the spot. He took a few moments to pet Benton appreciatively before his gaze shifted to Sylvia. Pointing at Melvin in her arms, he asked, "Is this one of the other animals that could be part of the program?"

"This is Melvin. But, he's sorta mine," she answered meekly. Yet she promptly regained her boldness. "So, what do you think of the idea, sir?"

He inhaled, rubbed his chin, and paused.

Charles walked back to his chair and sat, guiding Benton beside him.

Mr. Ginley exhaled, folded his hands on his desk, and leaned forward. "Jungilo has been pretty rough on the inside these days. I'd really like to see that change. I think we'll go ahead and bring in some of your animals, give this a try."

Sylvia jumped to a standing position and thanked him. Sylvia, Charles, and Rebecca each took a turn at shaking his hand vigorously. Rebecca gave him the business cards and explained that Rinalda Delany was the shelter director who could coordinate the logistical details with him.

Sylvia and her parents left the prison feeling exuberant from the successful meeting. They piled into the car with Benton and Melvin and drove back to the SPCA.

When he parked the car in the lot, Charles said to Sylvia, "We'll wait right here again for you."

"Can I leave Melvin in the back seat for a minute while I bring in Benton?" Sylvia asked while helping Benton out of the car.

"That's fine," Rebecca consented.

Sylvia heard her parents beginning to discuss something as she walked away from the car, but her attention was more focused on the sweet mutt at her side. She rubbed his ears and spoke to him as she led him inside the building. "You'll see that nice warden again very soon. You were such a good boy today, Benton, such a good boy." She put him in his cage, secured the lock, and patted his head gently through the metal grating. "You'll have a home soon, Benton, where you'll be helping people who really need you. Bye, sweetheart," she whispered.

She left the shelter with a lump in her throat. And not for a moment did she acknowledge Sara, perched behind the front desk, theatrically gabbing on her cell phone. When Sylvia returned to the car, her parents had a surprise for her.

Rebecca said, "We need to go run some errands around town. If you'd like, you can bring Melvin. You deserve a special treat today. We're so proud of you! And I'll be fine. I've got my meds with me for the whole day."

"Cool! Thanks!" Sylvia buckled up, picked up Melvin, and held him out in front of her. She peered into his eyes, wondering if it would be OK for him to delay his trip home even longer.

Seeming to magically know her concern, Melvin meowed once, while bobbing his head up and down.

She grinned at him and winked.

# CHAPTER FIFTY-THREE

It was pushing noon, the gas tank was at a quarter, and Ron was getting hungry. It was time for a break. He exited the highway at a rest stop. After fueling up, he parked the car in front of the minimart. Twisting sideways, he was rifling through the glove compartment, searching for some small change, when a piercing scream caused him to flinch and shudder. He snapped his head around to see Cedric's mouth open, his eyes widened with fright. "Shut up!" Ron yelled. He grabbed the rag beside the car seat and pushed it into Cedric's face.

Ron breathed heavily when Cedric fell silent. He could feel his heart racing. How the hell had the little brat woken up so fast? Up until then, throughout the trip, Cedric had been either unconscious, or in a sleepy haze. But a minute ago, the runt had nearly given him a heart attack with that scream, for Christ's sake.

"I'm supposed to kill you, not the other way around," he muttered at the unconscious Cedric. Laughing at his clever remark, he was able to shake off the lingering tension, and his growling stomach reminded him that it was time to eat. Leaving Cedric in the car, he headed up toward the minimart.

\* \* \*

Ron hadn't noticed Amelia Day. He hadn't been aware that she was watching his abominable behavior. The car to the right of his had appeared to be empty when he'd parked. However, an elderly woman sat in the rear of the car, on the passenger side, but coincidentally, the moment Ron had glanced her way, she was bent forward, picking up a gum wrapper from the car mat.

Amelia, a small, frail, seventy-nine-year-old, had already finished using the rest room, and was waiting in the car for her daughter and son-in-law. Her daughter, a chiropractor, had installed an orthopedic cushioned seat in the back for her, which greatly eased the pain in Amelia's hip. She never would have imagined that waiting in her comfy seat would subject her to such a contemptible scene.

The car windows were all a few inches open, so when the child screamed, she heard it loud and clear. She saw the long-haired man shove a cloth into the child's face until the screaming stopped and the child passed out. She watched the man walk toward the minimart, leaving the assaulted child alone in the car.

Appalled, Amelia called the police from her cell phone. They asked for her location; a physical description of the offender; the color, make, and model of the offender's car; and the car's license plate number. Amelia answered all of the questions from her seat, except for the last. For that, she got out of the car, walked over to view the license plate, and read the number.

"Good. Now can you look inside the car and describe the child in the car seat?" the dispatcher asked.

"He's a little black boy," she said. "Oh, my!" she gasped. "I saw an AMBER Alert for a missing black toddler! The suspect was a bald, white male, but maybe he's wearing a wig! Maybe it's him!" She waited for a reply, but it was her daughter's voice that broke the silence first.

"We're ready to go, Mom." Amelia's daughter sat down in the driver's seat, and, with a bag of food, Amelia's son-in-law plopped into the front passenger's seat. Amelia returned to her cushioned seat behind him. A moment later, the police came back on the line, apologized for the slight delay, and confirmed that the call was complete. Amelia hung up her phone, hoping with all her heart that the police could save that poor little child.

# CHAPTER FIFTY-FOUR

Brenna sat at the kitchen table finishing up her lunch. She gazed lovingly at the three puppies, heartily feasting from their bowls on the floor. Anthony had been one hundred percent correct. Since she had taken in the pups yesterday afternoon, she was feeling more like a human, less like a zombie. She was keeping a schedule for their meals, and thus, her own. She was getting out of the house with them, breathing the fresh air, and stretching her legs. Of course, she was petting and playing with them, and they were deluging her with licks and nuzzles.

Cedric was always in Brenna's thoughts. Nothing could prevent her from worrying about him. Still, caring for the affectionate, vivacious puppies who now depended on her was helping her in weathering her suffering. She was enduring better than she ever could have without them.

Brenna got up and loaded her dishes into the dishwasher. She saw her friends licking their bowls clean, and her lips curved into a tiny smile. She was glad they all had such healthy appetites.

She walked out the kitchen door to the backyard. "Come on!" she called, holding the door open. The puppies ran outside with her. Squatting down in the grass, she doled out her affections among them.

Last night she had decided to name them, based on their unique qualities. The pup with one ear tinier than the other ear, she'd called "Teensy." The pup with one closed eye, she'd named "Winky." And "Pokey" was the pup with the weak back leg who was the relative slow poke of the group—but not by much. His crooked gait notwithstanding, Pokey very nearly kept up with his zippy siblings. She thought about how Cedric might react to the puppies' unusual features, and was reminded of how he used to play so nicely in the park with his albino friend, James. Tears welled up in her eyes.

Through the open kitchen window, the sound of the phone ringing startled her. With a jolt, she arose. It could be the police, or maybe Anthony calling a little early. Wiping her eyes, she headed for the door. The pups swiftly followed her into the kitchen.

She caught the phone on the third ring. "Hello?" she panted.

"Is this Mrs. Brenna Tormeni?" a deep, unfamiliar voice inquired.

"Yes," she said, feeling a flash of apprehension. She had picked up the phone so fast, she hadn't checked the caller ID.

"This is Officer Patrick Jennings, Tucson PD."

"Oh...yes?" she barely managed to utter, her breath caught in her throat.

"We caught Ron Camm. A tip came in, led us right to him. Your son Cedric is safe and sound."

Brenna could hardly comprehend his words. They seemed too good to be true. She was stunned. It felt as if her vocal cords were frozen.

"Your boy's in the hospital for now, but the doc said he'll be just fine."

Her vocal cords thawed slightly. "In the hospital?" she strained.

"Yes, ma'am. He was drugged up, so the doctor had to check him out."

"He's...ALIVE!" It was finally sinking in. Simultaneously laughing and bursting into tears, she repeated, "He's ALIVE! He's ALIVE!"

"Yes. Yes he is," Officer Jennings said with a small quake in his voice. He paused and cleared his throat. "I've got the hospital number for you, so you can talk to his doctor, and I'll give you my cell number, too."

"Yes, thank you; one second," Brenna said, sniffing.

She quickly got a pen and paper. He relayed the numbers, and she jotted them down.

"I know we're quite a ways from where you are, but we'll help you to get here and bring your son home."

Cedric was coming HOME! It was REAL! Brenna wept more intensely.

Officer Jennings hesitated, and then offered, "If you'd like, you can let me know which airport you fly out of, and our volunteers at the station can look into what's available for you to come and pick Cedric up. A few airlines work with us and give discounts in situations like yours. I can call you back in an hour or so with some options. How does that sound?"

"Wonderful! Wonderful!" Brenna told him of her closest airport, lavished him with thank-yous, hung up, and sobbed some more. After calming down enough to speak again, Brenna called the hospital. Dr. Layla Tong affirmed that Cedric wasn't seriously ill, and that he was being carefully monitored, hydrated, and fed. She said she saw no problem with releasing him whenever Brenna could arrive to pick him up. Dr. Tong also suggested that Brenna consult with a local, holistic doctor regarding a nutritional detoxification program, to help Cedric's body rid itself of the residual chemicals from his consecutive days of drug exposure. Brenna agreed with the recommendation and proposed hopefully, "If he was sedated so much, maybe he won't remember anything from the ordeal."

"It's possible," answered Dr. Tong, "but we can't know if he had any short periods of alertness in between being doused. His behaviors in the coming days and weeks will tell you more."

Brenna thanked the doctor, got off the phone, and shuffled into the den. Sinking down onto the floor, with her back leaning up against the couch, she melted into her habitual spot for letting the pups climb into her lap, which they now did. Gently stroking them, Brenna bawled without restraint, her emotions raw. Although right now, Cedric was in a hospital across the country, he was COMING HOME.

She could breathe.

Soon, she would hear Cedric's high-pitched giggle, and the mispronunciations of his blossoming speech. She'd be watching him play, so full of animation and delight. Their goodnight hugs and kisses and his breath on her cheek would warm her heart again. She'd see him, curled up, peacefully sleeping, his blue blanket rising and falling rhythmically. Every time he said, "Mommy," she would be bursting with gratitude and love.

Gratitude and love were all she could feel now. For Cedric. For the police. For the doctor. Gratitude and love, beyond compare.

She heard the phone ringing again. For a split second, she contemplated not answering it. But then, she realized—it was afternoon, after lunch. ANTHONY! She sprang up, rushed over, and picked up the receiver.

"Hey, beautiful." The sound of Anthony's voice was sublime.

"He's coming H-HOME!" she stammered. "Cedric is c-coming HOME!"

"They found him?" he asked in shock.

She gasped for air between her sentences. "Yes...A tip came in...They caught Ron Camm...and saved Cedric!"

He sputtered, "Thank...God!"

For a long while, they simply cried with joy together.

# CHAPTER FIFTY-FIVE

When Sylvia winked at him, his tiny feline heart squeezed in two extra beats. And for the entire day, he was as happy as an alien cat could ever be. Sylvia's parents took them shopping in an outdoor village, where the streets were lined with quaint, artistic shops and cafés. Some store owners kindly permitted Sylvia to carry him inside. Ogling the arrays of Earthly tools, appliances, garments, and decorative knickknacks was fascinating. But, even when store owners denied Melvin's entrance, he and Sylvia amused themselves with window shopping while waiting for her parents.

For lunch and dinner, indoor admittance wasn't an issue; both meals were enjoyed at cafés with outdoor seating. Sylvia's parents ordered Melvin cooked fish each time, telling him they were royally spoiling him for the day.

After they finished dinner and were riding in the car together, Sylvia's parents said they wanted to stop off at the SPCA because Sylvia should try to admit Melvin again.

"When you tried in the past, you'd been carrying him all the way from the park," Rebecca said. "But tonight, we'll drive you right up to the front door. He won't have much of a chance to squirm out of your arms."

"OK; I'll give it a try." Sylvia looked at him and mouthed, "Run away."

His eyes met hers, and his head bobbed up and down.

She mouthed, "Meet me in my room."

He nodded his furry black head again, and she smiled.

Their skit went off seamlessly.

* * *

Sylvia closed her bedroom door behind her and turned on the stereo. Stanlin had invisibly transported to her room and slipped on his invisible garment, which he'd planted in its usual spot before that morning's departure.

"Hi," he said, becoming visible.

Sylvia's hands were on her hips. "Now they're worried about you— Melvin—on the loose still. I'll have to come up with something to tell them. I don't want them upset for nothing."

"Do they know that Melvin's used to the outdoors?"

"Yes, yes." She folded her arms across her chest. "I guess I could remind them that while the weather's warm, there's lots of time to rethink how to get Melvin into the shelter. For now, that'll have to do."

She walked over to her desk, rotated the chair around toward her bed, and gestured for Stanlin to sit. He did so, and she sat, Indian style, on her bed. "Now, for the bigger question: How're we going to know if what we did yesterday and today makes any difference to the future? Do I just wait and pray that no one gets that disease and dies?"

Stanlin thought about how miserable a state of prolonged, fearful limbo would be. He wouldn't wish that upon an enemy, let alone a close friend. Maybe a super quick trip, only to give her a message, could potentially be finagled. He said, "It'll be extremely hard for me to come back to Earth again after today. I can't tell you if or when I might be able to. But I promise you, I'll do everything I can to try and pop in, to give you a brief update, as soon as I know something. And if it's impossible for me to make the trip myself, I'll send a mailing robot to your window with a note."

Then he began fretting. How in the heck was he going to know something? He had told R he wouldn't ask to use his Probability Sphere again.

But he needed to see it! Could he possibly sneak into the teacher's office in the middle of the night? That might work...check the Sphere's forecast for Earth, and give Sylvia a midnight update. His parents probably couldn't keep watch on him all night, every night, to prevent him from transporting, could they?

"Thanks! Any updates at all would be great," she said, her eyes sparkling.

He smiled. He would have to find a way. No lame note. No robot.

"And thanks for coming with me to the prison and to Mrs. Tormeni's house, too, Stanlin. I really liked having you here," she said appreciatively. Her cheeks were a little flushed.

Exulted, he replied, "I was really glad to stay." He thought, "And I wish I could stay even longer." But he didn't say it; instead, he said something else equally true. "By now, though, I know my parents are really worried, and probably really mad. Plus, I have to find out an update on Earth's forecast for you. So, I do need to get back to Capton."

Sylvia nodded. "Hey, listen!" Her back straightened up and her eyes widened. "It's our favorite song on the radio again!"

Stanlin heard the familiar, upbeat song from the night before thumping through the speakers. They listened together as it played through. He tapped his foot, and she subtly moved her head in time with the music.

When the song finished, he asserted, "That group is definitely superbly super."

"Yeah, they are. But Rick is the coolest," she said, eyeing the poster. "The scratchiness in his voice during those low notes totally makes the song. And it's funny—almost every girl has a crush on him."

Stanlin didn't think it was funny. She sounded almost giddy; he was feeling irked.

"Oh! Crush! Ha, ha, ha!" she giggled. "That's one of those words that has more than one meaning."

It took all of his energy to refrain from rolling his eyes.

She went on. "Sometimes it means to squash something, but in this case, it means to like someone; you know, to think they're really cute and hot."

"I know what a crush is," Stanlin thought petulantly, pressing his lips together to keep silent. If only there was a punching bag in front of him now, he would pulverize it. And any boxing opponent would be toast.

"You're getting all quiet on me," Sylvia said lightly. "You know, Rocklore has this other really good song. I have it downloaded. I can play it for you, so you'll have one more good tune in your head for the long trip home," she joked. Sprightly, she hopped off of the bed and over to her computer.

"OK," he assented reluctantly. At the moment, Rocklore was making him want to gag, but her computer fiddling was already underway.

"This song is a ballad," she explained. "It's slower than the other song, but it's beautiful. I love listening to it lying down with my eyes closed, 'cause it's soooo soothing." She hit a few more keys on her computer, turned off the radio and the lights, and lay down in her bed.

"Something soothing would be good now." He could at least say that much with honesty. "I'll listen to it lying down, too." He climbed into the crate and stretched out amid the Earth animal replicas.

"Cool," she said, clearly tickled that he was participating in her little ritual.

The ballad felt like a lullaby, relaxing both of them.

A few bars into it, Stanlin was so impressed with the melody that his inner beef with Rick of Rocklore was pretty much forgotten. He simply couldn't deny the band's talent. "You're right. This is a beautiful song," he admitted.

"Yeah. I thought you'd like it, too," she chimed. "It's so awesome that we're from different galaxies, but we can still love the same music."

"Yeah, it is pretty wild," he agreed, smiling. The serene song and Sylvia's merriment were imbuing him with a very peaceful feeling. Listening to this entrancing melody with her was a nice way both to finish this visit and to steady his nerves for the upcoming confrontation back home. He folded his hands over his abdomen.

Only, the song was just a little bit too relaxing.

Before the last note sounded, the two of them were fast asleep.

# CHAPTER FIFTY-SIX

The Capton Governmental Council was in a special session. Typically, meetings were held weekly. Occasionally, however, when pertinent news arose, an additional meeting was called to order. Such was the case this week.

Munin, today's orator, addressed his colleagues. "Thank you all for coming. I requested this supplemental meeting to discuss an astonishing update, which I viewed in my Sphere. As most of you know, I've been using Probability Spheres for about thirty years now, ever since the first one was created." He flashed a quick smile at Nixar, who responded in kind. "In all the years until this point, whenever a prediction was greater than 92 percent probable, I've always seen it play out. But, for some odd reason, yesterday evening, as I prepared to leave the office, I felt an impulse to check my Sphere about the lethal disease that was predicted for Earth during our last meeting. And what I saw, and also what I didn't see..." He shook his head. "Well, suffice it to say, I was excited—and baffled. My Sphere didn't depict the sick animals and humans like before. It revealed a swirl instead."

Nixar concurred. "I checked my Sphere this morning about Earth and saw the same."

"Last night, I did too, and I also saw a swirl," Cadence piped up.

Initially, gasps resounded, but within moments, applause broke out. Members rose from their chairs, embraced one another, and cheered. They were ecstatic that Earth's deadly pandemic had somehow been averted. Everyone knew that a swirl in the Sphere wasn't a troublesome forecast; it indicated that the future was wide open, with multitudinous possible outcomes.

Once the festive reactions subsided, Munin spoke in earnest. "I suggest we try to figure out what caused this incredible turnabout. Maybe then, we can learn to harness that element to purposefully overcome other negative predictions or challenges."

There were shouts of agreement: "Yes!" "Here, here!" "Absolutely!"

"Does anyone have any theories brewing already?" Munin inquired hopefully.

When his colleagues were quiet, Munin probed further. "Has anyone heard of any dealings with Earth initiated by other planets this week? Maybe during communications with your intergalactic committees?"

Everyone appeared thoughtful, but no one spoke.

"Please bring this up with your committees then, and keep your eyes, ears, and minds open to whatever surfaces. Let's all meditate on this, too." Pensively, he added, "It's so dramatic a change, it's as if someone intentionally subverted Earth's disaster." He rubbed his brows with his fingertips. Lowering his hands back to the podium, he asked, "Are there any last comments or questions?"

"What about the ban on visiting Earth? It's no longer necessary, right?" Nixar queried.

"Correct. I'll announce on the radio this morning that the ban is lifted," Munin said.

\* \* \*

By midmorning the meeting was adjourned.

The Council members filed out of the room, and Ramaway was deep in thought. When Munin had said it seemed as though someone had "intentionally subverted" Earth's disaster, Ramaway thought of his student

Stanlin. Earlier that week, the young Rampont had been to his office, twice, to view the Probability Sphere. Stanlin had seen a disturbing forecast initially, and then had come back, hoping to learn of ways to alter that prediction. Stanlin had been trying to *subvert something.*

Ramaway's forehead creased. But surely the boy had been using the Sphere for personal matters. Why would a fourteen-year-old care much about Earth, or any other planet, for that matter? At that age, didn't one's thoughts revolve primarily around peers? Or, on the far out chance that Stanlin had, in fact, viewed something about Earth in the Sphere, Earth travel had been forbidden all week. Stanlin was a good lad, not a lawbreaker. No, he couldn't have affected the changes in Earth's forecast.

Irrespective of his best cognitive reasoning, Ramaway's intuitive, inner pull persisted: He should check the Sphere's logs and find out what Stanlin had viewed. Ramaway transported to his office, manifesting in front of his Sphere. He fixed his eyes at its center. "I wish to access the records," he pronounced. The Sphere turned bright pink. Ramaway focused on the date and time of Stanlin's first visit to his office, and mentally requested to see what Stanlin had viewed.

A lovely young Earth girl was depicted, being closed up inside a casket, which was then lowered into the ground. The prediction was to occur in three months with 95 percent certainty. Ramaway swallowed, trying to ease the tightness in his throat. It didn't help. That poor young girl looked about Stanlin's age. Stanlin had probably been observing her; no wonder he'd wanted to see if he could change the future.

Ramaway stated his intent to access the records again. He thought of the date and time of Stanlin's second visit to his office, and mentally requested that the Sphere show him what Stanlin had viewed. An image of a shelter housing various animals appeared. One cage in particular became the focus. Inside it were three puppies, each with an unusual feature. One pup's right eye seemed permanently shut, another pup's left ear was small and misshapen, and the third pup was holding up his right rear leg, as if it was lame.

The picture of the puppies began to fade, and in its place arose a huge brick and cement building with very few windows. "Jungilo Maximum Security Prison" appeared in black lettering above the front doors. A man inside a prison cell came into view. He had long, dark hair and a slim, strong-looking physique. He was alone and talking to himself in a way that didn't seem like merely thinking aloud; it was more like he truly believed someone else was there. Ramaway shuddered, and the Sphere defaulted to its cream color.

He had no idea what those influencing factors were about, but there was one thing he was sure of: He needed to stop by and ask Stanlin about everything. He felt comfortable enough going to Stanlin's home; impromptu visits were fairly common on Capton. He had also met Karilu and Andrigon in student/teacher conferences and considered them to be pleasant, likeable folks. He verified the address in his student records.

An instant later, he manifested on Stanlin's porch. Rampont homes had mini speakers on their front doors, which guests used to announce their arrival. He leaned in close to the thumb-sized, square device. "Ramaway here to visit Stanlin."

"Hello, Ramaway," Karilu said in a frail voice as she opened the door. She looked worn down and pale.

"I dropped by to ask Stanlin about something, but, Karilu...are you alright?"

"Stanlin hasn't come home for the past two nights," she answered wearily.

Ramaway's jaw fell open.

"He sent us a message that he's not hurt, and is tending to something very urgent. That's all we know," she said with worrisome eyes. "Please come in," she added awkwardly.

"Yes, please come in, Ramaway," Andrigon said, walking into the room. "I'm working from the house until Stanlin gets back," he explained.

Ramaway readily accepted Karilu and Andrigon's hospitality and sat with them in their gathering room. He told them all about Stanlin's recent visits to the office, and what he had seen with his twofold usage of the Probability Sphere.

# CHAPTER FIFTY-SEVEN

A bird chirped loudly outside her window, awakening Sylvia from her deep slumber. She sat upright in bed and looked at the clock. Her eyes bulged. It was 10:22 a.m.! Her eyes darted over to the crate, and she saw Stanlin, still visible in it, sound asleep. She leaped out of bed and barreled over to him. "Stanlin! Stanlin! Wake up!" she whispered urgently.

"Huh?" he muttered, as he turned over and gazed at her with half-open eyes. In his barely alert mind, he thought, "I like the mussed morning hair look. Why does she sound so agitated?"

"We both must've conked out listening to that song last night! You hafta get home! It's morning already—it's 10:22 a.m.!"

Her words began to penetrate, and his morning fog rapidly dissipated. "Oh!" He rustled up and climbed out of the crate. "Yes, I've got to go! Like we said, I'll give you an update as soon as I can."

"Right! OK!"

"Bye!" he said.

She was waving as he left.

He manifested in his garden spot in the backyard and cautiously entered the house, hoping his parents were still in their bedroom. No such luck. He found them sitting in the gathering room, and he was shocked to see R sitting there with them.

Karilu saw him right away. "My dear boy!" she cried out, running to him and embracing him.

Andrigon rushed over to hug him also. "Are you alright?" he asked.

"Yes, I'm fine, and I'm sorry if I scared you guys. But, there really was—is—something urgent going on." Seeing R, right there, was too much; Stanlin was unable to control himself. In frenzy, he blurted out, "Please let me look at your Probability Sphere one more time, R! I know I said I wouldn't ask again, but I have to see if the good deeds changed anything!"

Andrigon glared sternly at Stanlin. "You need to tell us everything—and I mean everything—that you have been up to before you get one ounce of information."

"Yes," Karilu concurred resolutely.

His parents were right. They, and R, were entitled to understand why he had been gone, and what was so incredibly pressing. He sat down with the three of them and divulged his whole Earth saga. They were spellbound throughout the tale, and incredulous when he finished.

"I can already tell you, Stanlin, that Earth is out of imminent danger now," R said. "Whatever that disease was, it's not a looming threat anymore. The Sphere is showing that Earth's future is anything but set; the possibilities are wide open. The Council lifted the ban on Earth travel this morning."

Stanlin jumped up from his seat. "Really? Really?"

"Really and truly," R confirmed.

"Superbly super! I've gotta go tell Sylvia!" Stanlin exclaimed. When he saw the looks on his parents' faces, he qualified, "What I mean is, I can tell her the update and be back in five minutes. I swear it. I just don't want her panicking about everyone dying anymore."

"Three minutes," Andrigon said.

"Or less," said Karilu.

Stanlin agreed. "Three minutes or less," he repeated, and then transported to Sylvia's room. "I'm back," he announced, becoming visible near her.

"That was fast," she mused happily. "I didn't think I'd see you again for days, or even weeks."

"I can't stay, and I don't have the details yet, but I wanted to let you know that as of now, the Sphere says that disease isn't going to kill everyone anymore!"

"Really?" She flung herself forward and hugged him.

The speed and force of her movement made her form overlap slightly into his. Although he felt the typical uncomfortable pressure sensation, Stanlin wasn't about to complain, especially because the hug also sent a wave of euphoric chills through him that were far more potent than the pressure.

"Yes, what you did with those animals must have changed the influencing factors in all the right ways. I'll come tell you more as I learn it, but now, you don't have to be worried in the meantime. Unfortunately, I do have to get back now though," he said regretfully.

She stepped back and looked at him, gently disengaging from the hug.

Up this close to her, he could see dark and light flecks of shading in her breathtaking eyes. He swallowed hard.

"OK. I understand. I'll see you...whenever you can make it. But, I'm soooo glad you were able to stop by and tell me the wonderful news! Thank you, Stanlin! Thank you! Bye." She was looking aglow, and waving at him.

"Bye," he said, waving back. As he disappeared, he wondered if he had just detected a glimmer of attraction in those lovely flecked eyes. He quickly concluded it was wishful thinking. For goodness sake, she was stunning, and he was skinny, bald, and blue. He couldn't keep himself from grinning, though.

When he manifested into the family room, barely two and a half minutes after he'd left, Andrigon nodded in approval, and Karilu smiled widely with relief. R winked at him. Stanlin sat down and thanked them all for allowing the quick trip.

"Now that we're all present again, we have some planning to tend to," R began. He nodded at Stanlin, and then addressed his parents with the utmost delicacy. "Andrigon, Karilu, I would like to take Stanlin as my guest to a Governmental Council meeting, one week from today. In three days, at our next meeting, I'll inform the members and set it up. I think everyone will learn a lot from what Stanlin accomplished on Earth.

Yes, he will be reproved for his unlawful behaviors, but, undoubtedly, the members will see the whole picture and won't dole out unreasonably harsh punishment."

Stanlin fidgeted, repeatedly lacing and unlacing his fingers. Undoubtedly, huh? Not unreasonably harsh? R seemed authentically convinced, which was somewhat pacifying, and R's supportiveness was obvious, which was also encouraging. But what exactly would *reasonably* harsh punishment entail? Stanlin rubbed the side of his neck and slowly exhaled. Becoming a jittery basket case wasn't going to change anything. Whatever the verdict, he'd have to suck it up, period. He had broken laws, after all. And, thank The Highest Authority above, it had been one hundred percent worth it.

R's considerate phrasing notwithstanding, Andrigon and Karilu were well aware that Stanlin's actions needed to be judged before the Council. Stiffly, they stood up, and Stanlin and R followed suit. With uncharacteristic choppiness, Andrigon replied, "Of course. Yes, Ramaway. We understand about the meeting. Completely."

"Good," R responded pleasantly.

Karilu's voice quaked with her question. "Ramaway, may Andrigon and I attend that meeting, also?" Andrigon reached for her hand and interlaced his fingers with hers.

"That would be a pleasure," R consented, bowing slightly toward them. He turned to face Stanlin, his eyes shining. "Your friend Sylvia's actions were outstanding. You behaved commendably, too, by giving her the information and supporting her but never dictating her choices. You upheld the Free Will Decree, while seeing to it that the Sphere's insights were put to use. And, together, the two of you saved planet Earth! Ah! Phenomenal! Young Rampont, you're a real hero!" He shook Stanlin's hand heartily. "I'll come by next week to pick you all up for the meeting." He specified the time they should be ready, bid a fond good-bye to all, and left.

"Come here, my little hero," Karilu said, tearfully pulling Stanlin into a hug.

Andrigon put his hand on Stanlin's shoulder. Speaking slowly, he said sincerely, "You are becoming an adult now, but, at the same time, your youthful idealism, your belief in the goodness of a human girl, helped in saving billions of lives. It's mind-boggling. And very impressive." He bent forward and kissed the top of his son's head.

Seeming to sense the love in the room, Mini-G, who had been curled up on the floor by the chairs, joined the huddle at all of their feet. They chuckled and pet her together.

As Stanlin smoothed the fur on her neck, he speculated about his parents. As pleased as he was that they were proud of him, it was odd that they weren't addressing his pending punishment at all. The elephant in the room couldn't sit there with them indefinitely, for crying out loud. He strained, "I know R thinks the Council won't discipline me to the fullest extent, but that doesn't mean they won't still send me to prison for a while."

His parents kept petting Mini-G with their eyes fixed on her. Both appeared deeply troubled and uncertain what to say. A long silence ensued.

Stanlin noticed a tear trickle down his mother's cheek. "If I end up having to go to jail, I'll be OK," he said, trying to be comforting. He had never seen his parents so disquieted.

"Yes, but we don't want you suffering through that." Karilu's voice cracked.

"The Ramponts in the prisons are..." Andrigon trailed off. "We know that some punishment is necessary and understandable, but prison..." he paused a second time. "It feels like we're all at the Council's mercy," he concluded vulnerably.

"Whatever they decide, we know where your heart was, and what you helped to achieve on Earth," Karilu said.

Andrigon and Karilu's eyes met, and his grew alight. "And to commemorate that achievement, to celebrate all of the rescued lives and Stanlin's bravery, I'd like to take our family on a special vacation. How about we go to that beautiful new resort by Aeenut? I hear there are walking paths, sporting events of every kind, and gourmet meals."

"I think they allow pets there, too," Karilu added, petting Mini-G's head.

"Sounds fantastic! Thank you! Thanks!" Stanlin was delighted and honored, in equal measure.

"I'll send a message to the office that I'm taking time off. We can pack up and leave tonight, which gives us almost a week there," Andrigon said, rubbing Stanlin's shoulder.

"Superbly super!" Stanlin exclaimed.

Karilu enthusiastically nodded and smiled, cupping Stanlin's cheek in her hand.

Stanlin couldn't restrain himself from a small joke. "Hey, Mom, now we'll really get to take that long walk with Mini-G."

Surprising him, she jested back, "We'll have to stop off at the library on our way back."

# CHAPTER FIFTY-EIGHT

Yesterday afternoon, after officer Jennings first called Brenna, the volunteers from the police station had assisted in booking her flights. Last night, she was already touching down in Tucson. One of the volunteers picked her up at the airport, brought her to the hospital to get Cedric, and dropped the two of them off at a hotel where Brenna had reserved a room for the night. The next morning, the hotel's shuttle service took Brenna and Cedric to the airport.

On the home front, prior to her trip, Brenna had also enlisted help. She'd asked her next-door neighbor Mary to come over to feed, let out, and play with the puppies on Thursday night, after Brenna departed, and again on Friday, in the morning and afternoon, before Brenna and Cedric's return that evening. She'd also specified that Mary be there at 2:00 p.m. on Friday to answer Anthony's call, and tell him that Brenna and Cedric were flying home together.

While the logistical arrangements for picking up Cedric were smooth, handling him in his listless state was not. When Brenna had first arrived at the hospital, he'd cried and hugged her, which she had expected. Yet after those initial tears dried, he became withdrawn and was dull and distant thereafter at the hotel, on the airplane, and in the car riding home. The entire time, she wasn't able to entice him to talk or play, and his avoidance of eye contact stymied her efforts all the more. It was all she could do to restrain herself from screaming in frustration and anguish. She understood that he'd been drugged, and that his body and mind had been under duress for days, but it was still devastating seeing her normally vibrant boy in such a stupor.

It wasn't until they arrived home from the airport that Cedric spoke at last. Brenna was holding her suitcase in one hand and holding Cedric's hand with the other. They were walking up toward the front door when Cedric stopped in his tracks and started wailing.

She dropped the suitcase, squatted next to him, and embraced him. Brenna sensed it was the comfort of seeing their home again that had let him feel safe enough to finally vent his emotions. She knew that the sooner he let out his feelings and worked through them, the faster his psychological recovery would be. "I'm here. I'm here, sweetheart. Tell me, what is it? Tell me, please," she coaxed.

"The bad man, it was the bad man, the bad man!" Cedric howled, sobbing heavily into her shoulder.

Brenna's eyes welled up as she held him close and rocked him. She was shaken. It was clear that Cedric had recognized his loathsome tormentor. The earlier years of abuse he'd suffered at Ron's evil hands were resurfacing in his tender memory. Poor Cedric had been alert, at least some of the time, during his abduction. She pressed her cheek lovingly to his.

They embraced in front of the house for a long while. Cedric continued crying and saying, "the bad man" many times, and Brenna patiently repeated soothing reassurances. "Yes, he is a very bad man, but the police have him now. He can't hurt you anymore. The police are locking him up in jail, so he can't hurt you or anyone else, ever again."

Finally, when Cedric's tears subsided, they went into the house together. Because of the baby gating, the puppies were contained in the kitchen, but their welcoming yipping and barking could easily be heard from the foyer.

"Mommy, dat sounds like puppies!" Cedric perked up with excitement. "Is dat puppies?" Not waiting for an answer, he took off in the direction of the sounds.

Quickly setting down her suitcase, and laughing joyously at Cedric's spiritedness, Brenna followed him.

"Mommy, dats puppies in da kitchen!" he announced, staring and pointing at them.

"Yes, honey. They are our family's new puppies!" She opened the baby gating, letting the pups freely inundate Cedric with licks. While he petted them all, giggling and smiling, she described how their names suited their unique features and helped him practice the pronunciations.

She could see how Cedric instantly loved his new canine friends. To Brenna, the pups were like furry little angels. They had helped her in her most trying hours, and, by extension, they had given Anthony more peace of mind during that time, too. And now, they were uplifting her Cedric, bringing back his adorable smile and his glorious, high-pitched laughter—such sweet music to her ears.

Later, when bedtime could be delayed no longer, Brenna let the pups outside briefly and then gated them in the kitchen for the night. She carried a dozing Cedric up to his bedroom, but she could not bear to leave him there alone. Not yet. His bed was large enough for the two of them. She set him down on the mattress, got her pillow from her room, and placed it next to his pillow. She also moved the three stuffed animal puppies that Anthony had given Cedric for his third birthday from atop the dresser into the bed.

She climbed in. Cedric stirred and wakened. Brenna playfully positioned the three stuffed toys on his chest.

Touching them, Cedric murmured, "From Daddy."

"Yes," Brenna whispered. "It's funny how he got you these three little puppies almost a year ago. It's like Daddy knew we'd be getting Winky, Pokey, and Teensy." She was half talking to herself, but Cedric was attentive to her words.

He picked up one of the toys and folded down one of its ears. "It's Teensy!" he said with a giggle.

Brenna laughed, "Oh, yes! I see!"

Encouraged, Cedric set that toy down and picked up another. Covering one of its eyes, he exclaimed, "Winky!"

Brenna laughed harder. "Yes! Yes!"

Gleefully, he put down that pup, picked up the third, and maneuvered it in a pretend limp. "An' Pokey!"

"You are so creative," Brenna praised.

They giggled and cuddled, and soon, they were peacefully asleep.

\* \* \*

The next morning, Brenna had an idea. While Cedric was still sleeping, she got out her sewing kit and added defining characteristics to each of the stuffed dogs. She sewed an eye patch on one, snipped an ear smaller on another, and on the third, she sewed a mock bandage around one of its hind legs. She replaced the toys on his chest. Twenty minutes later, he woke up chuckling.

Later that morning, she and Cedric were in the backyard playing with the puppies when the phone rang. Brenna ran inside and snatched up the receiver.

It was Madeline, from the adoption agency. "Good morning, Brenna. I heard the update to the AMBER Alert on the news. Thank heavens Cedric is alright! You must be so relieved. I'm so happy for you!"

Brenna hooked the phone up to the headset and went back outside. She sat in a cozy lawn chair and watched over Cedric and the pups as she talked. "Thank you. Yes, words can't describe how happy I'm feeling. Oh, and thank you for helping out the police, and for your kind phone message."

"Of course," Madeline replied. "Thankfully the police caught that awful man. I just wish the prisons had solid therapy programs for people like him."

"That monster doesn't deserve any help," Brenna snapped. The image of a caring counselor treating Ron Camm altruistically was repulsive to her.

"I understand," Madeline said compassionately, "but you may want to consider it this way: If more prisoners were reformed, there would be fewer victims in the future. Isn't it such a waste, that after all their time in prison, so many of these perps just go back to doing the same despicable things all over again?"

Brenna was stunned into silence. Madeline did have a point. She stewed a moment before saying somberly, "*If* they could somehow be rehabilitated, yes, it would save a lot of innocent families a lot of pain. But I doubt if someone like Ron Camm can ever really change."

"The possibility is there, Brenna," Madeline countered gently. "I don't know if I mentioned it to you before, but the main reason Claire was strong enough to leave Ron was that she'd been attending group therapy sessions. In abusive relationships, there's a lot of denial going on. It's easier to first see others' problems in the group, and later, to admit one's own. Therapy groups for abuse victims are helpful, and so are therapy groups for the abusers themselves. And the absolute best results for changing abuse-related behaviors come after using a combination of group therapy and individual counseling sessions. It's true, researched and documented. "

"Hmm," Brenna murmured, mulling things over.

"Speaking of counseling, I would like to extend a few complimentary sessions to Cedric, to help him overcome what he's been through."

Brenna gratefully accepted the offer. She explained that the hospital doctor had estimated that Cedric was sedated each day while he was abducted. But she also told Madeline of Cedric's tearful outburst about "the bad man."

"It does sound like he glimpsed Ron at some point, but, with the repeated sedations, Cedric probably didn't see or hear a whole lot of disturbing things, which is good," Madeline inferred. "And children, bless their hearts, tend to be much more resilient than adults. I think after a few sessions with me, and lots of love from you, he'll be in great shape."

Brenna agreed, reporting how Cedric's mood had been catapulted by seeing his new pets.

"Yes, very encouraging," Madeline agreed.

They scheduled a therapy session for Cedric the following week, and said their good-byes. Brenna popped inside, replaced the phone and headset, and returned to her lawn chair. But Madeline's words stayed with her long after hanging up the phone.

\* \* \*

After lunch, when Anthony phoned, Madeline's comments became even more relevant, although not until the end of the call. At first, Brenna turned on the speakerphone, and Cedric went on about each of the new puppies and how Mommy had made each of his three little toys look like one of the puppies. Brenna and Anthony were beside themselves, hearing the merriment in his little voice. Ever since that first day, when they'd seen him holding the ceramic dog in Madeline's office, his pure affection toward animals had always been beautiful for them to witness.

When Cedric's lively chatter wound down, Anthony said he needed the last few minutes to talk with Mommy about boring grown-up stuff, and said good-bye to Cedric.

Brenna put on the headset and shepherded Cedric into the backyard, so he could play with the pups while she sat in her lawn chair. "What's up?" she asked Anthony.

"I learned about something amazing today, from Kent, one of my colleagues. I was talking to him about Cedric being saved and Ron Camm being caught. He went off about this new prison project that's going on in Europe. Apparently, there's this machine called a SPECT scanner that analyzes how the brain is working. Depending on which areas of the brain are lighting up in the scan, doctors can tell if parts of the brain are malfunctioning. Kent said that with a lot of the prisoners scanned so far, one or both of the temporal lobes weren't working right. The doctors started prescribing antiseizure-type medications and some cognitive therapies, and the prisoners are getting better. SPECT rescans have started normalizing, and behavioral problems have been improving. Kent said the European prisons using this technology have been seeing the best success ever in rehabilitating their prisoners."

"That really is amazing," Brenna replied. Then she shared with him what Madeline had said about group and individual therapies helping abusers and their abused partners.

Anthony was intrigued. "Hmm, I guess it is easier to first see what other people are doing wrong, before facing your own demons and hashing through them," he speculated.

A tingling coursed through Brenna's body; a sense of purpose was taking root deep inside. It seemed too serendipitous to be coincidence that on the same day, both of them had learned of potential ways to reduce recidivism. She said boldly, "I want to prevent other families from going through what we went through. I want America's prisons to incorporate group and individual therapy sessions, and the SPECT scanning program like they have in Europe. It just makes sense."

Anthony immediately supported her. "I'm with you. I'm all for it!"

They decided to initiate a letter campaign, in addition to visiting with local congressional representatives. For preparation, Brenna committed to researching the various types of therapies and SPECT scanning, and Anthony offered to pass on to her whatever additional tidbits he could wheedle out of Kent about the European prisons' successes.

"Once I know this stuff backwards and forwards, I'll write the letter," Brenna said. "After I present the letter to our representatives, I'll send it to everyone else I know and ask them to send it to their own representatives, and to everyone else they know!" Brenna was alight and inspired.

"That sounds incredible. You'll be turning what happened to Cedric into a positive force to help so many people," Anthony projected proudly.

"Yes, I think you're right," Brenna agreed. She found herself crossing her fingers but unable to sit still in her seat. Though her superstitious nature was intact, she realized that some of her husband's starry-eyed idealism seemed to be rubbing off on her.

# CHAPTER FIFTY-NINE

At the Governmental Council meeting following Ramaway's visit to Stanlin's home, he coordinated bringing in Stanlin as his guest for the supplemental meeting at the end of the week. He arranged to be the orator for that meeting, and received the approval to admit Stanlin's mother and father.

Stanlin, his parents, and Mini-G, had a splendid getaway at the resort and were back home on schedule, the night before the meeting. The next morning, as planned, R picked up Stanlin and his parents and escorted them to the Council Headquarters meeting room. He led Andrigon and Karilu to two seats in the audience, and instructed Stanlin to sit in a chair on the stage.

R stood at the podium and addressed his colleagues. "As discussed in our last meeting, I've brought my student, Stanlin, here with me today, because he was pivotal in changing Earth's forecast. This young Rampont creatively stayed in compliance with the Free Will Decree, by helping the humans to help themselves."

Faint whispers were audible throughout the room.

"He did disregard some laws in the process, however. He traveled to Earth after it was forbidden, and he interacted with a human girl. Please note, I was not aware that these rules were breached until after the fact," R stated.

Stanlin's throat felt dry. He squirmed in his seat.

The members listened closely as R went on. "Earlier, prior to the ban on traveling to Earth, during Stanlin's educational pursuits, he had observed a kindhearted human girl named Sylvia. When his parents informed him of the impending disaster in Earth's future, he feared for the girl; he didn't want her to be killed."

Stanlin could feel himself blushing, and he hoped that his being on the stage and far away from everyone else made it less apparent.

"He asked to use my Probability Sphere twice, during which I allowed him complete privacy. First, he checked to see if Sylvia would die, and it was predicted that she would. Next, he asked me if the Sphere could provide guidance for changing a perilous future. I let him use the top of the Sphere, to view the influencing factors."

"Did you see the puppies in the shelter and the man in the prison?" Sillu asked Stanlin.

"Yes," Stanlin said from his seat.

"He didn't understand the images," R continued, "but he described them to Sylvia. He gave her no instructions, except to say that positive actions toward those influencing factors might alter Earth's destiny. On her own, the human girl came up with good deeds relating to the images."

The fascinated Council members began whispering to one another again.

"We've already seen that Earth's overall future has transformed into a swirl, but now we can also see what will happen with the two influencing factors." R asked Stanlin to approach the Sphere on the stage, and Stanlin did so. R directed him, "First, please picture the puppies, and look into the center of the Sphere."

Stanlin obliged. An instant later, Mrs. Tormeni, Cedric, and a handsome man whom Stanlin assumed had to be Mr. Tormeni appeared in the Sphere and on the mounted screens. Mr. Tormeni set down suitcases in their home's foyer, and then Brenna and Cedric excitedly led him into the kitchen to see the puppies. A second scene of the three of them laughing and playing delightedly with the three puppies followed. This image was gradually replaced by the words "Nine months from now, with 98 percent certainty."

"Hmm. Let's check the other factor," R said. "Stanlin, please picture Jungilo Maximum Security Prison and that particular inmate, while looking into the Sphere's center."

Stanlin proceeded as R instructed. They all viewed a statistics sheet being printed, which documented declining percentages of violence within the prison. The lean, muscular, foreboding young man with the long, dark hair was depicted next, being introduced to an older-looking dog with gray fur. When this image faded, the words appeared: "Six weeks from now, with 98 percent certainty."

R scratched his temple thoughtfully. "The pictures look good. The puppies have a loving home, and violence is diminishing in the prison. I don't know what to make of that one inmate, though, and I don't understand how these factors affected the course of that deadly disease." He looked at Stanlin inquisitively.

"I was there, and I don't get it either, sir," Stanlin replied, shrugging. "I did recognize the dog, though; his name is Benton."

Light laughter arose.

"What we do know is that giving just a small amount of information to the humans made an immeasurable difference for them. If we ever foresee a disaster for Earth again, it seems the only moral thing to do is temporarily suspend the Non-Interaction Law. And, we can divulge, as Stanlin did, hints from our Sphere's technology, while allowing the humans to act as they see fit," R proposed.

Many members called out their support.

R turned and faced Stanlin. "I'd like you to come up to the podium now, and tell the Council what your friend Sylvia did to positively influence the puppies and the prison." R stepped down.

Stanlin situated himself there, center stage, seeing his parents and all of the distinguished Council members looking up at him. He felt his heart pounding. Speaking in front of others was always stressful. He hoped the right words would come to him.

Forcing himself to begin, he said, "Sylvia really loves animals. She volunteers at this shelter for strays that helps find homes for them. The three puppies we saw in the Sphere each had an unusual physical feature, which most of the humans considered flaws. But Sylvia thought Mrs. Tormeni and her family would still accept and love the pups, even with their flaws. She brought the three puppies over to Mrs. Tormeni's house and asked her to adopt them, and Mrs. Tormeni said yes. Sylvia had also read that animals could help people with depression, and Mrs. Tormeni had been very depressed at the time, because her son was missing and her husband was away.

"At the Jungilo Prison, Sylvia initiated a program of adopting a bunch of the shelter's older dogs and cats there. The older animals weren't getting adopted from the shelter as fast, so Sylvia thought the prison would make a great home for them. She had read that feeding, grooming, and exercising animals could teach prisoners compassion, and could also help reduce internal violence at prisons."

To Stanlin's pleasant surprise, his sentences had flowed effortlessly. Sylvia's kindness had inspired him and pacified his nerves.

Lively chatter filled the room.

"Thank you, Stanlin." R got up, motioned for Stanlin to return to his chair, and resumed his position behind the podium. "Clearly, animals have a positive effect upon the humans. The Sphere showed us all how jubilant the Tormeni family was, playing with those puppies." R lowered his voice an octave. "We all also know that the humans are morally evolving, and oftentimes face difficult choices. It stands to reason that if increasing the humans' contact with animals makes the humans happier, it will help in steering them toward more altruistic choices, both consciously and unconsciously. We have seen proof, with the statistics of prisoners at Jungilo fighting less after the animal program is underway.

"The humans can feel calmed and soothed by animals as well. Stanlin discovered this because, originally, he befriended Sylvia by shape-shifting into a cat. She felt so at ease around his feline presence that she requested he accompany her, as the cat, for moral support when she propositioned Mrs. Tormeni and the prison warden about the adoptions."

Stanlin was blushing again, and, judging by the temperature of his face this time, everyone else could see it.

R gazed beseechingly at his colleagues. "Considering the evidence of animals uplifting the humans, I propose that the Non-Interaction Law be modified such that both silent, invisible observations and silent, shape-shifted animal visitations to Earth are legal."

Mumblings of consideration resounded.

Nixar stood up. "I have a question for Stanlin." He looked squarely at the young Rampont. "Were you aware of the penalties for breaking the Non-Interaction Law and the ban on traveling to Earth?"

"No—and yes. I'll explain," Stanlin answered nervously. "When my class first visited Earth, the teacher allowed us to leave out our auditory plugs to hear some Earth sounds, and it was safe and fun. I used that day as an excuse to downplay the plugs' importance in my mind. Then I accidentally lost my pair and thought that, since I was doing fine without them, replacing them wasn't a big deal. Also, I was rationalizing that I wasn't actually a visible Rampont interacting with the human, Sylvia, because I was technically a cat."

Amid snickers and stifled laughs, Nixar repressed his own chuckle.

Mortified, Stanlin admitted, "I've had a big crush on her, and she became one of my best friends. I always loved visiting her so much that I guess I didn't want to see the whole reality of what I was doing."

It was Nixar's turn to blush, and he coughed unnaturally. Only Munin noticed.

Stanlin pressed on. "The same day that my parents told me about the Sphere's predictions for the disease, my dad woke me up to the seriousness of the Non-Interaction Law. He told me it was a crime to violate it, and the punishment was one year in jail. He also told me that breaching the ban on Earth travel was punishable by imprisonment for a term as long as the Council decided."

"And those consequences did not deter you?" Nixar asked pointedly.

"All I could think about was that Sylvia was going to die. I knew I needed to help her, no matter what happened to me. I was, and still am, willing to go to prison for what I did," Stanlin said plainly.

Nixar rubbed his chin with his fingers and sat down. He glanced at Munin, seated beside him.

Munin leaned toward him. "Reminds me a bit of a good friend, back in his younger days," he whispered.

Nixar gave a tiny smile, and his gaze veered back to Stanlin.

Andrigon squeezed Karilu's hand, which he'd been holding from the moment they were seated.

"Stanlin has fully acknowledged his transgressions for us. But, I'd also like to reiterate to everyone that if Stanlin had not done what he did, Earth would be mired in death and disease only a few months from now," R defended.

Twenty-five minutes of discussion followed, during which the Council members formally ratified both of Ramaway's earlier propositions regarding the Non-Interaction Law: It could be suspended if Earth was in peril, and silent, shape-shifted animal visits to Earth would be permissible. The Council still believed that human observations should not be the primary focus, though, so the corollary to the Non-Interaction Law, The Educational Prioritization Standard, remained unchanged.

Stanlin's punishments were also issued. He was mandated to write an essay, backed by historical research, discussing the reasons why, under normal, non-emergent circumstances, Ramponts should wear auditory plugs on Earth and abstain from conversing with the humans. Stanlin also had to sign a contract, agreeing to immediately consult the Council if he ever felt a reason to break rules again, so that he could receive government assistance with whatever the problem was. The document further specified that should Stanlin violate any laws again, the repercussions would be maximal. Finally, he was required to assist Ramaway with research projects for at least one hour each day after school, for the next three years.

Stanlin readily agreed to comply with the reprimands, which he knew were extraordinarily fair. But he did have one request. He asked for the Council's consent to visit Sylvia one last time, as a visible, speaking Rampont, so that he could inform her of the Sphere's newest readings. He was granted the permission, and the Council members excused him from the meeting.

R escorted Stanlin and his parents through the exit doors. Outside the room, Andrigon and Karilu hugged and kissed Stanlin, telling him how relieved they were at the Council's decisions. They wholeheartedly thanked R for being Stanlin's advocate, and for allowing their attendance at the meeting. After the joyful exchange, Stanlin asked his parents if they would mind if he met them back at the house a little later. "I'd like to talk with R for a few minutes and then think through some things for a while," he explained.

"Not a problem," said Andrigon.

"Sure, honey," said Karilu.

Stanlin's parents each shook R's hand, thanked him again, and left.

"What did you want to talk with me about?" R asked Stanlin.

"I know my parents thanked you, but I need to, too. Thank you times a thousand for letting them be here, and even more for bringing me here as your guest," Stanlin said. "Coming on my own would have been..." He paused. "Scary" would sound too wimpy; he settled for "really bad."

"Well, I reckoned that everything would turn out for the best the way we did it. And look, the Non-Interaction Law was improved, we all learned from your courageousness, and the small, ah, disciplinary matters were dealt with." R smiled.

"Yeah," Stanlin agreed. His face flushed with heat, but only for a second. He added happily, "The after-school research won't be a chore at all. Research is cool. I read scientific journals for fun sometimes."

R raised his eyebrows, looking quite pleased.

"But, sir," Stanlin said, his voice becoming softer, "I'm not sure if I'm smart enough to be your assistant." Since chagrin had dominated his morning anyway, he might as well say what was on his mind.

"Someone who can combine compassion with ingenuity is exceptionally intelligent in my book," R extolled, shaking Stanlin's hand.

"Thanks," Stanlin replied, feeling a bit stunned. No teacher had ever said something so complimentary to him. He left the building in a haze of gratitude and swarming thoughts.

R said good-bye and returned to the meeting. The Council members agreed upon one more issue: They would nominate Stanlin for the next Annual Rampont Peace Prize, recognizing that he was instrumental in saving billions of lives on Earth. While he had broken Capton rules, he had never intended to harm anyone. His motivations had evolved from infatuation, to friendship, to pure, unselfish love. And Stanlin was ready and willing to endure any and all of the consequences for his actions. He was a young yet worthy contender for the prestigious prize. It was also understood by all that, should Stanlin wish to apply to the Governmental Council in adulthood, this award nomination would seal his acceptance.

# CHAPTER SIXTY

As Stanlin walked away from the Council building, his thoughts and emotions were spinning. He ambled through the local streets, trying to organize the whirlwind inside his head.

He was incredibly thankful and relieved to have aired out his whole story, without receiving a prison sentence. He was also honored by R's praise and excited about being his assistant over the next few years.

But his breathing was labored, and his heart felt like lead. His chest was physically sore and seemed to have shrunken down a size. He was soberly realizing that, after one more visit, he would never again be able to speak to Sylvia or hear the sound of her voice talking to him. Although it would be legal to visit her in silence, invisibly or as Melvin, after all they'd been through together, he couldn't imagine feeling good about doing either.

Secretly and invisibly observing a stranger to learn about a culture was one thing, but doing that with Sylvia, a real friend, would be an invasion of her privacy. He would feel like a spy.

On the other hand, if he were to explain the situation to her on their last speaking visit, and then attempt silent Melvin visits in the future, she would, without a doubt, be disappointed too, knowing that Melvin was Stanlin but that they could never talk. And what if, while trying to be a quiet Melvin, he lost control? What if he broke down and started talking with her—and got caught? It was way too risky to put himself into a position of temptation like that. His contract stated that he'd be maximally disciplined if he violated any more laws.

Stanlin shook his head back and forth and groaned. It was clear: All mute visits to Sylvia would be fruitless and would feel like leaping backwards, like regression rather than progression, which just wasn't right. Life didn't move backwards!

He began speculating about where Sylvia's life on Earth was headed. She had loving, supportive parents, a best friend, and good grades in school. High school and college were right around the corner for her. She was purposeful now, helping out at the shelter, and later on, as an adult, she would contribute positively to society with whatever she chose to pursue. Stanlin was certain of that.

He reflected upon where his own life was going. In the coming three years, his scholastic demands would continue increasing; plus, he would be staying later at school doing the research each day. After that, his studies would become more specialized. He planned to concentrate on Universe courses, like R had. When he graduated school at twenty-eight, Highest Authority willing, he wanted to become a Governmental Council member.

He sighed. Things were marching onward, for both of them. He understood it. Their lives were inevitably diverging. It was logical. And it was natural. It still sucked.

Blowing off steam, he sprinted down the street and kept on running until he'd thoroughly winded himself. Catching his breath, he walked again, contemplating some more. One last, real visit with Sylvia was permitted. They would be able to freely banter, laugh, and interact. It was a precious gift. He pledged to make the final visit count, to say and do whatever he felt he should, without abandon, and to have no regrets.

On Earth it was between breakfast and lunchtime, as good a time as any to see if she was home. Thinking she might be outside enjoying the sunshine, Stanlin transported himself and arrived invisibly in her backyard.

It was raining out, so he checked her room, where he found her sitting at her desk, busy on her computer.

He became visible beside her. "Is it an OK time to talk?"

She gasped, jumping in her seat with one hand over her heart. "You scared me for a sec there, but yeah, it's good." As usual, she started up the background noise first, and raced back. Standing in front of him, agog, she asked, "Did you find out how what we did stopped the disease?"

"What *you* did," Stanlin corrected her. "You were the one who did all the work."

"Couldn't have without your help!" she shot back brightly.

He smiled. "I did learn some more from the Sphere, but, unfortunately, not everything."

Her beautiful eyes were fixed on him.

"It showed Mr. Tormeni coming home, and then he and Mrs. Tormeni and Cedric all playing with those three puppies."

"Yes! That totally sounds right, because the police found Cedric! He's home now. And Mr. Tormeni will be home from overseas in the spring."

"Terrific," Stanlin replied, so grateful to hear the confirmation that the little toddler who'd fawned so sweetly over Melvin was safe. "The Sphere also showed a statistics sheet documenting less violence inside Jungilo," he relayed, "plus that one spooky-looking prisoner meeting with Benton."

"Way cool—that sounds right, too! Karen called a couple of days ago, saying her mom already met with the warden, and they brought over Benton and the first few animals to get things rolling."

"Superbly super!" Stanlin exclaimed.

"I still don't know who the spooky prisoner could be though," she said, befuddled.

"Me neither, and I can't figure out how the influencing factors and the positive changes prevented that deadly disease. Honestly, I don't know if we'll ever find out. I wish I could tell you more."

"I was really curious," she admitted. "But what's most important is everything's better now for the future."

"Yes," he agreed.

"Thank God you came to Earth to help out."

"I got into some trouble for coming, and for talking with you, though," Stanlin said. He told her about his punishments: the after school research, the signed contract, and the essay about the Non-Interaction Law.

"Why does Capton forbid Ramponts from interacting with humans?" Sylvia asked with sad confusion.

Stanlin didn't want to upset her further by telling her that Ramponts saw the humans as morally inferior beings. He was also not fully informed and needed to research all of the motivations behind the creation of the Non-Interaction Law. "I don't completely understand why," he said truthfully. "To write that essay, I'll have to read about the history leading up to that law."

He didn't specify that it was still legal for Ramponts to silently visit the humans when invisible or when shape-shifted into animals. He simply couldn't bear to rehash for her all of the reasons why he'd determined that mute visits would sorely disappoint them both.

She said wistfully, "So the bottom line is, we can't hang out anymore, right?" Her eyes were becoming watery.

"That's right," he confirmed somberly. "But I have some time right now that's legal," he added with a tiny smile, trying to lift both their spirits.

She bounded forward and hugged him tightly, her arms overlapping into his semisolid form.

He felt the familiar pressure sensation, but also the fabulous, fluttery chills he'd felt when she'd hugged him before. Then it dawned on him that the pressure sensation was totally unnecessary. "Hold on a second," he said. "I want to become fully solid for this. It's the best contact sport ever!" He solidified and hugged her with zeal.

Sylvia chortled and sniffled. "It's so nice hugging you solid like this."

Stanlin peered up at the Rocklore poster on her wall. What he was preparing to suggest made him feel ridiculous, but he didn't care. He'd decided to say and do what felt right—ridiculous or not. He continued holding her in his arms but backed up his torso enough to look into her eyes. "Sylvia, I was thinking, since this is our last visit..." Realizing his voice was about to tremble, he paused to compose himself. His face felt like hot coals, and his heart was thumping so loudly he could swear he could hear it, and feared she could, too.

"Yes?" she encouraged.

"Just say it," he thought, and said aloud quickly, "Well, I was thinking I could shape-shift into that lead singer guy from Rocklore, and you could kiss me." He wanted the kiss to be as tempting as possible for her, and he knew she fancied that singer.

Her silence unsettled him, so he tuned into her thoughts. Sylvia was feeling surprised, and a bit overwhelmed, but was contemplating what it might be like to have a 3-D Rick from Rocklore there in her room, kissing her.

Assuming it would be welcomed, Stanlin swiftly morphed into Rick and brought his Rocklore-Rick lips toward hers. But the second their lips touched, Sylvia pulled away from him. They were still standing very close, but she disengaged from the embrace, appearing confused.

Perplexed himself, he tuned into her thoughts again. She was thinking that this wasn't really Rick. It was really Stanlin. Stanlin, who'd first befriended her as Melvin, and who, later on, was the blue boy who had supported all of her ideas. The friend who had come to save her life, and who had helped in saving her whole family, and even planet Earth as she knew it. It was a lot to grasp.

Stanlin had always made her feel at ease and comfortable. He cared about her, and really listened to her when she talked. His close attention to her had made her feel very special. And although she could not really describe it or understand it, when she looked into his large, dark eyes, there was a strange cuteness about him, and she felt a little melty inside. "Stanlin, I don't want to kiss Rick," she said finally. "I want to kiss *you*."

Stanlin's heart felt like it was jumping on a trampoline. He morphed back into himself and wrapped his arms around her. Pulling her close, he passionately pressed his lips to hers. Disregarding the aborted previous attempt, this was the first kiss for both of them. With all of his studies, and his interest in Sylvia, Stanlin had never kissed a Rampont girl, and Sylvia's parents had insisted that she be in high school before dating.

Maybe it was because it was their first kiss; maybe it was the special bond they had formed; maybe it was the wildness of them being different species from different galaxies; or perhaps it was a combination of everything that made their kiss so magical. A euphoric blend of nervousness, caring, and unique attraction swept over them.

When their lips parted, he said, "I stand corrected: This contact sport is way better!"

She chuckled, and he kissed her again.

He edged back, lightly ran his fingers through her hair, and looked into her eyes. "No regrets. None," he thought. Cupping her face in his hands, he said, "You're the most beautiful girl I've ever seen. And you're just as beautiful on the inside. I love you, Sylvia."

She looked shocked.

"It's OK. You don't have to say it back. Really," he immediately assured her. He knew that he had known her on a different level than she had known him. She hadn't been tuning into *his* thoughts all this time—thank The Highest Authority! He didn't expect her to share in the depth of his feelings.

Still, he couldn't help himself from listening to her thoughts as she tried making sense of her emotions. She was taken aback, because her feelings for him were stronger than anything she had felt for any boy at school. Her heart fluttered and melted in her chest from his compliment about her beauty. His kisses and hugs, and his hands in her hair and on her face felt so warm and caring. And the way he looked at her with such unabashed affection enveloped her with a mix of giddy happiness and soothing peacefulness. Her crush on Rick from Rocklore seemed like a game in comparison, because she didn't know the faintest thing about Rick's personality. Stanlin, on the other hand, she did know, and he was so nice and so uplifting to be around. She realized how very much she was going to miss his visits. She was wondering if all that she was feeling could, in fact, be love. "I think I might love you, too," she said softly.

"You don't have to know," he said understandingly. He was thrilled with her thoughts about him, just as they were.

She suddenly giggled.

"What is it?" he asked.

"I was just thinking, Karen would *never* believe me if I told her about this!"

They laughed.

Stanlin thought for a minute and said, "Corimo would believe me for sure!"

They laughed more.

"I wish I could stay here with you," he lamented as their laughter quieted.

"Me too," she sighed. "I don't know how to thank you...or...how to say good-bye," she said, her eyes filling with tears.

"We could take a picture together, you know, to remember each other by," he suggested, trying to lighten the mood. "I've read up on Earth culture. I know you all keep picture albums in books and on computers. We take pictures on Capton, too. Our cameras are made differently, and our photos look more like what you'd call a hologram, but still, it's the same basic idea. I think photos are really cool." He bit his tongue to stop the babbling already.

"Yes, they are! OK, let's take one," Sylvia consented, brightening up. She retrieved her cell phone from her desk and positioned herself beside Stanlin. Draping one arm over his shoulder, she stretched out her other arm in front of her, angling the phone for the photo. "Smile," she said, and snapped the picture.

She hooked up the phone to her computer and downloaded the photo, printed two copies, and gave one to Stanlin. "Even if Karen saw this picture, she wouldn't believe it was real. She'd just think I got high-tech and created the whole thing." Sylvia snickered with amusement.

"Corimo would be really jealous if I showed him this picture," Stanlin chortled.

She reddened and cracked a shy smile.

"Let's take another one, where we're smooching! Corimo will be raving jealous!"

"No!" Sylvia objected, turning scarlet.

They were both giggling.

Becoming more serious, Stanlin said, "I know you'd feel weird telling anyone you kissed an alien, so, if you want, I'll keep this to myself, too. Today can be our little secret."

She gazed at him tenderly. "Yeah, I'd really like that."

He knew in his gut that it was the right time for him to go. He'd never actually be ready to say good-bye to her, but their lives and the laws sadly required it. They shared their final kiss and embrace, which was, like their whole relationship, utterly unforgettable for each of them.

"Last chance to come back with me and live on Capton," he joked, his eyes stinging.

She shook her head, smiling, her green eyes shimmering.

They waved good-bye, and, with a lump in his throat, Stanlin transported home.

# Spring, 2033

# CHAPTER SIXTY-ONE

Surprisingly, as the country's officials had predicted it, the security lockdown in South Africa was lifted in the spring of 2033. The date of Anthony's trip home from his one year assignment there was precisely on schedule.

Brenna stood waiting for him at the baggage claim, holding Cedric in her arms, resting his bottom on her hip. At four years old, he was almost too big to be held, but she felt she needed her beloved little man snuggled up next to her right now. It was so hard to believe that her other beloved man was finally coming home.

Over the past months, she and Anthony had had many enterprising phone conversations. Their congressional letter campaign was progressing rapidly, and she loved conferring with him about each new development. She'd made fast friends with her local congressman, and had inspired her friends and family to actively campaign the cause. She had engendered endorsements from several civic organizations, and had requested that they contact as many of their branches as possible, all across the country, to appeal to their local representatives.

Although she'd cherished every call with Anthony, one of her most favorites had been early on, when she'd described a special new addition to their original letter. At the project's inception, when Brenna had first discussed the cause with Rebecca and Rinalda, they'd told her about Sylvia's budding animal program at Jungilo and had asked if Brenna could add a clause in the letter, encouraging more animal shelter adoption programs in prisons. Brenna had readily agreed and done so.

When she'd told Anthony about it, he was all revved up. "That's outta sight! We're gonna make history with this!" he'd exclaimed. His unbridled fervor never failed to boost her own.

Currently, Anthony was updated about everything, except the most recent leap forward, which she would surprise him with in person. One of National Public Radio's regular guest commentators, Dr. Clarissa Faulksman, was a staunch advocate of the prison reform cause, having learned of the letter campaign from her fellow Lion's Club member, Rinalda Delany. At that week's Lion's Club meeting, Dr. Faulksman had said that she had secured thirty-five nationwide public service announcements to educate the masses about the cause. The first announcement was set to air this Saturday morning. Brenna could hardly wait to see the look on Anthony's face when he listened to their letter being spouted over the airwaves. And hearing it for the first time herself, with Anthony by her side, was going to be fabulous!

She was also overjoyed that Anthony would be seeing how Cedric had grown and changed. Sure, she had described Cedric's skill with a Frisbee, and his near-perfect spirals with the Nerf football, but she knew the light in Anthony's eyes when he watched his son in action would be priceless. And the sight of Cedric romping around in the yard with Winky, Pokey, and Teensy was more adorable than her words could ever convey.

There was so much to look forward to. Together again as a family. At long last.

"When's Daddy coming?" Cedric asked, bouncing up and down on Brenna's hip.

"Any minute now, sweetie," she answered. "He'll be walking through those doors right there." She pointed at the double doors several yards away from them.

As if on cue, the doors opened, and passengers from Anthony's flight started coming through.

Then, they saw Anthony.

"Daddy! Daddy!" Cedric yelled gleefully.

Brenna's eyes filled with joyful tears, and a colossal grin overtook her face. "Daddy! Daddy!" she chimed in.

Anthony's eyes and smile reflected hers as he ran toward them.

Years ago, in her wildest dreams, Brenna would never have thought a day could be happier than her wedding day. Then, later on, the day that she and Anthony had brought Cedric home seemed to be the pinnacle of bliss. She could not have fathomed days like those to ever be surpassed.

But today, they were. As Anthony hugged and kissed her and Cedric, Brenna knew this was truly the most wonderful day she had ever known.

In the past, whenever she'd felt fortunate, she'd also nursed fears of some mysterious curse creeping in and wiping away her blessings.

But today, she did not. Her fingers were not crossed; she was not thinking of jinxes or wishing she could find some wood to knock on. Instead, her outlook was pragmatically rosy. Many golden, sunny days were awaiting them. So were the inevitable challenges. But as a loving family, they would treasure every goodness and would, through their joined efforts, eventually surmount every obstacle. She was not distressed, guessing, or hoping.

Today, she knew.

# Late Spring, 2033

# CHAPTER SIXTY-TWO

Stanlin brought his most recent data compilations into R's office. Handing over the cylinder, he summarized, "More about gravitons and gravitational forces, more about sequences of streaming photon emissions, some tips for reconfiguring electron spins and fiddling with quarks inside protons and neutrons, and extra detail about varying the nuclear force outputs from gluon and W and Z particles."

For nearly ten months now, ever since his research assistant duties began, Stanlin had been pooling together all of the available information about the inner workings of the Probability Spheres. According to the Council's reprimand, he was obligated to research for one hour after school each day, but quite often, two or three hours would pass by before he finally wrapped up a session. His fascination with the Spheres, and his respect for R, made Stanlin all but tireless when fact finding, and his reports were almost impeccable.

While collectively, the Council members were perpetually refining the Sphere's technology, R had been working feverishly on his own pet project. He hoped to boost the Sphere's sensitivity to thought frequencies to a threshold where it would yield more detailed predictions and influencing factors. Several months earlier, after making significant strides in his research, he had beseeched additional help at a Governmental Council meeting. Munin and Nixar had volunteered to assist him. Since then, the three of them had been persistently tinkering with R's Probability Sphere, applying the information that Stanlin was bringing them.

R inserted the cylinder into his Rampont Reader. "Ahhh. This looks very good," he mused, looking through Stanlin's report with keen eyes.

Stanlin was glad that his teacher could make clear sense of the baffling stuff. Though Stanlin's knowledge of physics had been expanding tremendously, when he read the data, he usually felt an odd amalgam of enlightenment and confusion. The concepts were profoundly complex, and he was never completely certain of his level of understanding. His frequent talks with R, when they related the scientific principles to real life analogies, helped him the most, and from this, Stanlin's ability to orally convey his ideas had improved dramatically. Nevertheless, he always wanted his comprehension to be ever deeper and more concrete. "I wish I really got all this, like you do," he said to R.

"In a few years, you will. What you're being introduced to is highly advanced material, Stanlin. The fact that you're grasping as much as you are now is phenomenal. You'll have a real leg up on your peers in the coming years." R winked.

Stanlin smiled broadly.

R resumed scanning through the report. A few minutes passed before Munin and Nixar strode into the room.

After the usual greetings were exchanged, R said, "I have a great feeling about today. I think a few more modifications, based on this," he waved the Reader in the air, "just might boost the Sphere's sensitivity to the threshold we need."

Stanlin was fidgeting, hardly able to contain himself. He believed in R's feeling about the day, because he had it, too. He'd sensed a pending breakthrough the moment he'd completed his report.

"What've we got?" Nixar inquired. R handed him the Reader, and Nixar and Munin began reviewing the material together.

Following a quiet spell of reading and contemplation, Munin observed, "According to this, not only can we make the Sphere much more receptive to our thoughts, but we can also vamp up the frequency of our thoughts themselves."

"Our thoughts can be made stronger?" Stanlin asked, intrigued. He hadn't been able to draw that conclusion from his report on his own.

"Yes. The data implies that thoughts accompanied by positive feelings produce more intense signals," Munin explained.

"That's why once we make the Sphere more sensitive, *and* we send it positively infused thought signals, the new images we'll see should be absolutely exquisite," Nixar said. Transitioning to the work ahead, he suggested, "I think we should toy with the quarks first."

Munin and R agreed, and the three brilliant Ramponts commenced toiling away at the Sphere.

Stanlin shifted between watching them, trying to comprehend their jargon-filled dialogue, and rereading the information he'd brought them. He had made up his mind to hang around for as long as the elders worked today, to witness their advancements. Plus, he couldn't help but wonder if the refined Sphere might somehow be able to show him how Sylvia's actions had saved planet Earth; that miraculous turnabout had remained a mystery.

For a few moments, he stared ahead vaguely, with unseeing eyes, conjuring up Sylvia's lovely face in his mind. Although it was pushing a year since he'd last seen her, her beauty, sprightliness, effervescence, and kindness were still etched into his heart. If he was able to see her within the Sphere today, and learn more about her good deeds, it would be bittersweet emotionally, and gratifying intellectually. So the waiting was worth it to him. And it pressed on.

About two and a half hours later, the calm, concentrated atmosphere in the room took a dramatic turn. Throwing both fists up in the air, R loudly yelled, "Ah! Yes!"

"That should do it!" Munin concurred.

"Let's test it!" Nixar goaded.

R strode over to Stanlin and put his hands on Stanlin's shoulders. "Your hours of research gave us what we needed for this. I don't want you just watching. You should test the Sphere with us."

Munin and Nixar readily nodded their consent.

"Thank you!" Stanlin said to R. "Thank you!" he repeated to Munin and Nixar. He was practically hyperventilating.

"We'll let you ask the Sphere the first question," R offered. "What would you like to see in splendid detail?"

After working alongside them for so long, Stanlin wasn't shy about telling them exactly what he wished to know. "I'm still curious about the particulars of how Sylvia's animal adoptions saved planet Earth. But since the Sphere views the near future, and that question involves the past, is there any way the Sphere can help?"

Nixar said, "The Spheres do have records of their past predictions."

"That's right," Munin agreed with vim. "Each Sphere automatically records everything it shows into a permanent log."

"And each of those logs becomes part of a shared database among all of the Spheres," said R. "I've accessed the records before, though we rarely need to do it."

"That's what Nixar was counting on years ago, when *he* peaked into an Earth girl's future," Munin teased.

"You did?" Stanlin asked in disbelief.

"Let's just say you're not the first Rampont to have cared about a human girl, and we'll leave it at that," Nixar answered. He shot a warning glance at Munin, who was unsuccessfully restraining a goofy smirk.

"Maybe we'll need to review those logs, eh, Nixar?" R joked. "I'll have to get the scoop on that later. No, but seriously, retrieving old predictions isn't complicated. You look into the Sphere's center, announce your intent to access the records, and then focus your mind on what you want to look back on."

"Will the logs be superbly detailed from your work today, just like the other thought-based images will be?" Stanlin inquired.

"I bet," R conjectured.

Nixar and Munin heartily agreed.

With zeal, Stanlin said, "Hopefully, with the extra detail, we can piece together what really happened on Earth and figure out how what Sylvia did stopped that disease."

"Let's give it a go!" Nixar urged.

R led Stanlin to the Sphere, and the four Ramponts encircled it. R was as exuberant as a lad himself as he directed Stanlin. "When I cue you in, focus on 'Earth's dire future prediction, as of summer 2032.' And when you send your thoughts, remember to add positive emotions to amplify the signal. Love or gratitude intensifies the best. The more detail we can squeeze out of this, the better."

"Got it," Stanlin replied.

R fixed his gaze at the Sphere's center. "We wish to access the records," he announced. The Sphere changed from its cream color to a vibrant pink, and R pointed at Stanlin.

Stanlin focused his mind as R had instructed, and suffused the thought with all of his love for Sylvia. The images that followed dumbfounded them all: The definition and clarity of the pictures themselves was wondrous, and the story that unfolded was enrapturing.

They watched a prisoner escape Jungilo Maximum Security Prison by clutching the underside of a medically marked helicopter. They saw him drop himself down into thick brush below and begin running through what looked like a forest, distancing himself from the prison gates. The Sphere's perspective changed to an aerial view, revealing that the vast woods eventually abutted the border of a park, which a sign delineated as Ashbury Park.

Stanlin's words tumbled out hurriedly. "That prisoner was an influencing factor! Remember? At the meeting after Earth had been saved, the Sphere showed him meeting with a dog. He hadn't escaped the prison. And that park—Ashbury Park—it's where I used to meet up with Sylvia." He felt a sudden pang of sorrow. He had so many fond memories of their time together at that park. But this was not the time or place to dwell on missing her. He forced his attentiveness to the present.

R uttered a quick, "Yes, thank you," to acknowledge Stanlin's comments, but all of their eyes stayed fixed on the Sphere. The scene changed to three coughing puppies in a cage at the SPCA.

"Those three puppies were also influencing factors!" Stanlin blurted out. "Remember? Sylvia adopted them out to her neighbor." More quietly, with bewilderment, he added, "But wait a second; I don't remember them coughing. Sylvia and Karen had said there was a canine influenza virus, but it typically spread in the autumn season."

"Don't forget, this was the prediction of what *would* have happened if Sylvia had *not* had those dogs adopted," R emphasized.

"And this image could easily be from the autumn season," Munin inferred.

"True," said Nixar. "We don't know the exact dates of the Sphere's images."

They all drew silent again and watched a teenage girl, on duty alone at the shelter, trying to feed the three puppies while she was distracted, talking on her cell phone. With their cage momentarily open, the puppies capitalized on the girl's inattentiveness and bolted out. They careened through the front door, just as a few people were entering. The girl tried to pursue the fleeing pups, but couldn't get around the incoming patrons and out the door quickly enough to catch them. The three puppies continued running through the local streets and into nearby Ashbury Park.

They ran all the way to the border of the park and into its adjoining woods. The Sphere showed the sun quickly set and rise a few times, indicating that on their third morning of running, they seized and consumed a wild turkey. The pups died afterward. An injured fox then ate some from each of their small carcasses, and died after as well.

The man whom they'd seen escaping the prison was depicted eating the fox's remains, but he did not die as fast. In the following scenes, he was very ill, coughing and spitting but purposefully spreading his infirmity in public places. People and animals all across the Earth passed the sickness to each other and perished from it. Stanlin had to avert his eyes when Sylvia and her family appeared. At last, the evil escaped convict succumbed to the disease, too. When the deathly images faded, the Sphere became pleasantly cream again.

"That disease," Stanlin murmured. "It's unthinkable." Seeing its devastation so vividly rattled him to the core.

"Such an atrocity that almost was," sighed Munin.

"After seeing those images at our Council meeting last year, I wanted to know more about diseases on Earth. I found out quite a bit about interspecies flus," said Nixar.

"Yes, I've read up on the topic as well," said R. "Here, why don't we all talk more comfortably." He walked over to his desk, pulled up additional chairs, and everyone seated themselves. "Interspecies flus often begin with diseased fowl. It seems that the turkey initiated the chain reaction," R surmised.

"And beforehand, the puppies were already coughing, maybe with that canine influenza virus, when they were in the shelter," Munin pointed out.

"Most likely, the canine influenza combined with the avian influenza in the bodies of those pups, after they ate that infested turkey. RNA strands began swapping, and the disease began mutating. The genetic reassortment process continued further in the fox, and still further in the man. The noxious mutations grew increasingly contagious and lethal," Nixar theorized.

"I wasn't aware that flus on Earth could swap species like that," Munin commented.

"The avian influenza virus has been mutating to humans and other mammals very slowly for over a century," R said, "but in the last decade, the rates of these mutations have skyrocketed."

"Correct," Nixar concurred. "Hundreds of influenza variations have been developing in recent years on Earth. Interspecies flus have become more common because both the outer capsule proteins and the inner genomes are being altered. But the flu strains so far have yielded very low mortality rates, unlike the one that almost formed."

"The chain reaction couldn't get started," Stanlin observed, "because when Sylvia brought the puppies to Mrs. Tormeni to adopt, they weren't stuck in the shelter anymore, so they didn't need to break out, run away, and eat that diseased turkey."

"Not to mention that Sylvia got them out before they ever caught that canine flu," Nixar added.

"Yes," R acknowledged, lacing his fingers together. "Now, on to Sylvia's adoptions at the prison: Could those animals have somehow prevented that convict from escaping? As you said before, Stanlin, after Earth was saved, the Sphere showed that man and a dog within the prison."

"Right," said Stanlin. "But in the prediction log we just saw, the convict escaped by holding onto a medical helicopter. How could the adopted animals have changed that?"

"Let's start by thinking about what the animals did change," Munin suggested.

"They decreased the fighting between the inmates," Stanlin replied.

R pitched in. "If you recall, at the Council meeting Stanlin attended, when we checked upon Jungilo's status, the Sphere revealed statistics about the prison's reduced internal violence."

"Less internal violence means fewer injured prisoners, and fewer medical helicopters. That convict's escape vehicles dwindled fast because of Sylvia's animals," Munin reasoned.

"And since he couldn't escape, he couldn't become a host to the viral mutations or spread the disease," R concluded. "So, from both of Sylvia's animal interventions, Earth was doubly protected from doom."

"A mini miracle worker, she was! Quite a gal, that Sylvia." Munin playfully raised his eyebrows up and down, looking at Stanlin.

Nixar and R chortled.

"At least it all makes sense now," Stanlin said, trying to smile yet failing and feeling wistful. But suddenly, an idea began forming, which started to ease some of his sadness. "We've seen the enhanced detail in the Sphere's recorded logs, so how about we view an enhanced future prediction, too?" he asked.

His mentors consented.

"I take it you have a topic of interest already," R said with apparent amusement.

Stanlin blushed slightly. "I am wondering if Sylvia's animal programs might catch on in other prisons, too. Could we check on the future of prisons on Earth?" It was a risk. He didn't know if more Earth prisons would initiate such programs, or if Earth prisons would be run any better in any way at all in the future. But he was betting with all his heart that they would be.

"Earth prisons are disasters," Nixar grumbled.

"If nothing else, I guess it might be, uh, interesting," Munin said tenuously.

"I don't see any harm in checking," R conceded, sounding tentative about the request himself.

The four Ramponts encircled the Sphere once again. "Remember, we'll get more detail if you blend the focus of your inquiry with positive feelings," said R.

"How am I going to accompany a thought of prisons with positive feelings?" Stanlin wondered aloud.

Munin posed, "Try this: Think, 'I want to learn about Earth's prisons in the future, and I'm so grateful that animal programs have proven helpful so far.'"

"OK." Stanlin focused his mind as Munin recommended, and exquisitely defined pictures arose. The US Capitol building in Washington DC appeared. Mr. and Mrs. Tormeni were there speaking to personnel, presumably congressmen. A bill came into view proposing that animal shelter adoption programs be implemented in federal prisons. This faded, and a second bill came into focus proposing that federal prisons use SPECT scanning to evaluate prisoners' brain functioning, and to guide the doctors in prescribing medications and cognitive therapies. After this, a third bill, calling for group and individual counseling services to be incorporated within the prisons, was depicted.

A legislative agenda then appeared, with the three bills scheduled for House debate. The image was replaced by the words, "One year from now, with 56 percent certainty," and the Sphere slowly turned cream again.

Stanlin was ecstatic. "You see! The humans aren't immoral! The good ones are trying really hard to fix up the bad ones! And maybe, with the right help, some of the bad ones will get better." From writing his essay about the Non-Interaction Law, he'd learned in greater depth how morally corrupt the Ramponts perceived the humans to be.

"It's only 56 percent certain that these bills will go to the House, which is just a baby step in an arduous, equivocal process," Munin said skeptically.

"It's highly doubtful that these bills will ever become law," Nixar droned in concert. "Political reformation procedures on Earth are pitiful."

R and Munin nodded in somber agreement.

"But doesn't it count for something that they care enough to want to improve themselves? Doesn't it prove their morality is intact because they're trying to make things better?" Stanlin challenged.

The three elders exchanged pensive glances. Evidently, Stanlin's optimistic perspective had given them a little food for thought.

Stanlin struggled to suppress the grin that threatened to reveal itself. His mentors wouldn't understand his current satisfaction. But in his mind, he had just tilled the soil and planted seedlings toward his future goal. In time, when he became a Council member himself, he would convince his colleagues to repeal that absurd Non-Interaction Law and its corollary, altogether.

# About the Author

Cynthia Hey is a chiropractor and a certified fitness trainer, who lives on Long Island with her husband. Her position paper, "Complementing Chiropractic Philosophy with Science," was published in the June 2007 issue of *The Journal of Vertebral Subluxation Research*. *Stanlin and Sylvia* is her debut novel. Send your comments to cynthiahey@yahoo.com, or visit her on Facebook.